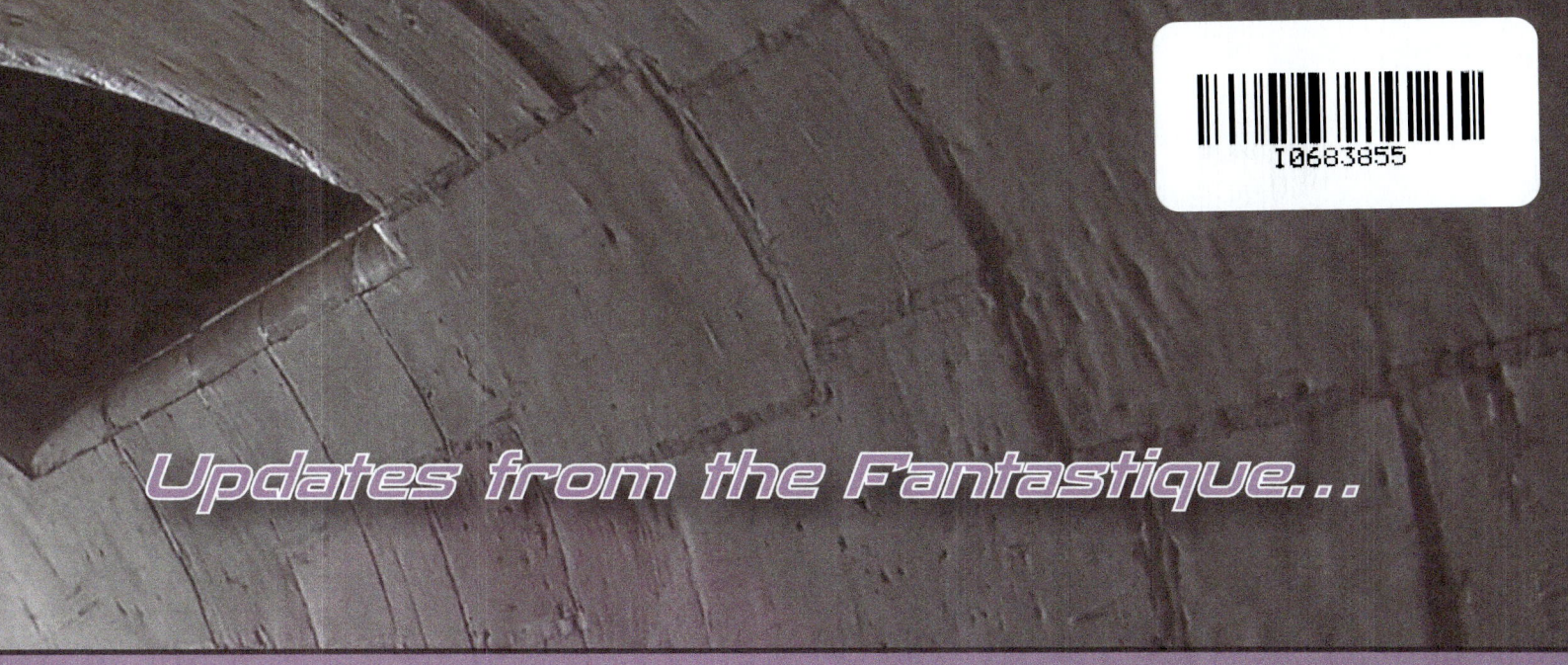

# Updates from the Fantastique...

some of the more metaphysical aspects of the Transhuman concept, while the stories elevate the idea to brand new heights of imagination.

Versatile science fiction, fantasy and horror author Lisa Tuttle gives us a glimpse into the terrors that transhumanism offers to future femininity, in bizarre and unnatural ways; Nebula Award-Winning science fiction writer Gregory Benford shines the theme of this issue through an extraterrestrial lens; Paul Di Filippo describes an unlikely job occupation in the future, and the strange creatures that go along with it; R.B. Payne presents an action-packed transhumanist version of *The Fast and the Furious* genre; the virtual gaming world is transformed into a terrifying and violent reality in John Shirley's inclusion; and finally, John C. Wright draws the theme into the age-old battle between the powers of good and evil—in this case, the technological advances of science vs. the illuminating qualities of spirituality.

On the nonfiction side, we have a wonderful article by Mike Lester on Hubbard, Parsons, and Scientology, and two pieces on the phenomenon of transhumanism by myself and scholar Egil Asprem. These latter two articles do included some overlap, but I think you will find that they complement each other nicely, and together offer a well-rounded perspective on the implications of transhumanism.

John Palisano gives us an entertaining recap of the 2015 World Horror Convention and Stoker awards ceremony. There are new interviews with Neil Clarke and Paul Di Filippo, and plus we have an intimate virtual fireside chat with best-selling science fiction writer and futurist David Brin. We return with our "Horror in a Hundred Stories" feature, three short pieces of horror fiction chosen out of a hundred submissions and selected from our Hellnotes community. And the Transhuman is explored by our usual stable of columnists including Donald Tyson whose column Murmurs in the Dark evaluates the enhancement theme through Mary Shelley's classic novel *Frankenstein*.

So, are you ready to see what it's all about? Jetpack your way through the pages that follow, but be sure not to lose your humanity...

—Aaron J. French
Editor-in-Chief

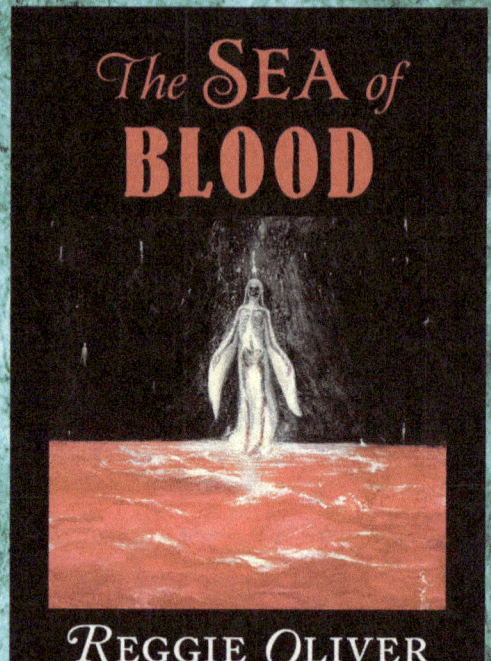
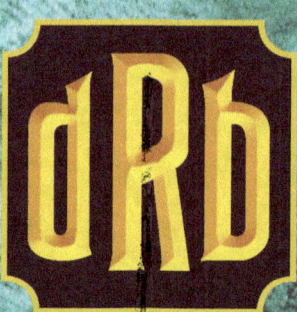
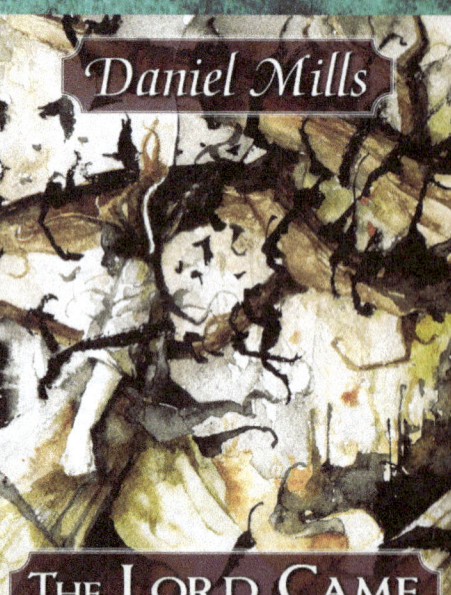

# DARK DISCOVERIES

Spring 2015, Issue Number 31, www.DarkDiscoveries.com

**Publisher**
JournalStone Publishing, LLC

**Editor-in-Chief and Art Director**
Aaron J. French

**Contributing Editor**
K. H. Vaughan

**Assistant Editors**
Nancy Kalanta (Reviews Editor)
Russ Thompson (Senior Submissions Editor)
Stuart Conover (Assistant Reviews Editor)

**Layout and Design**
Paul Fry

**Contributors**

Lisa Tuttle
Gregory Benford
Paul Di Filippo
R.B. Payne
John Shirley
John C. Wright
Mike Lester
David Brin
Neil Clarke
Aaron J. French
Nelli Kowalik
(Cover Model)

Bizarro Pulp Press
T. Chris Martindale
K. H. Vaughan
Egil Asprem
Robert Morrish
Yvonne Navarro
Richard Dansky
Michael R. Collings
Aaron J. French
Leah Jung
Donald Tyson
John Palisano

**Founding Publisher and Editor**
James R. Beach

**Special Thanks**

Mike Lester
Egil Asprem
David Brin
Nelli Kowalik

Neil Clarke
T. Chris Martindale
Leah Jung

**Contributing Artists/Photographers**
Bradley Thornber (Cover Photographer)
Steve Santiago (pg 5 & 21)
Greg Chapman (pg 49 & 65)
Luke Spooner (pg 33 & 81)
John Palisano
Cecile Grimm-Cabeen

---

**DARK DISCOVERIES**
(ISSN 1548-6842) is published (Qtrly) by
JournalStone Publications
439 Gateway Dr., #83, Pacifica, CA 94044

**Christopher C. Payne**
**JournalStone Publications**
**439 Gateway Dr., #83, Pacifica, CA 94044, U.S.A.**
**christophercpayne@journalstone.com.**

Please make check or money order payable to: JournalStone Publishing and send to the address above. Credit/Debit cards via Paypal at: **christophercpayne@journalstone.com.** Advertising rates available. Discounts for bulk and standing retail orders.

## FICTION

| | |
|---|---|
| Dissecting the Alien by Gregory Benford | 05 |
| 2-Dava by Lisa Tuttle | 21 |
| That Part of the Brain by John Shirley | 33 |
| The Herple is a Happy Beast, or, "Neighbors are Delicious!" by Paul Di Filippo | 49 |
| Spark by R.B. Payne | 65 |
| The Scepter of Nowhere by John C. Wright | 81 |

## FEATURES

| | |
|---|---|
| "A Virtual Fireside Chat with David Brin: Intelligent Aliens and What it Means to be Human" | 17 |
| "Hubbard and Parsons—Spiritual Machines: A Brief Introduction" by Mike Lester | 31 |
| "Introduction to Bizarro" by Bizarro Pulp Press | 40 |
| "A Conversation with Paul Di Filippo" by K. H. Vaughan | 43 |
| Horror in a Hundred Stories | 57 |
| "The Magus of Silicon Valley: Ray Kurzweil's Transhumanism as Contemporary Esotericism" by Egil Asprem | 59 |
| "Trans-Beauty: An Interview with Nelli Kowalik" by Leah Jung | 71 |
| "The Future Event of Global Transcendence" by Aaron J. French | 78 |
| "The World of Neil Clarke" by K. H. Vaughan | 89 |
| "World Horror Convention 2015 Wrap-Up" by John Palisano | 95 |

## COLUMNS

| | |
|---|---|
| Murmurs in the Dark: "Frankenstein Transcendent" by Donald Tyson | 14 |
| Double X Chromosome: "Metawoman" by Yvonne Navarro | 27 |
| "What the Hell Ever Happened to…T. Chris Martindale" by Robert Morrish | 74 |
| "What Makes Not-So-Good Horror…Not So Good" by Michael R. Collings | 92 |
| "Transhumanism and Video Games" by Richard Dansky | 100 |

## REVIEWS

| | |
|---|---|
| Hellnotes/Horror World Reviews | 103 |

# Editorial

reetings, Earthlings, and welcome to the newest issue of *Dark Discoveries*. This time around, our theme is Transhuman; while this is, in effect, our sci-fi issue, rest assured it is dark sci-fi. Transhuman explores what it means to go beyond being human, whether into realms of the extraterrestrial, the cybernetic, the virtual landscape, or the artificially intelligent machines. The theme is inspired by the recent movement known as transhumanism, which has gained in popularity over the years. Transhumanism is essentially described like this: with advancing technology, eventually the machines/computers will become smarter than human beings, so we will have no choice but to merge with technology and become cyborgs. That's transhumanism in a cybernetic nutshell.

However, with *Transhuman*—the theme of this issue—we broadened the horizon to include ideas about transhumanism but also virtual reality, A.I., aliens, spiritual scientific topics, and really anything involving technology or scientific discourse aimed at enhancing the human being to go above and beyond itself.

But is this horror? We think it is. If one of the basic ingredients of horror is encountering the unknown, then the thought of going transhuman ought to evoke immediate dread, if only for the sole fact that it points to an unknown outcome. What will it mean for human beings to become more than what we are, to become immortal, super intelligent, and virtually indestructible? Sure, a lot of good might come of this, but so will plenty of inherent opportunities for things to go horribly wrong.

Take for instance the Gray Goo Scenario, an entirely probable situation in which the nanobots injected into the human bloodstream inadvertently start self-replicating exponentially until they reduce all the matter on planet Earth to nanofied gray goo. This potential outcome has actually been posited by academics, and it was recently used for the highly successful *Wool* books and *Silo* series by Hugh Howey. And how about the Skynet scenario of the *Terminator* movies? Or *Transcendence* with Johnny Depp, where the main character, Dr. Will Caster, uploads his consciousness to a quantum computer?

These are undoubtedly works of science fiction, however the scenarios they depict for the future of human beings are truly horrifying.

The writers for this issue of *Dark Discoveries* have set out to explore these horrific and sometimes awe-inspiring potentialities for the future of humanity. They offer intelligent and disquieting glimpses at the nature of being human, and where we all are headed in a few years' time. The articles in this issue introduce readers to, perhaps,

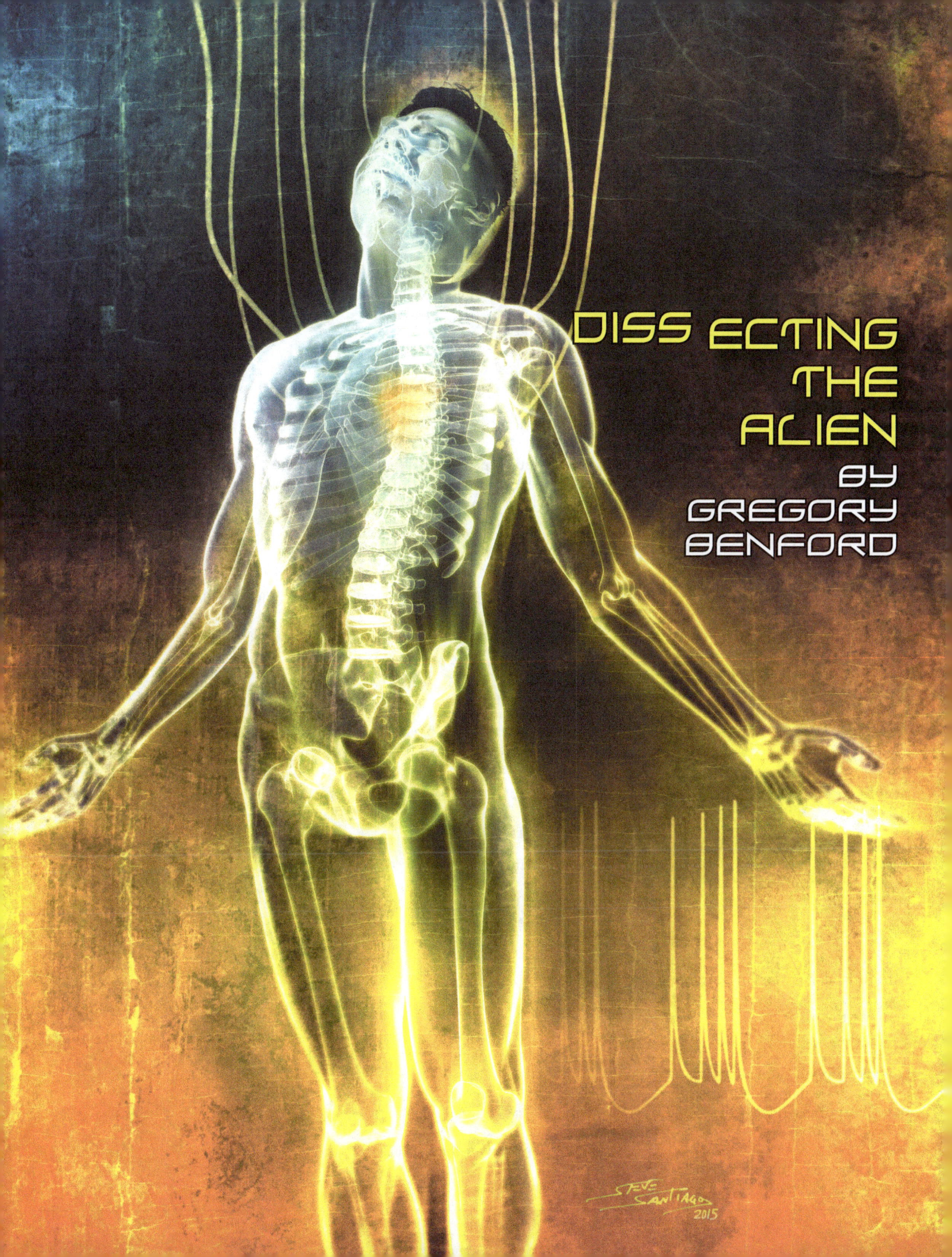

DISS ECTING THE ALIEN

BY GREGORY BENFORD

A primate, quite clearly. Hairless, pale, large head, trivial genitalia. No claws, dull teeth, essentially defenseless. The alien proved to be more surprising when taken apart.

They held it aloft. It squirmed. The two intelligences regarded it distantly. They preferred to watch it in the infrared, where the creature emitted its waste heat, but to assess it they began reading its shimmering electrical patterns first.

***

Such agitation. Yet witness,
the connections in its head
cycle only a few hundred tiny
voltage steps per second.

So slow! And they still can register real-time events. It does surprisingly well with such an affliction. Notice how it looks around so energetically.

Perhaps it had difficulty
adapting to this position?
We are suspending it upside down.

It thrashes its head around because its eyes are all on one side of the head. So much energy, just to see. A curious choice of construction.

Look! It is using pattern matching
to scan its surroundings. It makes
a standard picture. Odd!

I can measure the data-flow. The brain processor is strongly linked to the eyes, so several times in each second it compares what it is seeing with a standard image it remembers.

If I move quickly—yes, see?
It picks the best matching pattern,
estimates possible danger. That tells
it what response-script to follow.

How governed it is by past experience! It keeps twitching as though it could get away.

Apparently in the past it *did*
escape that way. Look at all the
bone and muscle devoted to locomotion.
Is it used to being picked up
and dangled?

No—so it redoubles its effort if the situation is unusual. I register high chemical levels squirting into the blood stream. See, they affect brain performance.

More programming from its past.
It seems to want to run away.

Its legs certainly do.

Here, I will put it rightside up.

Confirmed! It tries to run.

Slow learner. It cannot outrun us.

But that must have worked for it in the past, you see. It has no other immediate strategy.

No wonder. Gaze upon the neural
firings in the upper brain. (Curious,
putting all the most important networks
on top, where impact will most likely
injure them.)

Such slow circuits! Artful patterns, though. It is learning only a few data-droplets per second. Only $10^7$ in one of its years!

So it simply cannot reason out a
fresh strategy for dealing with us
in short times. It lacks the
computational speed.

Now it waves its arms.

Non-random, though. Simple
symbols, I suspect.

Of a very simple sort.

'Primitive' is a better word.
Notice how abstracting functions,
which must have evolved later, are
simply layered over the older areas
in the brain.

Definitely not. It knows very
little of what goes on in its mind.

All the rest must be a mystery
to it. See, down below it is
digesting some crude chemical
food—but does not think about
the act at all.

Trace this spray of winking light
in the head.

I see. Down below, in the
under-brain, now coming up
to its limited awareness.

That is how ideas come to it?
A surprise.

How confusing, to never know
what is going on inside yourself.

They find out what they think
by speaking?

What a long word this is.

Meanwhile I see below its
top-brain the motor muscle
commands are—caution!

Retain it for inspection. The creature
became very excited—see the gaudy
streamers of thought-webs!

Or controlling it.

This poor thing has been hampered
all through its evolution by these
pitifully torpid synapses. They are
a million times slower than ours!

Do not try to manufacture beauty

That shows forward-seeing, adaptive behavior.

Promising. Its brain is made of organic compounds entirely. So-called 'natural' development.

The entire brain design is retro-fitted! Surely this thing is not truly conscious.

Watch the flashing patterns. It senses only what occurs in the very topmost layer of its brain.

It does not even know that it is mixing acids and massaging the bolus.

Neurons firing. It is framing a new idea.

Now the idea erupts into the over-brain. Spreads. Pretty, in a way.

Whereas to us, it is more like fog condensing.

They speak the same way. Series of sounds emitted acoustically, without their knowing what they will say.

Access its acoustic emissions! It is stringing together bursts—"words"—to deal with us.

That is a scream, actually.

There! I caught the weapon. A simple chemical-discharge type. Amusing, the presumption.

Nearly all below the over-brain, so it does not truly know that it is feeling them. Yet the thoughts cause organs to squirt chemicals into the blood. What a curious way of talking to yourself. Not sensing it directly.

It still wriggles in our grasp. What slow neurons!

But beautiful, in their serene way.

out of mere necessity.

Clearly these sluggish neurons forced such creatures to use parallel distributed processing.

See it dance! Is that "anger?"

Similar patterns, I see. Confirmation—they run in parallel.

See, while it believes it is thinking about getting away from us—

What pleasure-fiends they are.

They do everything at once, that is their secret. The same brain cell can be idea-making and at the same time, helping it digest food. How difficult!

All with the same cells, tied together.

I am amazed that the tiny thing can concurrently walk and talk.

So ungainly! Even a sentimentalist like you will have to admit that.

Then head on the floor!

A risky one. Most sensible animals use four feet. We, of course, employ six.

I believe I understand this curious method of parallel distributed thinking. Notice that when a brain cell dies—see there, a feeble light just winked out—their internal computation still goes on.

But it also does not know it is losing brain cells.

This parallel thinking masks so much and—look out!

This design was *necessary*?

How horrible.

Apparently. Their literature speaks of such a response. They do it often. See, "anger" is coded much like those orange-white filigrees now spreading through its mid-brain.

Watch it try to have a new idea! See, they decide what to think by adding up many thousands of brain cell triggers. And those same brain cells are at the same time tied up in other parallel problems.

Yes!—a small submind is meditating upon a sexual adventure it had, quite some time ago. And the submind enjoys its recallings.

I wonder that they can get anything done at all.

Meanwhile, other decisions are trying to get made. They have to wait in line!

Incredible!

Simultaneously, yes—but not very well.

True. Delicate neural circuits atop the head. Feet go forward, it starts to fall, then catches itself with the other foot. What if it did not?

What a movement strategy.

Notice how afraid it is of falling. It devotes much brain space to avoiding that.

You are right! See, this anger-reflex is fading, turning blue, seeping down into the circuits which control its digestion. A cell dies, but the pattern-flow continues. So the creature is usefully redundant.

No point in that, I suppose. This unfortunate being cannot replace the cells anyway. Poor design.

They *are* quick at some things. Its armored feet are powerful.

Are you damaged?

Actual physical damage! How quaint. I have
never seen it before.

I doubt that they can even
read us.

Dramatic! Frustration seizes the
entire brain, so that it cannot
think of anything else.

I gather that most of its brain
has no choice but to go along.

Apparently. Torn by emotion.

Ah! It injures me, too.

Thanks be to you. It ripped away
my microwave antenna.

How could you? It did not know
itself until a fractional moment ago.

You mean, when they do not grasp
themselves the reasons for their
own actions?

No, I believe it thinks that
*it* is the ruler.

And it cannot choose to stop
the spreading. Or the chemicals
that the web makes spurt into the
body.

You mean they do not even know
why we are destroying them?

There is some small truth in that.
We machines need mass and energy.
But we avoid frothy organic life
forms such as this creature.

They are so liquid, and shot
through with desires.

They embrace the process.
They *pleasure* in it.

But such strategies designed

Only temporarily. My inboards will refashion a patch of my carapace.

Apparently they cannot directly attack our circuits.

Look how frustration-webs spread through it. Down to the very base
of the brain.

And other parts of its brain do not know how the decision was made
to *be* frustrated.

It lives that way all the time?

Most of what it decides, the rest of it cannot know! Emotions must
appear to govern its actions without obvious cause. Oh, look—

I shall seize it afresh.

I should have detected its plans.

I am beginning to understand the data files we captured. The term
"free will" must refer to this method of thinking.

That must be it. This little thing believes it has an inner self which
directs its actions—a ruler it cannot see directly.

Of course, you are right. But it cannot govern itself. See, its frustration-
web spreads anew.

I doubt that we should regard such an odd construction as truly
conscious.

No doubt they have a theory. Probably that evolution makes all life
compete for resources.

Indeed. Poor company at best.

Far down in this one, a sub-program keeps thinking of reproduction.

Evolution programs them to.

for living on planetary surfaces do not work in the long run. They will outstrip their resources.

So that is why they struggle so!

Now I see why you wanted to study these. What a fate they face!

If they cannot read themselves, *to* themselves...

This creature is trapped forever within a single brain.

So if this one—oh!

*Eiii.*

Lock-web it!

Momentarily. I have blocked that area now. What a vicious little thing.

Because they cannot self-copy?

Death makes them hurt others?

They cannot fabricate backups. I wonder what it is to live that way. To...die that way.

All of it? All these messy chemicals held together by carbon and calcium?

They salvage it all because they know only "This is Jocelyn?"

The name of this mite. Since they cannot directly read each other, either, they need tags.

Incredible, yes.

Watch it—the creature has fashioned a fresh weapon.

So fast, it is.

Augh!

Got it. Are you damaged further?

I can see your damage from here. Vexing.

It still emits acoustically.

Nature compensates. This tilt-walker vertebrate has a very short life span.

True, they have little to lose. They will be dead soon anyway.

See their dilemma?

They cannot copy themselves.

No copying, if this unit runs down.

Irksome, no? Here, I constrain it further.

Pesky—

Did it pain you?

They gain their fervor from their mortality.

It is the way of all flesh.

You miss a point. To avoid death they do what they must.

Since they cannot read their internal states, to save themselves they must therefore save their structure.

At least the head. They may be fond of the rest as well.

"Jocelyn?"

One word to describe a self?

How do they converse, then?

Ah! It burned my receptors down one whole side. Get it!

Even its acoustic cries injure. So loud, it is.

Evolution has much to answer for.

I will have to get outside service.

Troublesome. And with these jobs, it is not the parts, it is the labor.

Painfully.

Listen—bleeps and jots in
acoustic wave packets. Cries
for help?

You wax rhapsodic over these
crude blurts?

So coarse.

Obviously they have that backward
as well. Their talk is serial,
their thinking parallel. Nature is
a witless inventor.

So free of nuance. Where is the
cross-talk all intelligence requires?

I have read a slab of perception
from it, rather interesting.
Catch this data-group:

Exactly. They see in a narrow
little region of the electromagnetic.

They were designed by chance for
a specific environment and cannot
escape from that programming.

And about as predictable. No,
I fear they cannot be re-
engineered. Too clumsy.

Well, you must admit that is a
conspicuously dangerous strategy.
More pointless redundancy, like
their thinking patterns.

Yes yes, you could rebuild them.
But equally well, that copy can
be damaged by its surroundings.
Then you would copy a mistake.

Here, grasp the creature again.

Mortality lends energy, I suppose
Here—a slice.

Piled on top of each other.

I doubt that they do it often.
Probably evolution prefers to

And pitifully narrow-band.

The song of the genes.

Listen! Serial confabulation—so strange.

We know that thinking must be serial. But—connection? *Serially*?

Listen: their codes are so linear. Straight little sentences. Guileless.

This must make them grasp their world in a fashion utterly differently
from us.

Received, digested. They at least clasp visual pictures in parallel, I see.
But what a curious, stunted view.

A squeezed single octave in the optical range.

Surely a little tinkering? Look how it prowls the confines we have set
for it. Impatient to get out. Its neurons flare with plans, ideas, fitful
flashes that come and go like weather.

You are biased against them because they carry their complete
instructions with them.

In every cell they hold a set of their individual design plans. So from
any one tiny fragment—

Admittedly, a flaw. I am happy my own copy is safely stored, not
dangling out here in the fearsome naturalness of it all.

Ah! It struggles so.

Tubes, motors, pumps—all squeezed together.

Every one different shapes and sizes. No common specifications. How
difficult they must be to repair.

build another one instead.

Growing a fresh copy, perhaps whenever they feel threatened?

Like plants.

"Growing." It must feel like bursting open.

I wonder if we could experience it. That would be a new stimulation.

Certainly that would make even thinking exciting. One would never know what one would discover next, even about oneself.

You mean, that our exposure of every thought to scrutiny is *bad*?

That would imply that our method of selfhood itself...

I find my own tapestry of thought quite lacy enough.

Foolishness. That would imply that such creatures would be inherently capable of more subtle strategies than we.

Careful. We have partially disassembled it. Primitives tend to dislike such activity.

Augh!

Pain, pain.

So much...

It was...

You are mobile?

I have lost many endpoints.

What could motivate such a tiny being to destroy itself, all to render damage to us?

I saw no clue to this.

Ah, their reproduction obsession. They use the plans they carry around in every cell.

They make a small one and then it enlarges from the inside out.

True, but a little smarter.

Do you suppose? How...horrible.

So would it be to comprehend this odd kind of stunted consciousness they employ. Can it be *better* to keep part of yourself secret from another part?

Do you suppose that is how they have done so well, despite such terrible limitations?

Could it be? These creatures seem to be inventive, creative...

Evaporates the fine-grained delicacy of a new concept, beneath a constant, lacerating inspection? ...That could be why we have fresh thoughts so rarely.

As do I. But not this fall-walker, I suspect.

Look. It is beckoning us to draw nearer.

I think discourse with such an enchantingly primitive and swampy mind would be a boon. We could copy its colloquy and transmit to the multitude, who would be—

Ah!

I must shut down my peripherals—

Damage, I am injured everywhere.

...a trap. All along.

I fear not.

I too.

Something you said...earlier.

And would cancel themselves entirely to do us harm? When we shall simply live on in our archive copies?

They believe in something beyond selfhood?

If we cannot soon get aid—

I suppose that is some consolation.

Perhaps it had something more?

Short life span. That is why...they struggle so.

Something about this species...

And we, who have copies safely stored, do not.

Our copies will be activated.

The little creature did not have even that.

What could that be? What could that be?

Beside them lay the finespun latticework of calcium rods that had been a rib cage. They sprawled amid meat and mess.

The shattered creature seemed to still embody a secret the dying aliens struggled to grasp.

Structures unraveled. Currents ran down.

On the barren plain only a single plaintive voice now called.

*What could that be? What could that be?*

"Obsessively dark and razorous, these graphic takes on life, faith, illusion and self-delusion open paths where you need to watch your step."
 – Tanith Lee, recipient of 2013 World Fantasy Life Achievement Award

"Aaron J. French leads his readers on dark and dangerous journeys, where the destination is never sure."
 Storm Constantine, author of the *Wraeththu* books

Aaron J. French

ABERRATIONS of REALITY

Available now in Hardcover, Paperback, and Digital formats

*www.crowdedquarantine.co.uk*

FRANKENSTEIN;

OR,

THE MODERN PROMETHEUS.

IN THREE VOLUMES.

Did I request thee, Maker, from my clay
To mould me man? Did I solicit thee
From darkness to promote me?——
PARADISE LOST.

VOL. I.

London:
PRINTED FOR
LACKINGTON, HUGHES, HARDING, MAVOR, & JONES,
FINSBURY SQUARE.

1818.

## MURMURS IN THE DARK:
# FRANKENSTEIN TRANSCENDENT

## BY DONALD TYSON

What was it that drove Victor Frankenstein, the main character of Mary Shelley's 1818 novel *Frankenstein, or the Modern Prometheus*, out of the well traveled throughways of conventional medicine to create a grotesque, stumbling monster that in the end destroyed his life? It cannot have been mere curiosity. Scientific curiosity is not strong enough to make a man cast off all of the conventions of his social class and religion to become an outcast, a freak, a pariah from his own kind. No, Frankenstein was driven by a devouring need to exceed the ultimate limit of the human species, a need to transcend death itself and endow mankind with immortality.

This irresistible need had its roots in his childhood, when Victor discovered and studied the occult philosophy of Cornelius Agrippa, Albertus Magnus, and Paracelsus. As he himself declared, "I read and studied the wild fancies of these writers with delight; they appeared to me treasures known to few besides myself. I have described myself as always having been imbued with a fervent longing to penetrate the secrets of nature."

All three men wrote about magic and alchemy, which were regarded in some quarters as the lost wisdom of the ancient world. Frankenstein became obsessed with the discovery of one of the two greatest goals of the alchemist, the elixir of life. The other goal is, of course, the

philosopher's stone that turns base metal into gold, but Frankenstein had no interest in riches.

When he went to university, the forward-looking professors of natural philosophy mocked his study of alchemy, and for a brief time he repudiated it, uncertain which path to pursue, but in the end he decided to combine the old with the modern and to make an entirely new path for himself. "So much has been done, exclaimed the soul of Frankenstein—more, far more, will I achieve; treading in the steps already marked, I will pioneer a new way, explore unknown powers, and unfold to the world the deepest mysteries of creation."

To be human is to be mortal. To be mortal is to die. To transcend humanity is to transcend death. This obsession drove Frankenstein to assemble his own version of a human being out of bits and parts he scrounged from dissection tables and slaughter houses. Because the human body is so finely detailed, Frankenstein was forced to construct his transhuman as a giant eight feet tall. This made it easier for him to work with the smaller nerves, vessels and other parts he stitched together.

Using some method of vitalizing his piecework gigantic corpse that is not explicitly described in the novel, Frankenstein galvanized it into a semblance of life. Its strength was prodigious, its endurance endless, its flesh immune from cold and virtually indestructible, but the question arose as to whether its motives were really human, or something other than human. In seeking to construct a man who was more than human, Victor Frankenstein began to suspect that he had created something less than human in those ways that matter the most—less in empathy for others, less in compassion, less in understanding and forgiveness.

The question naturally arises, can a man put together from the parts of corpses be said to have a soul of his own? Of course it is easy to dismiss this question merely by denying the existence of the soul. But call it what you will, a question remains. Is the essential being of such a creature a composite of the essences of the living men from whom its parts were taken? Is it completely new and original, divorced from the essences of those parts? Or, is this creature lacking something entirely that those who contributed to its body possessed during their lives?

The creature certainly was not lacking in intelligence. It taught itself to read. It learned how to conceal itself, to find food and shelter while living alone, and how to function on the boundary of human society, where it observed the lives of human beings. Stronger, more enduring, arguably more intelligent, was there anything the creature lacked that its creator had to a superior degree? The creature itself would have denied it.

One human drive was shared by Frankenstein's monster, the drive to live and to extend itself into the future through its offspring. The creature demanded of its creator that he construct a woman to be its mate. This, Frankenstein agreed to do, but the horror of what he might be unleashing upon the world caused him to destroy the female thing he was making before it was animated.

It is evident in the novel that the monster is seeking to transcend humanity by becoming the Adam of an entirely new race of intelligent beings. Indeed, Mary Shelley has the creature refer to itself as "Adam" so that this aspect of her story will not be missed by her readers. We can only speculate as to whether the new race would have lived in peace and harmony with human beings, but given the violent tendencies of the creature, this seems unlikely. In a war between the species, man would stand little chance against foes so cunning and so powerful.

The fatal flaw in the creature's intention was its dependence on Victor Frankenstein, without whose advanced scientific methods the new race of supermen and superwomen could not be brought into being. When Frankenstein refused to betray the human race merely to save his own life, he exhibited the selflessness of the human soul that the creature he created lacked. Denied its Eve, the new Adam saw no recourse other than to seek vengeance on its creator, by murdering those he loved and making him suffer.

At the end of the book the creature falls into a fit of remorse when it learns of the death of its creator. It voices its intention to burn itself alive on a funeral pyre and wanders away into the frozen waste of the Arctic. The reader does not actually get confirmation of its death. We do not know for certain that fire would kill the monster, or that it even had the will to attempt to kill itself. The fate of the monster is left open.

Most people today are familiar with the 1931 film version of Frankenstein's monster. This differs somewhat from the monster in the novel. In the film, the monster is larger than human-sized, but not much larger—it is a good deal less than eight feet tall. It is still grotesquely ugly due to its piecemeal construction from the salvaged parts of numerous corpses, and both scars and metal staples are visible on its head. Unlike the monster in the novel, it cannot talk.

In the film, we are relieved of the quandary over the creature's moral nature by the insertion, into the skull of the monster, of a brain that is criminal and abnormal. We don't need to wonder, as we do in the novel, if the soul of such a monster could be as compassionate or as loving as a normal human soul. We never get a chance to even pose the question, because almost from the first the criminal brain of the creature asserts its violent and malicious tendencies.

The movie monster is galvanized into life by lightning drawn down from the heavens. This was a brilliant concept on the part of the movie makers. Not only is it symbolically powerful, it also makes for spectacular visuals. The lightning is channelled into the monster by means of a set of intricate machines. These represent the ascendancy of science over nature. In the film version of the story, the scientific aspect, or one might almost say the engineering aspect, of the process of giving dead flesh new life is brought to center stage, and its alchemical aspect forgotten. The one part of the monster not cobbled from corpses are the massive electrodes that protrude from the sides of its neck. They represent the human-machine interface, and resemble more than anything else the poles

allow."

This sentiment was echoed by the writer H. P. Lovecraft in the opening paragraph of his story, "The Call of Cthulhu," where he wrote:

> The most merciful thing in the world, I think, is the inability of the human mind to correlate all its contents. We live on a placid island of ignorance in the midst of black seas of infinity, and it was not meant that we should voyage far. The sciences, each straining in its own direction, have hitherto harmed us little; but some day the piecing together of dissociated knowledge will open up such terrifying vistas of reality, and of our frightful position therein, that we shall either go mad from the revelation or flee from the light into the peace and safety of a new dark age.

This is the theme of the biblical story of the fall of Adam and Eve from the Garden of Eden, and as such is one of the most ancient and most primal of cautionary wisdom teachings of our race. The boundaries that must not be transgressed are explicitly set forth by God. The Serpent enticed Eve to transgress those boundaries, and she in turn enticed Adam. The consequences are horrifying in the conventional Judaeo-Christian interpretation of the story. But there is another interpretation, a Gnostic interpretation, in which the expulsion from the Garden of Eden is seen as the liberation from a prison of ignorance.

The modern reader and movie-goer does not understand the ancient concept of hubris, and does not believe in the existence of the gods, or of a God. He has no patience for boundaries. Like Victor Frankenstein before his unhappy realization of what he had accomplished, he wants only more and more and more, with no thought to how much is too much. Scientists promise us artificial intelligence, weather modification, extended life, the preservation of consciousness on computer chips. Indeed, they promise us the very stars themselves, and never does the question of hubris rear its ancient, hoary head.

Is the novel *Frankenstein* a promise and a foreshadowing of the brave new world that is to come, where we will all be made deathless and given bodies free of fatigue and sickness and infirmity, perhaps at the expense of our beauty, our grace, our humanity? Or is it a dire warning of the consequences of hubris—rash defiance of the boundaries set by God and Nature over the reach of mankind?

Will artificial intelligence supplant and replace us? Will the creatures we craft from dead things and animate with stolen celestial fire look down at us with contempt and despise us for our weakness and the brevity of our lives? Or will we merge with them and elevate ourselves to the stars? Only the future will provide the answer, but from the past we have the dire warnings of Mary Shelley, H. P. Lovecraft, and others to remind us that when our reach exceeds our grasp, we fall.

of a car battery.

The fire of the gods, the lightning bolts of Zeus, give the movie monster superhuman strength, superhuman endurance, and (it is implied) eternal life. It has literally stolen the vitality of the gods from heaven. However, the monster is hindered by its criminal brain, which is defective from the beginning and can never be made right. We get the sense from the movies that if only the monster had received a normal human brain, it would have been a compassionate, loving creature. This is not at all certain from what we are told in Shelley's novel. In the novel there is nothing wrong with the brain, but even so, the malice of the creature comes to the forefront and dictates its actions.

For the hubris of stealing life from death, of bringing down the vitalizing force of heaven to the earth, both the monster and its creator are punished. In a way, the story of Frankenstein is a kind of Greek tragedy. Victor Frankenstein is the modern Prometheus mentioned in the novel's subtitle, who for the affront of stealing the fire of the gods is condemned to eternal torment.

Frankenstein's fate was sealed the moment he dared to attempt to usurp nature. *For there are things man was not meant to know.* This is a common theme of early horror and science fiction movies. There are bounds man must not transgress, and secrets he is not permitted to learn, or use.

In her novel, Mary Shelley puts these words into the mouth of Victor Frankenstein: "Learn from me, if not by my precepts, at least by my example, how dangerous is the acquirement of knowledge and how much happier that man is who believes his native town to be the world, than he who aspires to become greater than his nature will

# A Virtual Fireside Chat with David Brin: Intelligent Aliens and What it Means to be Human

Photo courtesy of David Brin

**Do you believe that there are alien civilizations in the universe—or do you think we are alone?**

**DB**: Other worlds and aliens have long been story topics, first on the pages of science fiction pulp magazines from the thirties and forties, then more insightful explorations by Arthur C. Clarke, Ray Bradbury, Robert Heinlein and others—all the way to new generations, including my own novels.

I've been involved on the scientific side of this topic, SETI—The Search for Extraterrestrial Intelligence—studying what's commonly called the *Great Silence* or the *Fermi Paradox*. Why have radio astronomers detected no signs of extraterrestrial civilizations in the cosmos?

Let's dismiss from the start the popular notion of UFOs. If there *are* silvery guys coming down to disembowel cattle and kidnap farmers, they're still not 'intelligent life'—just look at their behavior. It's exactly the same meddling-mysterious bullying you see in the mythologies of old human tribes. Only, instead of outer space, they were from the deep wood. Instead of aliens, they were demons and elves.

But let's go back even further. For two billion years, our planet was prime real estate—ever since microbes made earth's atmosphere oxygen-rich, with nothing more than slime mold to defend the planet! Nothing to stand in the way of ET colonists. Yet, there are no signs, in the rocks, of ancient cities—nor any of the biological changes that would have come from colonization. One spilled alien toilet or dropped coke bottle…and we would see the signs today, all over the globe. It never happened, across two billion years.

And the puzzles continue. For decades, the SETI program has been searching for alien signals, and we've already eliminated one scenario—that advanced aliens would beneficently beam vast tutorial beacons to help us youngsters along. Those beacons, which pioneers like Carl Sagan and Frank Drake expected to find, simply aren't there! Nor do we see any traces of Dyson spheres or the dross from fusion power plants or any of the great works that we hope and expect our own descendants to produce.

That doesn't mean the galaxy is devoid of advanced civilizations. Indeed, the matrix of possibility includes a hundred or more hypothetical explanations for the Great Silence, ranging from some that are preposterous-but-not-impossible, through many that are merely improbable…to about a dozen that make some real sense.

What's not justified is leaping to conclusions. In fact, we still have very little to go on.

**So let's say that we find no signs of extraterrestrial life. Could it be that we're alone?**

**DB**: There's a tendency among all the bright minds who get involved in SETI to pick one single explanation—and declare that this is the reason for the silence. Perhaps Earth-like planets are rare. (That one seems about to topple, as we discover thousands of exoplanets, many of them almost Earthlike.) Or life is difficult to get started. Or intelligence rarely evolves—or becomes extinct at some point in the development of technology.

Or perhaps…the internet will evolve into such an addictive honeypot that we'll all get implants and remain plugged into a virtual world. Augmented life will be so god-like that no one will want to explore the universe. And yet…

…and yet in this business, one of the top things to

remember is that *the exceptions make the rules*. And there will always be exceptions. Even if 99.999% of humans become these cyber-gods, there will still be those, i.e. the Hell's Angels, who will have the urge to explore, build starships, set out, reproduce, and pass on that trait. Those exceptions alone would fill the galaxy. Calculations show they could do this in a mere sixty million years. An eyeblink.

**What are some other bottlenecks that might cause the Great Silence?**

**DB**: One that's in my top ten...*strong intelligence, capable of radio and/or starships may be rare.*

Oh, some degree of sapience does seem to come fairly naturally. Indeed, what about dolphins, apes, sea lions, crows, parrots—who show signs of linguistic ability and problem solving savvy? So many—even prairie dogs! It seems Mother Nature and/or Darwin are generous...up to a point.

On the other hand, they all seem to crowd against the same upper limit—a glass ceiling that none has ever broken through—except us. And we blasted through, by miles. Could we be a fluke?

(This is the basis for my speculations about "uplift" or giving the gift of full sapience to other species. In addition to novels like *Startide*, I gave a TED style presentation about this, at the Smithsonian.)

Want another? Our Earth skates the very inner edge of the sun's "goldilocks zone," which explains why just a smidgeon of extra greenhouse gas can cause such problems. Might this make Earth *unusually dry* for a water world, with more continental land mass? Then most abodes of life could have smart squid, dolphins and such, but very few capable of smelting metal into starships.

**But what if there truly is no alien life to be found?**

**DB**: If there's no alien life anywhere in this vast universe, then I would have to say that we're living in a simulation or an intelligent creation. Because in my opinion, the odds of there being no other lifeforms in a *randomly evolved universe* are virtually nil.

If we're totally alone in the cosmos, then the implications are *theological*. And our simulation's creators wanted to save on processing power by leaving aliens out of it.

It also implies that the galaxy has only one chance to fill with intelligence, and that had better be us going out there. It puts an even greater burden on us to make civilization succeed.

**But suppose that we do make contact, what happens to our civilization at that point?**

**DB**: One of the great dangers—and one reason why *they*

might keep humanity isolated in a zoo—is that as soon as we meet an advanced alien civilization, our unique human culture will be effectively over. We have seen this from examples of First Contact all across human history. Maybe they are keeping us isolated to find out what we can and will become.

That doesn't make their position morally right! But I parse this down to a dozen *hard questions for alien lurkers*, as just one of a zillion little side-items in my novel *Existence*. (Have a look at the amazing video preview-trailer for Existence on YouTube.)

**Is the public getting a clear view of all of this?**

**DB**: Well, better than before. Movies like *Contact* and shows like *The Universe* expose millions to many of these ideas.

Still, there are so many things kept shallow...like the widely held notion that ET will already have watched "I love Lucy" by now. It's not true. Even when Earth was noisiest, in the 1980s, it all faded to static by 1 light year out.

Indeed, SETI has become a pawn in the Culture Wars. There's a truly stunning piece of drivel in the Wall Street Journal. One Eric Metaxas argues that the Fermi Paradox—the absence of any evidence (so far) of extraterrestrial civilizations—means there "must be a God." Quoth he: *"As our knowledge of the universe increased, it became clear that there were far more factors necessary for life than Sagan supposed. His two parameters grew to 10 and then 20 and then 50, then 200, and so the number of potentially life-supporting*

DAVID BRIN

EXISTENCE

"Grand-scale SF . . . A tale that challenges the definition of humanity, the purpose of life, and the mystery of existence."—*Library Journal* (starred review)

A NOVEL

DAVID BRIN

KILN PEOPLE

"Intricate plotting, unflagging inventiveness, and a judicious sprinkling of puns and in-jokes: Brin keeps the pages feverishly turning."
*Kirkus Reviews*

whole lot bigger, more curious and more ambitious than the philosophy clung to by claustrophilic, narrow-minded Kindergarteners, terrified of the vastness of actual Creation.

**Let's turn our attention back to humanity—and the question of what makes us unique—our consciousness. You must have thought deeply about this question of personal identity.**

**DB**: Not as deeply as when I was eight. That sort of issue so boggled me that, like many people, I had to form calluses over it. One can't help looking in the mirror, asking, "What exactly am I looking at? What is this consciousness, this sense of self that I have?" Our intense emotions and internal drama that gives us our sense of subjective reality, as Plato and other philosophers talked about. You could speculate that evolution rewarded those

*planets decreased accordingly. The number dropped to a few thousand planets and kept on plummeting."*

Given that the article offers no citations, it is hard to trace what he means by "parameters" for life to develop. But as someone who has been immersed in this field for 35 years, I have to say that he must have pulled such a number out of thin air…or somewhere else.

In fact, every year the conditions for life in the universe seem *more* prevalent. Today scientists no longer believe you even need an Earth-like world in a "Goldilocks Zone" (and those zones are now much wider than we previously thought). Indeed, there may be a hundred "roofed worlds" or icy moons with sub-surface oceans, like Europa, for every Earth with its waters exposed to the sky.

No, what puzzles me is a matter of basic *logic*. Like why some clearly *want* Earth to be alone in the cosmos. Somehow, they have convinced themselves that a vast universe of quadrillions of stars and planets is somehow better and more reflective of a great and creative deity if…if it is entirely *sterile,* except for one teensy dust ball, floating in one obscure corner, that somehow was chosen to receive a spark granted to no other place in all of that immensity.

Let's leave out that it took the light from some of those stars billions of years to get here…

In the end, what depresses me is how immensely *insulting to God* their proposal is—that we should act all impressed with such a measly, small-minded, un-ambitious and teensy-parochial "creation!" When in fact the heavens are replete with glories suggesting that—well—*if He is out there* (and I ain't sayin'), then He/She/It is surely a

who considered their own lives to be important—if you were willing to fight to stay alive, then you were more likely to reproduce. There are so many different angles that you can look at. For instance, why do people so yearn for telepathy and other psychic phenomenon—but as a way to connect to other people, to escape the loneliness of our own mind? We can't help but wonder, "What's going on inside that other mind?" Empathy, the ability to extrapolate into somebody else's mind isn't just altruistic. Imagining what others are thinking is also a tiger's tool, a warrior's tool. You're a better warrior, a better predator if you can imagine and anticipate what another person is thinking.

The prefrontal lobes, these "lamps upon the brow" are what humans use for these thought experiments—what Einstein called the *gedankenexperiment*. They allow us to consider: "What might happen if I do this? What will be the consequences of my actions? How might that person respond?"

**You explore these ideas in your fiction.**

**DB**: Writing is more fun than pure philosophical speculation!

Consider the idea of extending the human lifespan— this usually involves adding more life linearly, tacking on more years at the end. But there's a reason why we die— to make room for our children! I suddenly realized—as I try to take on more and more roles in my own busy life— that what I really wanted was more lives in parallel! So in my novel *Kiln People*, I posit an invention that is used to create many duplicates of yourself. These are not clones—human beings who have their own rights—but temporary duplicates of yourself. A ditto who is good for only one day, who has all your memory and consciousness, who knows exactly what needs to be done that day. It goes off and does these tasks. One 'you' has to do the toilets, the shopping, all the gritty chores. But you've had days like that! Its only chance of continuity is if the 'you' in the original body chooses to download the ditto's memories of the day. If that happens, you're basically splitting up, reconverging, splitting up again. Now you have multiple days in parallel! What a dream…

But the whole notion arises of what this would do to your personality. This novel became a great thought experiment about how different personality types would respond to this opportunity. Some people would hate themselves; there are those among us who hate to look in the mirror. Who would never get along with themselves. Some who would probably kill each other. Some who would always cooperate. Some who might prefer the company of themselves to other people. There would be every range in between these extremes. It would be like a laboratory experiment in human identity.

**This reflects on the nature of human consciousness. Do we have a soul? As a science fiction author, how do you reflect on this?**

**DB**: One aspect of this quandary is the notion of the zero sum game. You don't gain unless you lose something. For instance, the common notion is that the soul is not divisible. But if you had many bodies, one might posit that the soul could be divisible…what if you could lay your template, your standing wave, into raw material, and have it be a duplicate from that moment of yourself, with the original unaffected? You could bring that standing wave back with the memories downloaded. Then we become more godlike…

**Is this a fantasy or is this theoretically possible?**

**DB**: When I'm wearing my science fiction hat, I am 90% artistically speculating, with perhaps 10% grounding in science. This merges over into other areas where I'm 90% grounded in science, with 10% speculation. In this case I'm saying… what if? In my scenario, I give my dittos total freedom; you can download your 'self' into fish-like bodies, and come back to experience what that life is like as a fish. You can launch a frozen body to space…and explore the surface of Mars.

This type of 'what if' scenario is the essence of science fiction—exploring

outside the parochial here and now that appears to be the nature of so-called mainstream literature. Science fiction embraces the concept of change, anticipating that society—and humans themselves—might change and evolve—and create a better future through our own efforts.

*** 

David Brin is an astrophysicist whose best-selling science fiction novels include *The Postman*, *Earth*, *Startide Rising* (Hugo winner), *The Uplift War* (Hugo winner), *Kiln People* and most recently *Existence*. His nonfiction book about the information age—*The Transparent Society*—won the Freedom of Speech Award of the American Library Association. This media interview is transcribed here for the first time. (http://www.davidbrin.com)

# 2-Dava

## By Lisa Tuttle

He went to take a shower, leaving her alone in his bedroom. At first, sated and drowsy, Iris just lay there, feeling happy. Already, although this was only the second night they'd spent together (they'd known each other for two weeks), she knew this was *it*. When she sat up, and pulled open the top drawer of the bedside table to see what he kept there, she felt entitled to her nosiness. Condoms, lubricant, cough-drops, ear-plugs, a box of fancy handkerchiefs, a clip-on book-light, a red plastic comb, a ball-point pen, some pennies, a clutter of old brochures and instruction leaflets.

Shutting it, she slid open the second drawer, and there it was.

Dark and flat, familiar in shape and size, an object of power, sinister in its stillness, she had expected nothing like it here, in the room where they'd been making love, and she had a moment of blank terror, the feeling that she was doomed and utterly helpless. It brought back a moment from her childhood, when she had walked out of the house barefoot, and nearly stepped on a copperhead.

Of course it had been all right—she'd seen it just in time to hop over it; then she'd rushed around to the other side of the house, more excited than scared, yelling for her mom to come and kill it.

And this was all right, too. It wasn't a poisonous snake, just a gun.

But although it couldn't hurt her, she didn't like looking at it, and she sure didn't want to touch it. Leaning away, stretching out a long, bare leg, she pushed the drawer shut. Then she sat still with her arms wrapped around herself, telling herself the goose bumps were from the air-conditioning, feeling ashamed. So her boyfriend had a gun; no big deal. What was wrong with her?

The sound of the shower stopped. She got back under the covers, burrowing down, hiding her face.

Iris had been born and raised in Texas; guns were no mystery to her. She had learned to shoot in her teens. Although she'd never owned a handgun, she had handled them often enough; her brother had several semi-automatics in addition to his hunting rifles, and she'd helped her best friend choose a revolver for self-protection. Her last boyfriend had a Kimber .45, a Glock 9mm, and two or three other semi-automatics, one of which he carried at all times, and he'd thought she was crazy not to have similar protection of her own—in fact, he had harped on about it once too often, and although it wasn't the *only* reason they'd split up (he'd been way too controlling and critical) it came to mind now, and offered a sort of explanation for her unease. She was so happy with her new boyfriend, she couldn't stand for anything about him to remind her of that tedious bully. Finding the gun had stirred unpleasant memories. Anyway, while she had nothing against legal firearms ownership, there was something nasty about importing them into a pleasurable, loving sex scene—but she had only herself to blame for opening that drawer and allowing her mood to be disturbed.

Thus, she managed to reason herself back to the present moment of sexy afterglow by the time her lover returned, a towel around his waist and a grin on his handsome face.

Later it would occur to Iris that the irrational fear she'd felt had been a premonition of things to come. But that was not until *much* later.

\*\*\*

She never said anything to him about her snooping. The subject of the handgun came up quite naturally a couple of weeks later, when he gave her a key to his house and explained how everything worked. Somewhere between the air conditioning and the entertainment system he showed her the gun.

The sight of it, despite her mental preparations, still made her stomach lurch. She worked to keep her voice sounding natural as she asked, "You always keep it there?"

"That way I know where it is. And now you do, too. You know how to handle a gun."

It wasn't really a question. "Sure, yeah, well, I used to...I haven't actually practiced in a long time."

"I go to the shooting range at least a couple of times a month. Maybe you could come with me?"

They were still at that stage of their relationship where every chance to be together was a fresh delight, and she nodded eagerly, returning his smile.

"Go on," he said, nodding at the weapon, and her mouth dried.

"Now?"

"Don't you want to look at it?"

She could not explain her reluctance, but the thought of putting her hand on that thing, actually holding it, made her skin crawl. "Is that the only one you've got?"

His posture changed, becoming a little defensive. "Well, yeah. Why would I need more?"

"I didn't mean it like that."

"Oh, you mean because—wow, I'm surprised you recognized it." He sounded impressed, and she was sorry to have to disillusion him.

"What do you mean? I've hardly looked at it."

"I *know*. What are you waiting for?"

She had to pick it up. It felt OK, much lighter than she had expected, almost like a toy. She turned it this way and that, looking at the symbol incised in the middle of the dark gray stock: some kind of fancy lettering. "What is it? F.N. Five-seven?"

"Are you kidding? Do you know what one of those babies *costs*?" Then he smiled. "This is something totally new. Called a Two-Dava—don't ask me why; there's a spiel about it in the company mission statement—company is OE, the initials of the two guys that set it up—Oliver Somebody and Somebody Edwards—just two young guys, small scale, and a whole new approach, so they're kind of controversial. At least, this gun is."

"Why?"

"One is the way they produce it—all new tech, bio-tech, I haven't looked into it that much, to be honest, but new methods are always going to upset the old guard, I guess. The other thing is that it's a smart gun, and lots of people don't trust that. But this is not like anything else that's been tried. It's really good; it totally works. It recognizes the owner's hand-print—it kind of bonds with you—so if somebody stole it, or took it away from me in a fight, they couldn't use it. Want to see?" He grinned wickedly. "Come on...point it at me and try to shoot. I've been wanting to test it out."

She threw it down on the bed, repulsed. "No way!"

He laughed at her, but gently, and then he hugged her. "You're smarter than me, babes, that's for sure! Now you're wondering how I can offer to share it when it's bonded to me? Thing is, the owner can add up to three additional print-recognition patterns to one gun. I'll update the chip, so you'll be able to use it, too. What's mine is yours, is ours."

***

He wasn't a gun nut, he was practical, a rational consumer, not easily swayed by fashion, but Ben did like the coolness factor of being on technology's cutting edge. He'd always had the latest phone, and now he had this gun. Part of the attraction was safety, much of it was the price—attractively pitched not too high, but not suspiciously low—but what sealed the deal for him was the feel of the gun in his hand. It felt good, and seemed to fit, as if it had been made to order.

When she had a chance to practice firing it, Iris was surprised by how right it felt to her, too. It was lighter and smaller than any other semi-automatic she'd handled, and the lack of recoil, the way it fit her hand, made her think it was what her brother would have called, meaning no offence, "a woman's gun." Of course she never said that to Ben, who certainly had bigger hands and a stronger grip than she did—but her own experience made her wonder how he could find it as perfectly right for him as it was for her. Firing the 2-Dava brought back the excitement and the feeling of empowerment that she'd known as a young teenager, just learning to shoot. It encouraged her to practice regularly, and soon she was not only comfortable, but really very skilled at using it.

For her birthday, Ben bought her a 2-Dava of her own.

The name, she discovered, was a corruption, or modernization, of Tudava, who seemed to have been some sort of legendary hero on the island in Papua New Guinea where one of the co-founders of OE had been born. As for the "controversial" nature of the handgun, as far as she could discover from internet searches, the gun was loved by the people who bought it, and hated by the larger, more established manufacturing companies, who did what they could to pour scorn and doubt on its usefulness and safety as they saw their own sales eroded. Some members of the anti-gun lobby argued that any "smart gun" could fail, and such a label gave owners a false sense of security. But she could not find any reports of failure in the 2-Dava's biometric recognition system. Tragic tales still appeared in the news on a regular basis of children who shot siblings, themselves, or Mommy with her handgun, but never was the gun in question an OE 2-Dava.

Iris couldn't think of a bad thing to say about it. Of course, she hoped she'd never be confronted by a 2-Dava, or any other type of weapon in the hand of a criminal who meant her harm, but if it *did* ever happen, at least she would be better-equipped to defend herself. She scarcely remembered the fear it had inspired in her the first time she saw it. The memory faded like a bad dream.

The *real* bad dreams started more than two years later, when Ben and Iris were married, and she was happily pregnant. She woke one night, screaming, out of a chaotic, terrifying nightmare: someone had broken into their house, had come to kill Ben and take her, and take their baby. And she couldn't do anything to stop it.

That was the horror. She had a gun and knew how to use it—she should have been able to protect herself and her family—but somehow, she was restrained, tied down, or they were too quick; the masked man held a gun to Ben's head, and she must do what the intruder said. It was different every time, but always it was terrible.

The first few times, Ben was able to calm her down. But the nightmare kept returning. Maybe it was because she was pregnant that she felt more vulnerable, but Iris found it increasingly difficult to sleep through the night, starting awake in terror at every sound, sometimes frightened by nothing at all. Her husband was stoic, heroic, getting up whenever she insisted—taking his gun—patrolling the house, and then returning, yawning, to reassure her that they were safe, no one had entered the house, all the doors and windows were locked just as when she had checked them before they went to bed.

They got an expensive new security system, and Iris went to the firing range three or four times a week, honing her aim and her speed. When Ben had to go out of town for business, she slept with her gun under her pillow. That would shave a few more seconds off her response time; it also meant she could get her weapon in her hand without alerting an intruder to what she was doing.

She went to see a counsellor about her fears. But although, in daylight, in a professional's bland, safe office, it was easy enough to agree that her fears were irrational, they came creeping back to take control of her mind whenever she was in bed. Having her sleep disrupted so regularly shattered her nerves, made it difficult to think or behave rationally. She didn't dare take sleeping tablets, because of the baby, but also because she was afraid they would slow her responses if anything *did* happen, if her fear turned out to have been justified.

And then one night it happened.

She woke with pounding heart as she did so often, for the second or third time that night (all these nights bled together) knowing she was not alone in the house. She heard footsteps. She stayed still except for the one arm, the hand that snaked beneath the pillow and found—thank heavens!—the solid comfort of that familiar shape, her protection against evil.

A man entered the bedroom. Although it was too dark to see his face, she thought he was wearing a mask; there was just enough light from the window to reveal how tall and massive he was as he paused in the doorway, and that he had a gun in his right hand.

Iris did not hesitate. She had rehearsed this moment too many times. In one swift sure motion she had the gun in her hand and was rising, arm outstretched. She fired.

He dropped like a stone.

She fired again, lower, just to be sure, and then rolled over and hit the light switch, just before she landed on her feet beside the bed, looked down, and saw that she had killed her husband.

Memory rushed back, hitting her with the emotional force of the bullet she had sent into his heart. He'd been out of town *last* night. Tonight, he had come back in time for a late dinner. She should have removed the gun from beneath her pillow, put it back in the drawer, relied on *him*...but she was so *tired*...she'd gone to bed early, slept for an hour or two...rousing when he'd slipped in beside her, and they had cuddled...she slept again, woke, tormented by nightmares; he'd tried to reassure her, but nothing would do but that he should get up and search the house... she had fallen back to sleep, still in the dark, and when she woke, only minutes later, all that was gone from her mind, it was a different night.

She stared down at him, so peaceful in death. Her aim was true. He probably never knew what she had done. She heard a howling, and realized it was coming from herself. She could not live with what she had done, would not live without him.

For once, there was no thought for the child growing inside her. (Or if there was, the thought was embryonic, too small to affect her action.)

She put her 2-Dava in her mouth and gently squeezed the trigger.

*\*\*\**

Later, much later, she opened her eyes to find that she was still alive.

She lay on her back, in a narrow but not uncomfortable bed. When she tried to move, she discovered she was under restraint, her wrists shackled to side railings. Her legs were free, and when she raised her head off the pillow and looked toward them she could see by the rounded dome of her sheeted belly that several months, at least, had passed since her suicide.

*Attempted* suicide. Somehow, her intention had been foiled. She was alive. Tears blurred her sight. She remembered everything, up to the moment her lips had closed around the hard barrel of the gun. She had wanted to die. She *still* wanted to die, only now, for the sake of the baby, she was glad she had failed, and only hoped that, after it was born, she would be executed for her crimes.

As the minutes passed she became more aware of her situation. There were several tubes in her body, including one up her nose that she felt uncomfortably in her throat when she shifted her head. She had been catheterized. She was in darkness, but the darkness was not absolute; she could see the outline of a door a few yards away, lit by a light beyond. She could hear the faint hum of electricity, and other sounds suggestive of activity in some more distant part of the building. She guessed it was late at night, and that she was in a hospital, maybe a prison hospital, if there were such things. In the morning, she thought, someone would come to tend to her, and she would find out.

Morning came, and as weak, grayish light entered through a series of windows set high in one wall, she was able to see that she was not alone, as she had thought, but that her bed was one of more than a dozen spaced evenly throughout the long, high-ceilinged ward. Her nearest neighbour was a woman with greasy black curly hair and a pale face, eyes closed, her breathing too low and slow to

be noticeable; Iris might have thought her dead, but for the evidence of intubation, and the restraints. She, too, was visibly pregnant.

Her skin prickled with horror at the realization that she was in a room full of pregnant prisoners. Had they all attempted suicide? Or were some guilty of other crimes, and only being kept here in a sort of hiatus from their sentence, until they had given birth?

No one made a sound. Was Iris the only one awake? She had no means of telling time; the day wore on interminably as nothing happened, and no one—no warders, attendants,

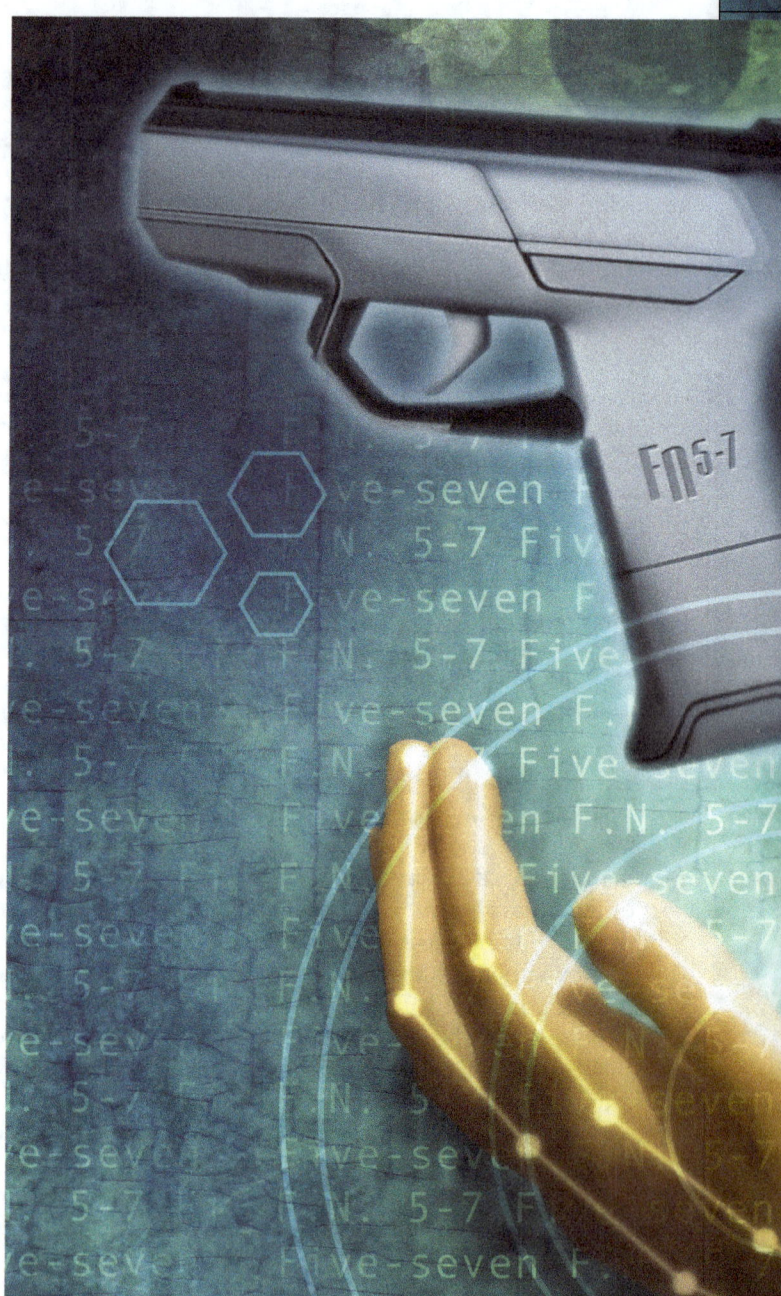

doctors or nurses—entered the room, and none of her fellow prisoners stirred.

When she tried to cry out, nothing happened.

She could breathe, and swallow, and hear the sounds she made in her mouth and nose—her breathing became harsher as she began to panic—but something must have happened to her vocal chords; she could not even groan.

Finally, as daylight from the high windows began to

fade, there was a fluttering click and a low, buzzing hum, and fluorescent lights came on in the ceiling. Sometime after that the door opened, and two people, anonymous in green hospital scrubs and large white surgical masks, came in. Iris's bed was nearest the door, and it was to her that one turned first, while the second went the other way, toward the far end.

She strained forward, raising herself up as much as she could to attract their attention, but the attendant (she could not tell if it was a man or a woman) seemed not to notice as they went about their business in silent efficiency,

removing the bag empty of nutrient solution and replacing it with a full one, removing the bag of urine and attaching an empty one, never giving her the slightest opportunity to catch their eye.

Only when they had left the room did she let herself collapse back onto her pillow, a silent sob forming in her throat as her eyes filled again with tears. She knew she deserved punishment, but did it have to be so cruel?

A few hours later—the windows now blank obsidian mirrors, the fluorescent light humming—another man came in. Like the previous visitors, he wore shapeless green scrubs, his head was covered, and most of his face hidden behind a white mask, but his sex was evident from his size and shape, and the bare fore-arms bristling with thick, black hair. He came straight to Iris's bed, pulled back the sheet, carefully prodded her belly, and then—without ever once looking at her face—he parted her legs, pushed them up, and gave her a quick vaginal examination.

It was not pleasant, yet under the circumstances, she found herself grateful for the attention—*any* sort of attention. At least they were concerned about her baby. It occurred to Iris that unconsciousness could be medically induced, and that she was awake now because her baby was soon to be born.

It did not happen that night or the next, but on the third day since her waking Iris felt something happening inside, and although she had never given birth, and she had nothing to compare it with and no one to consult, she was pretty sure she was in the early stages of labor.

She worried about all the things that could go wrong, and her inability to call for help, but by the time daylight faded and the lights came on again, the pains were still manageable, with several minutes in between. When the attendant came in as usual to change her bags he (she had decided they were all men) recognized her condition and went to fetch the doctor.

It seemed to take forever, but then it was over in no time at all. All at once, she was bearing down, she felt herself expelling something much too small to be a baby. She wondered vaguely if the placenta might have come out first. But the doctor, crouching, waiting between her legs, made a noise of satisfaction as he caught it.

He stood up, wiping something clean with a fresh white towel, murmuring, "You beauty." Then he held out the new semi-automatic handgun, displaying it proudly on the flat of his hand, smiling, as if it were all his doing. "Perfect."

Iris stared at the gun—similar to her own 2-Dava—its matte finish drinking in the harsh artificial light—thinking she must be hallucinating, or it was a cruel joke; trying to comprehend how her body could have produced anything like that, and wondering what had happened to her baby, until a new contraction, stronger than any before, took all her attention.

"Push—push harder!"

She tried to obey, tried to rise up to bear down, but it was impossible to move very far, bound as she was. Because she couldn't say anything about it, she could only wish that one of the three men at the end of her bed would notice, and unchain her—but all their attention was fixed between her open legs, on what was coming out of her body.

Another gun was wiped clean of her bodily fluids and displayed as before. Then another, and another, and another.

She lost track of how many she gave birth to that first time, before she fell unconscious.

# Double X Chromosome

BY
YVONNE NAVARRO

## METAWOMAN
© April 2015

Photo courtesy of Yvonne Navarro

For quite some time after learning the theme of this issue, I was perplexed about what to write. Yeah, I like science fiction, but "metahuman" sounds like more of a comic thing, or at least it seems to have originated there. I like some superheroes, but I have to admit I'm not much of a comic follower. There really wasn't money for collecting comics when I was a kid, and the magazines I wanted on a monthly basis took up most

of my meager allowance when they came out (think *Eerie, Creepy,* and *Vampirella*). More than comics, metahuman makes me think of robots, like in *AI* or *I, Robot.* A little research, however, started to expand my horizons about what metahuman means.

*More than human.*

Enhanced. Improved. Superhuman.

Oh, right. I got that.

A woman.

The 1950s image is gone. I'm not sure why, but there seems to be a resurgence of the pictures from that era, usually trim women with flipped hair, tiny waists around which are tied frilly-edged aprons atop a short-sleeved, below-the-knee dress. The stereotype prances around in high heels and a bright, lipsticked smile, likely as not brandishing potholders and a roasting pan full of perfectly cooked food.

Right.

At this particular moment, I'm sitting in the sunroom of a beautiful bed and breakfast in Jerome, Arizona. We're up here as part of a birthday weekend for my mother-in-law, and so far it's been a wonderful time—good food, great lodging, the wonderful company of my husband and my mom-in-law, whom I happen to love *and* like very much. If you aren't sure what any of that has to do with the metahuman theme, then you need to dig deeper and realize what's going on beneath the surface of me, or, perhaps, any woman you know or happen to pass on the street. Think of it as sort of a clockwork thing, or maybe steampunk. All those gears and cogs and chains working together, powered by an energy that often seems limitless, but at other times is dragged out of places unknown. That's when the gears slow down and the chains try to jump their tracks; the spinners catch and jerk, and the light behind the eyes starts to dim…

Until everything restarts.

The twenty-first century metahuman woman is an amalgamation of worker, wife, mother, daughter, sister, girlfriend, BFF. I don't know what goes on in other households, but I strongly suspect it's a variation on the same theme. I'm a secretary, supervisor, housekeeper, writer, gardener of both flowers and food plants, and laundress. I can use hand and power tools, and do it with a fair amount of not just success, but talent. I have built shelves, furniture, and a full-sized screenhouse to protect our plants from locusts. I've made clothes, repaired buttons and pockets and seams, and cooked for up to twenty-some people. I've canned food, painted rooms and houses, hung kitchen cabinets and installed plumbing, light fixtures, and floors. I've built block walls, cut down trees, written geology papers, studied martial arts, and been certified as a pool lifeguard. I've waited tables, taken care of the elderly, and given injections and subcutaneous fluids to dogs. I've built a trampoline, worked as a cashier at a Greyhound Bus Station, and slept all night on a Tennessee shoreline. I've been a bookkeeper, worked for the U.S.

government, been told secrets that I've never revealed by both friends and employers, and I can type 114 words a minute. I've found typographical errors in science books and on university English websites. I've refinished antique pianos, hung wallpaper, driven cross-country, edited reference books, and gone with a friend to Thailand so she could have surgery. I've installed baseboards and crown molding, written more than twenty novels, and reorganized everything from closets and pantries to legal filing systems. I've put an entire house into storage, then pulled it out again. I've moved two households, a working machine shop garage, a bookstore, and three vehicles from one side of the country to the other—all at the same time. I've buried too many people I love and still, *still*, haven't learned not to take it for granted that someone will be there the next day. I've had dogs die in my arms and held others as I made the crushing decision that it was time for them to go. I've worked and drawn and painted and written my way through three decades despite all the things that life wants to throw at a person, including loves and letdowns and broken hearts.

Because that's life.

And as we all know, life is nothing but chaos theory in motion. So a woman adapts.

Because she is metahuman.

Because she is woman.

She is *Metawoman*.

And she keeps on going.

No one does her work for her, no one organizes or

**Grendel (L), Goblin (R)**

cleans or cries for her. The things that she does, she must do herself. With empowerment has come responsibility and independence and *strength*.

I am surrounded by beauty as I write this, lovely music in the background, the wordless serenity of an Arizona vista that goes on for a hundred-mile view on the other side of a picture window. All this, yet inside my breast, my heart bleeds from sending, Goblin, my sweet old Great Dane, over the Rainbow Bridge the day before yesterday. After ten years of his companionship, of seeing his eyes light up every time I came into the same room as him, the chasm left behind will not heal so quickly.

But I must have strength.

We have two Great Danes left, but not for long. Both are blind, and one, a sweet-souled boy we adopted barely over a year ago named Grendel, has grown an inoperable cancerous mass in his chest. We will make him as comfortable for as long as we can, but sooner or later he won't be able to breathe and we will have to go through this all over again.

I must have strength.

There are a thousand other things going on, figuratively and financially, spiritually and emotionally. These are the things that power me, the things that keep me going. These are the things that keep any woman going, because she *must*. We must. *I* must.

Even though it has been scarred and split a thousand times, I am the woman with a heart of iron.

I am Metawoman.

~~~~~~~~~~~~~~~~~~~

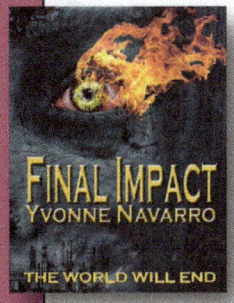

Finally available in ebook format! The award-winning *Final Impact* and its follow-up, *Red Shadows*. To order, visit the Crossroad Press Store at http://store.crossroadpress.com/ and search for "Yvonne Navarro."

Comments? Questions? Yvonne Navarro can be reached via her Facebook page (www.facebook.com/yvonne.navarro.001), or at her Dark Discoveries email: yvonne@journalstone.com.

# BIZARRO PULP PRESS

Necrosaurus Rex

Nicholas Day

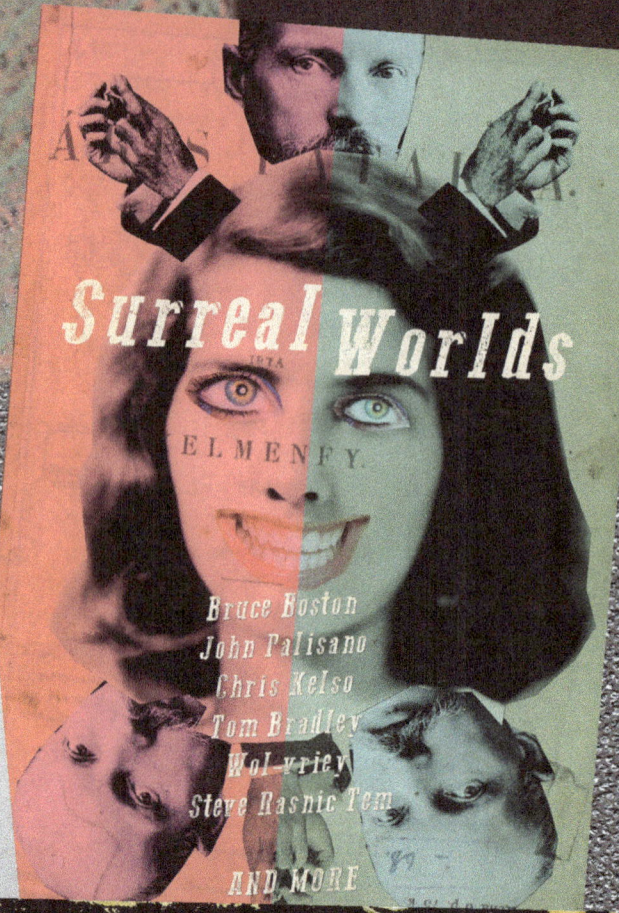

Surreal Worlds

ELMENFY.

Bruce Boston
John Palisano
Chris Kelso
Tom Bradley
Wol-vriey
Steve Rasnic Tem

AND MORE

2015

THE BOY WHO LOVED DEATH

HAL DUNCAN

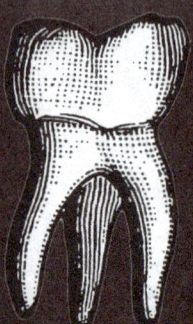

bizarropulppress.com

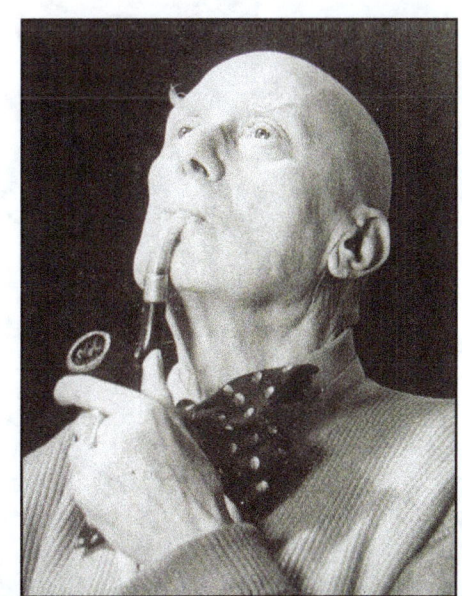

# HUBBARD AND PARSONS—SPIRITUAL MACHINES: A BRIEF INTRODUCTION

BY MIKE LESTER

The idea of the spirit, that organic essence of self, blending, merging with science to improve the state of mankind, indeed to achieve immortality or perfection, is an idea that has been explored in countless films and books; everything from *2001: A Space Odyssey* and *Blade Runner* to the writings of Isaac Asimov, among many others. We can look to Mary Shelley's classic *Frankenstein* as the forerunner of this "genre," a warning against man's dabbling in the arena of the Divine. This is a warning that has generally gone unheeded, both in life and art, as we shall see.

This concept has, in the last few decades, come to be embodied by the term *Transhumanism.* With the somewhat recent awareness of the concept has also come controversy. To some, the idea of spiritual perfection bringing about a pure humanity is a good thing, a perfection to be strived for in all areas of life—mentally, physically, spiritually. To others, the idea reeks of the worst totalitarian atrocities, particularly the Nazi eugenics program and the idea of the pure master race (and this may have something to do with the recent crackdown on Scientology in Germany). In the last decade or so, this criticism has increasingly been levelled against L. Ron Hubbard's Church of Scientology and the concept of the *Clear*. In short, a Clear,

or *Thetan* (which Hubbard defined as an awakened humanity), is someone who has managed to master and control their every action, being untroubled by id or ego, maintaining a constant focus on the present with vivid situational awareness, and the ability of perfect total recall, a perfected spiritual machine, a superman, if you will. The achievement of Clear status is the goal of everyone practicing Scientology. To some, this description of a Clear may sound almost like a description of a machine.

The influence of Aleister Crowley on Hubbard didn't really take hold until Hubbard was introduced to Jack Parsons, rocket engineer, founder of the famous Jet Propulsion Laboratory (JPL), and science fiction buff. Parsons was also a serious student of the occult and an adept of Crowley. Upon their meeting in 1945, both men were suitably impressed with each other. Parsons was taken by Hubbard's charismatic personality and sensed a deeper *Thelemic* presence within him (Thelema being Crowley's primary philosophy, or religion, whose main credo is "Do what thou wilt shall be the whole of the law," a parallel to Hubbard's later formulation of the pure Clear Thetan). Hubbard was equally impressed with Parsons, who had turned his Pasadena mansion into a Thelemic lodge of Crowley's Ordo Templi Orientis (OTO).

Hubbard soon found himself living at Parsons' home, and the two eventually undertook what Parsons referred to as The Babalon Working, the summoning of The Scarlet Woman (of biblical Revelation fame) and the creation of a Moonchild, or homunculus. Hubbard acted as Parsons' scryer, or scribe, during these rituals. After one such ritual conducted in the Mojave Desert, Parsons' Scarlet Woman had appeared to him. Upon their return from the desert, the two found one Marjorie Cameron ensconced in the Pasadena mansion. Cameron, with her flaming red hair and green eyes, captivated Parsons as Hubbard had earlier, and she was soon taking her part in the Babalon Working (Crowley later claimed that he had sent this woman, an elemental, to Parsons). While Jack and Marjorie engaged in ritual sex magick, Hubbard sat nearby and described what was taking place on the astral plane. After the prolonged and frenzied ritual, Parsons was sure he had succeeded and that within nine months' time Cameron would give birth to a moonchild, an incarnation of the goddess Babalon. Crowley, upon learning of the ritual, was unimpressed. He correctly understood that Hubbard was using Parsons for personal gain (stealing his girlfriend under the guise of "free love—Do What Thou Wilt" as well as ten thousand dollars), and soon Hubbard and Parsons parted ways acrimoniously. Within a few years, Parsons would be mysteriously killed in an explosion at his home. It is surmised that he dropped a vial of nitroglycerin during a chemical experiment and succeeded in blowing himself onto the astral plane.

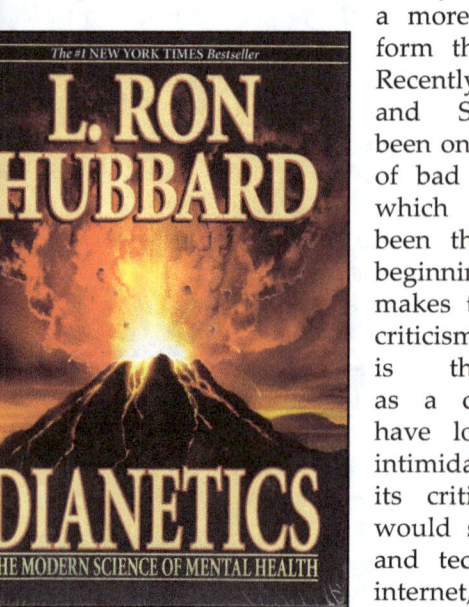

Though Parsons may have been out of Hubbard's life, the ideas and influence of Aleister Crowley stuck with Hubbard. Crowley's Thelemic religion basically became the framework for Scientology. The parallels are quite noticeable. Crowley insisted that the practice of ritual magick was a science, something he postulated in his book *Magick in Theory and Practice*. The science of magick then was about true knowledge of the self and the potential of the individual. Hubbard carried this idea over to Scientology with the concept of the Clear, a fully aware Thetan. A fully aware Thetan would be able to leave their body, to astrally project, becoming an all-powerful being. According to Crowley's Thelema, the point of ritual magick is for the magus to astrally project, and thereby be able to use any matter or any perception for their own ends. At this point the magus may then be able to control the universe, since anything perceived is also a part of the magus's will or being. Crowley's magus and Hubbard's Thetan are thus parallel supermen.

Hubbard, via Crowley and Parsons, has made popular, if not exactly mainstream, the idea that man perfected is a pure spiritual machine, an organic computer. Through Scientology and his book *Dianetics*, Hubbard has spread Thelemic teachings to everyone from movie stars to everyday seekers (most of whom would be squeamish in the face of Crowley's ideas, only to find a more easily accessible form through Hubbard). Recently, both Hubbard and Scientology have been on the receiving end of bad press, something which has always been the case from the beginning; however, what makes these most recent criticisms interesting is that Scientology as a church seems to have lost its power to intimidate and silence its critics. Ironically, it would seem that science and technology, via the internet, has allowed critics to more readily and freely express themselves. As for the future of the Church, who can say? One thing seems certain, however, and that is that Thelema will continue its course as it has always done, perhaps under a different guise, or perhaps back where it started, with Crowley himself.

# THAT PART OF THE BRAIN

## BY JOHN SHIRLEY

"Don't tell J-dad we won the contest, Philly," Dash said.

Philly shook his head. He didn't want to tell J-dad, but he felt like they had to. "He'll beat our asses if we don't."

They both looked down the West Oakland street, starting to cool now as the August sun dipped behind the rooftops and the shadows grew long. The row of small houses were catching the last light before the streetlamps came on; this time of day the peeling paint on the houses looked like feathers. The social worker lady, trying to sound nice, said the street's houses looked like miniature Victorians. Whatever a Victorian was.

Three doors down, the Gonzales family had their black metal barbecue out. Philly could see heat waves rising from it, could smell the charcoal and the lighter fluid. Rafe Gonzales, a stout guy wearing a short sleeved white shirt and jeans, like always, was poking at the charcoal with tongs. He had meat laid out on a tray table, still in its supermarket packaging to protect it from flies. That was good—Rafe would always give them a piece of meat in a tortilla, if they came around and stared at him. Philly and Dash had nothing to eat for two days but Sugar Squares cereal and the box was empty now and J-dad wasn't getting more anytime soon.

Aunt Treena wasn't around to feed them, she was on a meth run somewhere. J-dad was drunk in the bedroom, staring at the TV. Not a good time to ask about food. He'd throw something at Philly's head if he asked; probably an empty bottle. Last time a bottle had connected, Philly had gone across the street to ask the Chinese people for a bandage, because of the blood from the scalp, but somebody there called the cops so the CPS lady had come over and made noises about foster care.

J-dad, what mom called James, wasn't their dad at all, he was Aunt Treena's boyfriend. He'd worked as a bus driver, only they fired him for being drunk, and he had run through his unemployment checks. Aunt Treena was mom's sister, and J-dad was her boyfriend, and mom was dead, and their real dad was an unknown, so they could end up in foster care pretty easily. They heard brothers taken away by CPS were sometimes split up to different families, so Dash and Philly had pretended the bash was from falling on the sidewalk. They weren't taking any chances on being separated. Dash was Philly's hero; Philly kept Dash going. It was way past loyalty.

Dash and Philly liked to pretend they were ten-year-old twins, which might make it less likely that they'd be split up, but they weren't twins, Dash was a year older—a year and a half. Almost twelve. They did almost look twinny though, same blue eyes, same coarse brown hair cut by J-dad into mullets like his, same blue eyes.

"If we tell J-dad it came," Dash said at last, "he'll take the game away." He was watching closely as Rafe put the meat on the grill—one, two, three, four, five, six pieces of meat.

"He's the one who put us in the contest. We ain't old enough to be in it without he does that. He's going to find out."

"He don't have to know it came. We got to hide the console from him and the helmets and all. Because he will sell that shit."

"Maybe." Philly glanced toward the rhododendron bushes where they had hidden the box. "Wait one minute. Let me check what's up with him." Philly went around to the side of the house. He skirted the big rhododendron bush, glancing toward the half-opened cardboard box they'd stashed behind it, up against the house. He could see the special contest helmets inside the open box.

A leaning brown-painted wooden fence ran along the walkway between the houses; old broken toys Treena had gotten from an overfull donations box lay strewn like battlefield dead along the narrow walk between the close houses. Philly took a few steps, and the pit bull on the other side of the fence heard him and snarled, threw itself at the fence, making it crack and lean a little more. Philly liked dogs—Rafe had a good natured pit bull—but this one had grown up rough, and was kept in the back all the time, and barked with a lot of anger, a lot of hate.

"Shut up, Dre," he told it. The dog quieted to snuffling, knowing his voice. The people living over there, name of Johnson, had named the pit after Mac Dre. The Johnsons didn't like Philly and Dash or their peeps. All Philly knew about them was the dad had a night janitor's job, slept most of the day.

There were vertical support boards on this side of the fence, and one of them was splintered and bent so that Philly could climb up on the stub with his torn sneakers, walking his hands up the side of the house. Now he could see past the window blinds, which were crimped at the bottom; could see that J-dad, him with the potbelly and the torn green Oakland A's t-shirt that he wore most of the time at home, had fallen asleep watching that flat screen TV they'd bought from one of the Norteños up the street for sixty dollars. He was lying in there, mouth open, skinny pale legs sticking out of his boxer shorts.

J-dad usually got up for a while about one or two in the afternoon, drank forties till he got sleepy, then got up a few hours later and went out on errands he never explained. He hadn't been asleep long. That would give them plenty of time.

Philly dropped to the ground, ran to the back porch, got the long orange extension cord from under the stairs, lifted up the cover on the back porch's socket, plugged it in, and ran with the other end, trailing it carefully out to their hiding place by the front porch. Dash was already there, crouching over the box.

"He's asleep, dead out!" Philly said excitedly. "So I guess we could try it..."

"*Aight*, then." Dash took out the helmets, handed one to Philly, and poked through the box. It was a pretty big box, like four milk crates together. Packed in with Styrofoam pieces of random shapes were the light guns, and another more cryptic piece of gear. "I don't see how these light guns is going to work," Dash said picking them up. It looked like a miniature bazooka about the size of a submachine gun. "Contest said game didn't need a screen. Light gun shoots at a screen. Don't look like laser tag shit."

J-dad had an old X-Box and sometimes he let them take turns playing dual player with him, but he'd get mad when Philly or Dash won and then he'd send them away. They had played PC games at the community center, only they weren't allowed to be there anymore because J-dad used

34

to just leave them there unsupervised all day. Sometimes Treena took them to Cheesy Rat's, a kind of casino for kids, where you could buy a lot of tickets that let you play all kinds of games, including arcade videogames, and they'd learned videogames there, too, while she was down the street doing something.

Philly thought she was whoring when she left them there, but he wasn't sure.

Dash shook his head. "I don't see how it works without a..."

"Here's the directions," he said, taking a piece of paper from the box. "What, is that *all?*" Philly read it out loud: "'Charge the base box, it will communicate with the other game units, which will then direct you through the headsets on the helmets. And welcome to Dimension of Death!'"

They found a rectangular plastic box stenciled Base Box. At one end it had something like a transparent miniature satellite dish antenna sticking out; it had strips of metal inside it. The other end had an electrical socket. So they set it up on the dirt, plugged in the orange cord, and right away the little dish lit up...and a moment later so did green lights on the front of the helmets.

The crystalline muzzles of the guns lit up with a dangerous red light. Dash grinned. "Cool!"

\*\*\*

*...forty three, we've got activation. Subjects are prepping the device.*

*What about the* caregiver, *fifty?*

*Say again? Transmission was...*

*The caregiver, is he down?*

*He's out cold. The trank in the beer should keep caregiver down for about six hours, ought to get to stage two before then.*

*Caregiver, what a joke. James Derney, caregiver. Right.*

*You getting emo'tached to these kids, forty-three?*

*Fuck no. Okay, looks like helmets are going up. We have neuro reception...*

\*\*\*

Seeing the lights flash on the helmets, Philly and Dash instantly put them on and picked up the guns. They could see just enough to do this, through the darkened goggles, like looking through extra dark sunglasses.

Philly and Dash heard the same warm but business-like woman's voice in their ears, from the helmet headsets, saying the same thing.

"Please choose your gunner name," she said pleasantly. "Just say it loud and clear for voice recognition."

"Philly!" said Philly.

"Dash!" said Dash.

"Philly and Dash, my name is Sanguina! You will now notice a change in your field of vision."

It was true—the dim view through the goggles had vanished, replaced with a sharp-edged artificial image, a 3D scene showing a cratered and boulder-studded landscape picked out in luminous but dour green and deep-dark blue, a wasteland stretching out under a dull-red sky. Double alien suns, one bigger than the other,

glowered from above like angry mismatched eyes. A thumping electronica music was playing; eerie twanging sounds reverberated.

Calmly and sweetly, Sanguina said, "Here is your stage one battle scene—your entry into *The Dimension of Death* virtual reality that takes you all the way! For now, do not move from your real-world places as you play the game. Get comfortable and fire at the oncoming enemy, using your crosshairs. The first wave of enemies will come slowly and fall pretty easily, to give you a chance to get used to the weapon's aiming systems."

The monsters came at them then—six monsters, side by side. Instead of heads they had bruise-purple, human brains glowing as they floated steadily over naked, sexless, semi-human olive-green bodies. From the bottom of each brain extruded long, long stretchy tentacles. Mouths opened in the monster's bellies, wide screaming angry mouths, each mouth big as a great white shark's.

*"Fuuuck!"* Dash blurted. He fired his weapon, and they both saw its fiery-red beam zip out over the alien landscape toward the oncoming monsters, the ray sizzling right into a shrieking mouth. The monster staggered back. Dash fired at it again and the creature suddenly exploded into an expanding ragged cloud of bloody shreds and bone shrapnel. Dash laughed in delight.

Philly fired as the other monsters got within a few yards of him, and soon three of the creatures were mowed down. But the others were getting closer.

Dash and Philly fired again, almost at once. They missed one monster and its tentacles lashed out, showing serrations up close that made slashing marks over Philly's vision. And he felt actual *pain*, throbbing behind his eyes, from each slash. He fired the weapon again...

The creature exploded. The slash marks and the pain both ebbed.

"Dash—I felt that! It hurt when it got me!"

"It's like those buzzing things in the 360 controllers! But even more metal!"

"I guess..."

"Here comes another wave! Use the crosshairs, dude! Aim for the brains. That kills with one shot!"

\*\*\*

*...forty-three, we have clear-cut fix on Philadelphia Breedhouse. Dasher Breedhouse is still only partial fix. Both are in the cyberneuronal loop.*

*Dasher subject is closing in on pure fix. Still almost an hour to stage two, anyhow. What about perimeter interference?*

*We have our people in place, fairly close, in the neighborhood... Observation is ninety-two percent...*

\*\*\*

Philly and Dash had forgotten all about being hungry. They were filled with a glow of excitement, instead of food, and their palms were sweaty, the guns vibrant in their hands.

Dash had gotten a face slash, too; had felt the pain. He seemed to just accept it and Philly wasn't going to get all pussied out about it in front of Dash.

Wave after wave of monsters came at them...and then,

all at once, they were gone.

A chime sounded, and the sound of applause. A logo appeared in mid-air over the alien landscape, a symbol, slowly spinning in 3D—an image of a grinning skull wearing a Dimension of Death game helmet and goggles, and underneath it a rifle crossed with a light gun, like crossbones. The front of the helmet was imprinted with the letters *DoD*. When the symbol spun slowly around, in back the words *Dimension of Death!* lit up, complete with exclamation point.

Sanguina gushed, "You've done it, gunners! You've gotten through level one in record time! Our confidence in you is justified! Now, we're about to move on to Level Two! See anything familiar?"

What did she mean by "See anything familiar?" Philly wondered.

But after a moment's lag the landscape inside the goggles changed...and it *was* familiar.

It was their street, the very one they lived on, but seen from above. It was like a helicopter view from about fifty feet over the streetlights.

"Welcome to level two of the Dimension of Death!" said Sanguina. "If you want to adjust your virtual reality goggles, now's the time to do it!"

Both Philly and Dash stood up, took off their goggled helmets and wiped sweat from their faces. The goggles themselves seemed clear of moisture. Philly's head throbbed and the back of it felt hot, almost sunburned. He felt a little sick to his stomach, too. But he was fascinated, transported by the game, his pulse still pounding with excitement.

Standing up they could see over the rhododendron bush, and without the DoD goggles the street looked, somehow, more real than it ever had. It looked like a bright, living photograph. Philly could see Rafe taking meat off the grill, and across the street from him, three Norteños standing by the GTO, arguing with that Norteña, that girl Camila who was nice to them sometimes. She gave them Halloween candy every year even though they didn't have costumes. She was wearing those high heels that made it look like she was standing on tip toes, and a tiny little skirt and a blouse that showed her *chichis*. She was arguing with the taller Norteño, Salvador, about something, and holding her own against the gangster, poking him in the chest with her finger to emphasize her words. Farther down the street, a tall black guy wearing a Raiders jersey and a do-rag was playing the car radio as he washed his gold-flaked Hyundai. Some girl was rapping on the radio, probably Nicky Minaj. The sun was going down, and down some more...

Dash, always taking care of his brother, got the water hose that was attached to the spigot in the concrete foundation behind them, and started the water. When the splashing water was cooled off he gave the hose to Philly. They both drank deep. It tasted like hose but it felt good to drink it.

\*\*\*

*Forty-three, they've taken off their helmets.*
*They don't know how to adjust the goggles without taking*

*them off, I guess.*
*It's still hot out there too.*
*Just go ahead and amplify a request to return to readiness.*

\*\*\*

"I feel weird," Dash said, using his t-shirt to wipe sweat from the headband inside the helmet. "But this game is pretty tight. We fucking rule this, dude. Nobody else got one."

"How they got our street in the game?" Philly asked.

"Maybe it...took a picture of it or something...fuck, I don't know."

They heard Sanguina's voice, coming out of the headsets on their helmets. The voice was sort of distant,

without the helmets on, but they heard her clearly. "Please replace your helmets on your heads! Do not remove them without specific instructions!"

They immediately put the helmets back on, adjusting the chin straps. The goggles showed them their street, the animation aerial view of it...

But the view angle suddenly tilted, diving down to the level of the street, looking from the curb in front of their house... It really looked like their street, except that these were crisp videogame images of the houses, the parked cars, everything that was there, in the same sullen, slightly glowing blues and greens of the alien planet landscape. The sky was red, the glow of the sunset blue, like its own opposite.

The parked cars were familiar ones, but tinted in DoD colors. The old Seville belonging to those Chinese people was parked across the street, in the game view; Rafe's low-rider Chevy Impala was parked right next to the barbecue; there was the rebuilt GTO in front of the Norteño house, and that busted up minivan with the flat tires in front of the crackhouse way down at the next corner. He could see the big Harley belonging to the bearded mestizo guy who always wore the black leather vest, and there was that church lady's old Volkswagen.

There was Rafe, too, handing out food to a line of his four kids—all of them copied perfectly but in Dimension of Death colors. Camilla was driving by Philly and Dash now, passing in her small car.

She stared at them and frowned but kept going.

"Jesus, just exactly our street," Dash said admiringly, looking both ways.

Even the exact same little trees sprouting in squares of dirt, spaced evenly up the block, and the broken streetlight at the other end of the block—it was broken in the game view, in The Dimension of Death.

***

*Subjects Philadelphia and Dasher are both fixed, fully receptive, and transmitting, fifty. Move to target rendering?*

*That is a go, forty-three.*

***

Sanguina's voice sounded especially chirpy as she said, "Gunners Philly and Dash! Unscrew the glass cover from the guns!"

They both looked at their guns—and saw that their hands were "animated" or copied into the game world visual style on the guns. Dash unscrewed his light gun lens, and Philly followed suit. It was easy as unscrewing the lid from a jar.

"Put the glass cover in your pocket, please!" Sanguina said.

They obeyed, breathless, waiting for the next level to begin.

"You will soon see the enemy on the street! Open fire in the same way—but the ammo load-out is different now! You'll be firing *needle bullets*, which explode on contact, instead of laser bursts! Fire only at monsters! You each have forty-one shots so don't waste any! Aim carefully! Do you have any questions?"

"We can...we can ask you questions?" Philly said with surprise.

"Yes you can, Philly!" she replied sweetly.

"Okay, um—how come we're seeing our street in the game, like, where we live?"

"That's because contest winners had their street photographed and they are also monitored via satellite! All of this was rendered for the game, and continues to be updated."

"Um...okay."

"Ready to play?" asked Sanguina brightly.

"Yes!" said Philly.

"*Yay*-uh!" said Dash.

"Great!" chuckled Sanguina. "This time—don't stand still! You can now move down the block! The terrain is all yours! The entire square block has been added to the game! It's three-hundred-sixty degrees of *The Dimension of Death*! Good luck—and look out for monsters!"

\*\*\*

*Rendering fully completed, selections irrevocable, subjects fully receptive and transmitting.*

*How's power levels, fifty?*

*Good. Microwave transmission pick up is ninety-eight per cent. There should be no interruption.*

*Perimeter Interception team, are you in place?*

*We are in place, sir. PD has been decoyed, local phone transmission damped.*

*Coming up on targets...*

*Fifty, I'm a little worried about their pace, they seem reluctant to engage.*

*We expected that. It's just adjustment. Once the first target is engaged, amygdala pathways will open up, the hormones will flow, we'll be good.*

*That part of the brain is lighting up, right now—for subject Dasher. Subject Philadelphia is only showing partial...*

*Subject Dasher is taking aim, the targets are reacting, that should close the neural circuit for Philadelphia...*

\*\*\*

Philly saw the monsters turning toward him, and they were right where the Norteños had been. Same monsters as in the first part of the game but now standing on the sidewalk of Philly's street. One of the monsters appeared to be smoking a cigarette or maybe a blunt—lifting the smoke up to the brain that was floating over the naked, greenish body, inhaling, the smoke swirling between the brain and the body, then sinking into the body. A blurry yellow color appeared in the brain. The smoke exhaled from the mouth in the chest.

They could hear voices, ambient sounds from the street, a distorted echo of the car radio playing, and someone laughing. "What those fucking kids got?"

"Hey, you, kid, gimme that thing, little shit *nino*, I want to see what that shit is..."

Two of the monsters were coming toward them, one with hands extended. Laughter emanated from those floating brains.

The monsters were *coming to take away their game.* They were going to take their helmets and guns and The Dimension of Death.

Dash muttered, "The fuck you are!" and fired, the gun making a hissing sound; one of the monsters opened the giant mouth in its chest and screamed, and staggered—and then the monster exploded, red splashes, green-blue chunks of bony flesh spinning outward from unraveling entrails....

"Whoa!" Dash yelled. "Nailed him!"

Philly had to shoot too, at the other monster. He had to get his brother's back. The other monster had paused, turning toward the steaming wreck of its companion: a turn that made the brain a profile and a better target. Philly squeezed the trigger and the brain wriggled—and then exploded. The rest of the body dropped down, limp.

There were other monsters now, coming out of the gangbanger house, screaming and howling, big blue tongues drooping out of their oversized mouths, brains pulsating with fear; some were running away, some coming toward Philly and Dash. Dash fired, over and over. Monsters exploded.

Philly saw another monster coming out of the crackhouse. It had a shotgun in his talons, was waving it around. Dash and Philly targeted it and fired at the same time. The big toothy mouth opened to scream in the thing's chest, and then it flew apart in double explosions, one blasting low, one higher.

More monsters were coming out of that house, some running toward them, some away. Dash and Philly fired... again and again...

\*\*\*

*Now we've got full light-up for key neurological area, both subjects. They're committed.*

*Re-identification seems full; dehumanization complete...*

*They're not panicking, that suggests they'll be good candidates for relocation.*

*Let's not get ahead of ourselves.*

*Fifty, this is perimeter control, interception—we may have a problem.*

*What problem?*

*The caregiver—James Derney—he's heard the commotion, he's waking up—*

*Not possible, that drug should keep him down no matter what.*

*I'm being informed there were several bottles in the fridge and prep team may have missed one. He seems to have fallen asleep on his own.*

*That's major FUBAR, there, interception! If the subjects hear his voice it might break their commitment to the role!*

*We have another issue, we may have to evacuate—one patrolman, in the area. Not supposed to be here. I think he was getting head from a woman on the next street south, and our records indicate a history with this family, he's been trying to extort money from the caregiver—*

*We're going to have to close down and get the gear! If we have to take out the subjects—*

*Not necessary, fifty, the timing isn't bad, we've got recovery on hand.*

*Forty-three, don't argue with me, it'll go down when I say. No complications.*

*Respectfully, field work is all complications. We can get*

*Sanguina to order them to put the helmets down—*

\*\*\*

Philly heard J-dad shouting. Something like what the fuck, who the fuck, where the fuck—all of those.

Dash heard him too. They both turned and looked at their house.

There was a monster coming down the steps toward them. Its brain was bobbing a little with each step. The body-shape was familiar; that pot belly.

It was J-dad for sure.

"You little bitch ass lunatics, what, cops going to be all over us—fuck!"

Dash didn't hesitate. He aimed and fired. He hit the J-dad monster low, in a leg.

A moment passed with the big mouth in the J-dad monster's chest screaming, and then the right leg exploded.

The monster fell over, howling, waving its arms.

Philly had to back up his brother. He fired into that shrieking mouth in the monster's chest, and a moment later the creature exploded.

"Fuck J-dad anyway," Dash said.

"That's not really him," Philly said. But he was afraid to take off the helmet and look.

An amplified voice boomed at them from behind. "You two, put down the weapons!"

They turned to see a police car driven by a monster. It pulled up at the curb. The cop monster's brain was throbbing red. The creature was holding up a microphone for the car's loudspeaker in front of the space between the brain and the body. "Get down on the ground!"

It was a gravelly voice they knew, Officer Chernville, who was always hassling Aunt Treena and J-dad.

The monster was getting out of the car, pulling his pistol, and Dash fired. The monster raised the pistol—but exploded before it could use the gun.

Philly felt some of its hot wet fluids splashing his chin, his wrist. He could smell blood.

Hands shaking, he took off the helmet.

He saw what was left of the cop's body—the upper half mostly gone. Pieces of uniform were well mixed in with blood and torn flesh. The lower jaw was missing from the staring head. Legs were still twitching.

He turned to check out J-dad. Nothing much left of him. "Take off your helmet, Dash."

"Do not take off your helmets yet," Sanguina said. "New orders are coming through."

Philly's voice sounded strange in his own ears. "I already took off mine, Dash. Take it off and look."

"She said not to!"

"Dude, take it off..."

Something in Philly's voice convinced Dash. He took off the helmet, looked around, Dash catching his breath, gagging. Down the street they could see other bodies, and pieces of bodies. A siren wailed in the distance.

"Did we shoot...Rafe?" Philly asked.

"No. He's not there."

"Boys," said Sanguina, her voice a little muted now, coming from the helmets they held in their hands, "put the helmets under your arms. Prepare for extraction.

We're sending some help to rescue you, so you don't get arrested."

Dash gaped at Philly. Philly shrugged.

A white van was screeching around the corner on their left, and pulling up. A beefy man with short hair and dark glasses stepped out of the front passenger side, smiling. He had a military style camouflage uniform on, but the only insignia on it Philly could see was the symbol of the game. The skull in the helmet, and the crossed rifle and light gun.

The gun...

Philly looked down at it. A wisp of vapor rose from it and peering into the muzzle he could see the tips of skinny transparent bullets of glass. "Those...it fires real ammo, Dash..."

"Don't look into that gun, kid," said the man, voice gruff but not unfriendly. He opened the sliding side door of the van. "If that weapon goes off you'll lose your head right off your fool neck. Get in the van, and we'll get you out of here. Or you want to go to jail for life, or what?"

Philly looked at Dash. Who looked at Philly.

Dash licked his lips. He looked at the bodies on the street. He heard the sirens.

What else was there to do?

Anyway—the guy had the insignia.

\*\*\*

*Yes sir, we brought them in, no problem getting them both clear of the field test area. Gang-killing cover story took hold, once we made the payments.*

*All test goals met, fifty?*

*They were, Colonel, in terms of subject connection, commitment, target identification. I think it was a good idea to go with the easy conditioning of adolescents. It will extrapolate, sir, I'm sure of it. If it works on the street, with people they know, including the caregiver designate, it should work in combat, if our people show signs of reluctance to take out targets. We can go from real-life view to conditioning view, just like that, in the new combat suit-ups.*

*And you think these two will be okay to cultivate for special missions?*

*Oh yes sir. They were ready to get out of there, just any way they could get out. They were more than ready. We feed them regularly, we give them structure, we give them support, we give them what they need. They're going to do a great job for us, out in the field. I think they're going to show real enthusiasm.*

# INTRODUCTION TO BIZARRO

## BY
## BIZARRO PULP PRESS

Bizarro Pulp Press is a small publishing company that first opened its metaphorical "doors" to the world of fiction in January, 2012…

But that's not exactly right. That's not exactly right because it should be nigh impossible to figure out when the idea was put into motion as an event that could be shared with the world. Where does an idea begin? Maybe it begins the moment you can have ideas, because one idea creates another, as one experience influences an idea, and an idea may fester in dreams or some other corridor of the mind.

That's a load of crap, too.

Bizarro Pulp Press was purchased by JournalStone publishing
in the summer of 2014 when everyone was fishing
Thirty silver pieces and not a coin less
one strange monster like the loch ness
they've published authors from all over the world
international literature flags unfurled
I want to know what bizarro is
how does it fit into the publishing biz

Here is a list of strategies to figure out who/what Bizarro Pulp Press actually publishes:

1. Pretend to know what "kind" of genre bizarro "is"
2. Go to Wal-Mart

3A. Purchase five books
3B. Read those five books (it might take you two hours)
3C. Understand that Bizarro Pulp Press will never publish a similar book

What kind of fool would suggest that their books aren't mass-market material? Isn't that the goal of a publisher… to make money? That might be another publisher's goal, but it is not Bizarro Pulp Press's goal. Bizarro Pulp Press will publish books that might fit into any number of genres, because books that test the limits of what fiction can "do" will resonate with those readers who are in the mood for something completely different.

The great philosopher, Gurney Halleck, once suggested that mood is a thing for cattle and loveplay.

Most folks enjoy watching popular shows, like *Survivor: Lost in Mexico City* or *Keeping Up With Famous Millionaire Athletes*, and we can admit that those things have a place in our lives. Oscar Award winning actor (insert trademark symbol to prevent

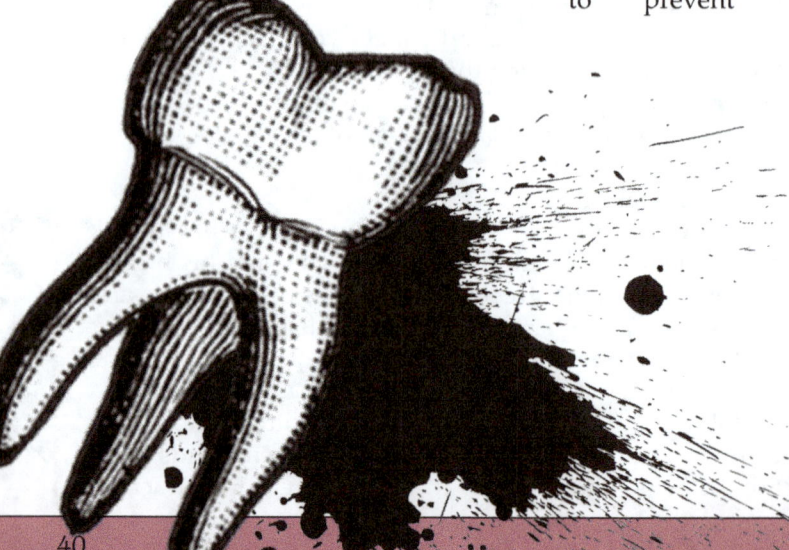

lawsuit) Nicolas Cage wouldn't keep making movies if people stopped watching them (or maybe he would just keep making movies that nobody watches). Pro sports leagues want to provide as much scoring and expensive merchandise as possible to keep us on the edge of our seats; in short, this is all cool stuff, and it's all popular. Sometimes, you might want to watch a movie that others have talked about, but isn't getting a lot of

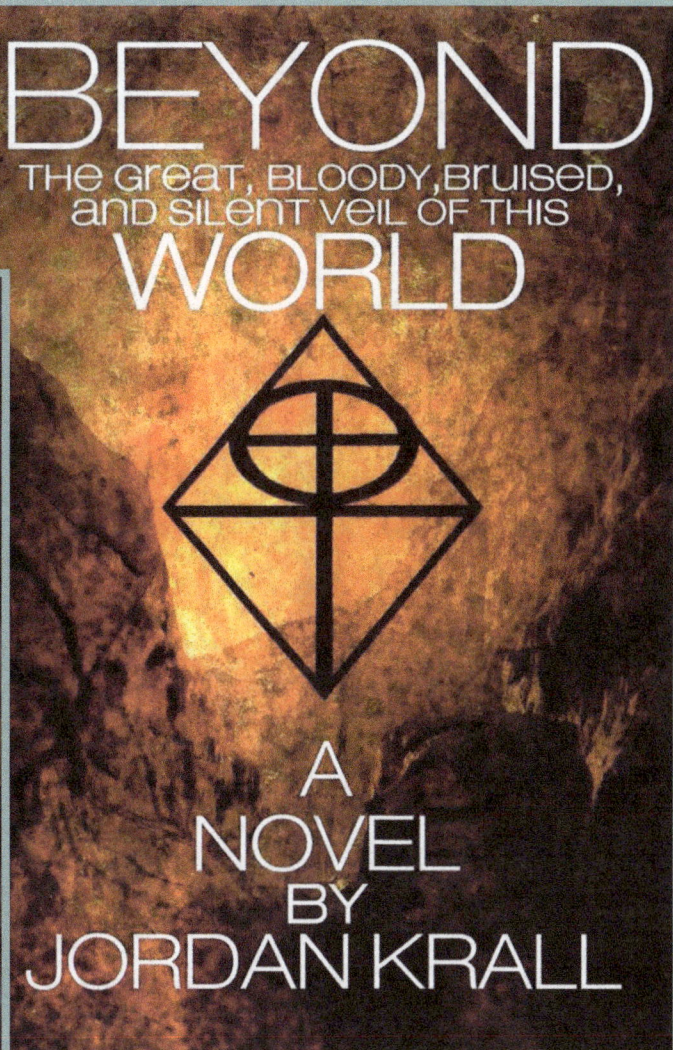

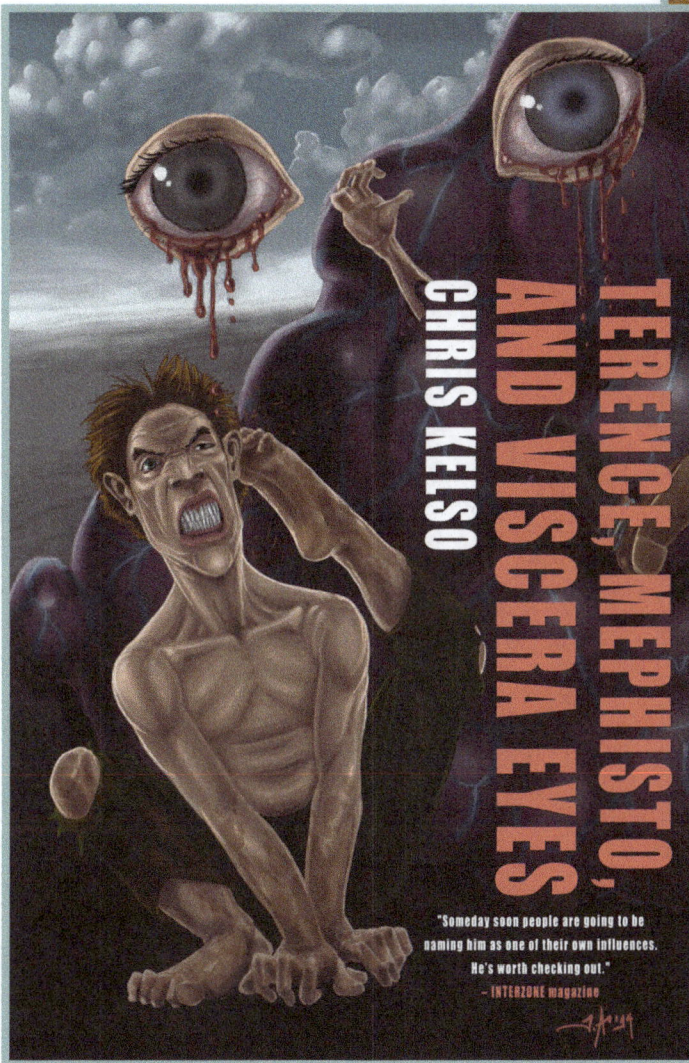

news. Maybe your friends found something on Netflix or Pornotube that you just have to check out because the plot is "Crazy, man, just unbelievable, you know, crazy, I don't know, it's weird, just… you gotta check it out."

Bizarro Pulp Press has published weird, gross-out fiction like *Fecal Terror* by David Bernstein and *The After-Life Story of Pork Knuckles Malone* by MP Johnson.

We've got surrealist journeys that take us into original, dreamscape worlds, like *All Art is Junk* by R. A. Harris and *Day of the Milkman* by S. T. Cartledge.

We've got B-movie, grindhouse-style horror-action like *Skinners* by Adam Millard, *The Fairy Princess of Trains* by Christopher Boyle, and *The ADHD Vampire* by Matthew Vaughn. We also got a cult film scriptwriter and actor named David C. Hayes with *Cherub* and *Cannibal Fat Camp*.

We've got metaphysical lyrical miracles, like *A Lightbulb's Lament* by Grant Wamack and *Necrosaurus Rex* by Nicholas Day.

Finally, we've got high-end speculative fiction genre-benders, like *Industrial Carpet Drag* by Bruce Taylor, *White City* by Seb Doubinsky, and *Terence, Mephisto, and Viscera Eyes* by Chris Kelso. We also like to publish poetry, like *Ascent* by Matt Bialer.

If you try to find out what the bizarro "genre" is by browsing cyberspace, you might be a bit confused. There's Anime-inspired metaphor fiction, celebrity satires, and one or two books that take themselves too seriously. Further research might reveal that the term was coined about seven hundred years ago in Venice, Italy, when a priest glanced at a translation of the Bible and thought it was "weird, a bit off somehow, not what people are used to." A bit deeper research into the internet might tell you something completely false about bizarro fiction: weird fiction was actually invented in the last fifteen years, and there was no such thing as non-mainstream, experimental, or otherwise "somewhat off" fiction that might feature talking animals on a farm as an extended metaphor for communism until the 21st century. In fact, satire wasn't invented until *Family Guy* aired on television, and satirical fiction was never published. If you have read "strange" literary fiction like *The Journal of Albion Moonlight* or *The Metamorphosis*, you actually haven't, because those things were never written. Trust me (TRUST US).

The person who wrote, or is writing, this article really seems pretentious. Who are they to have an opinion and

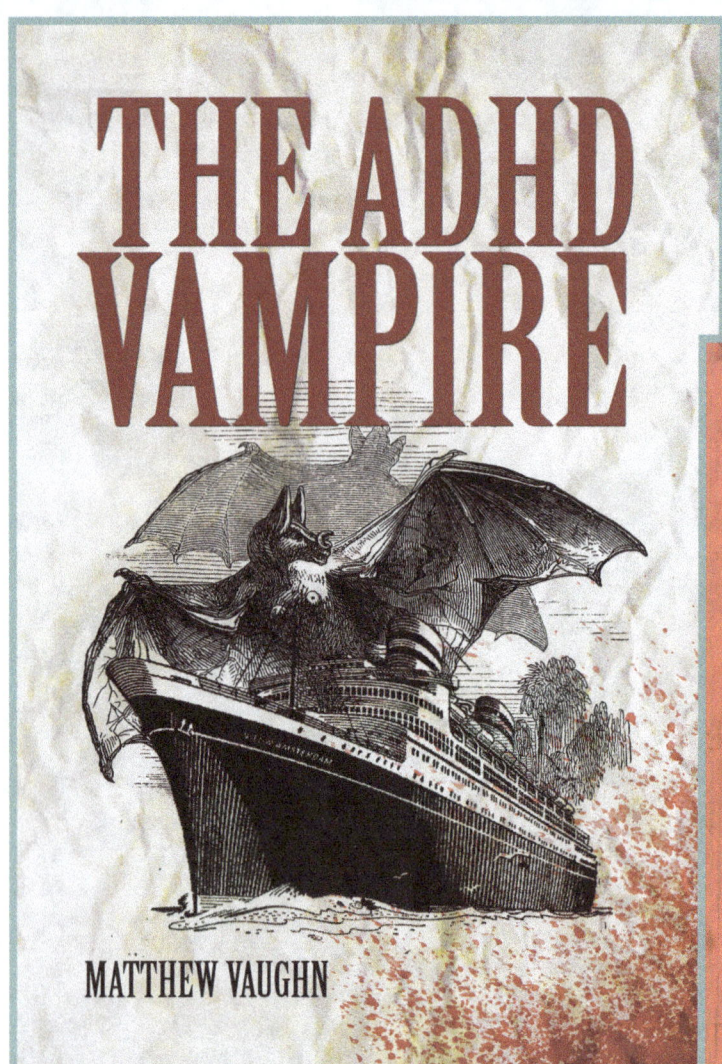

# THE ADHD VAMPIRE

MATTHEW VAUGHN

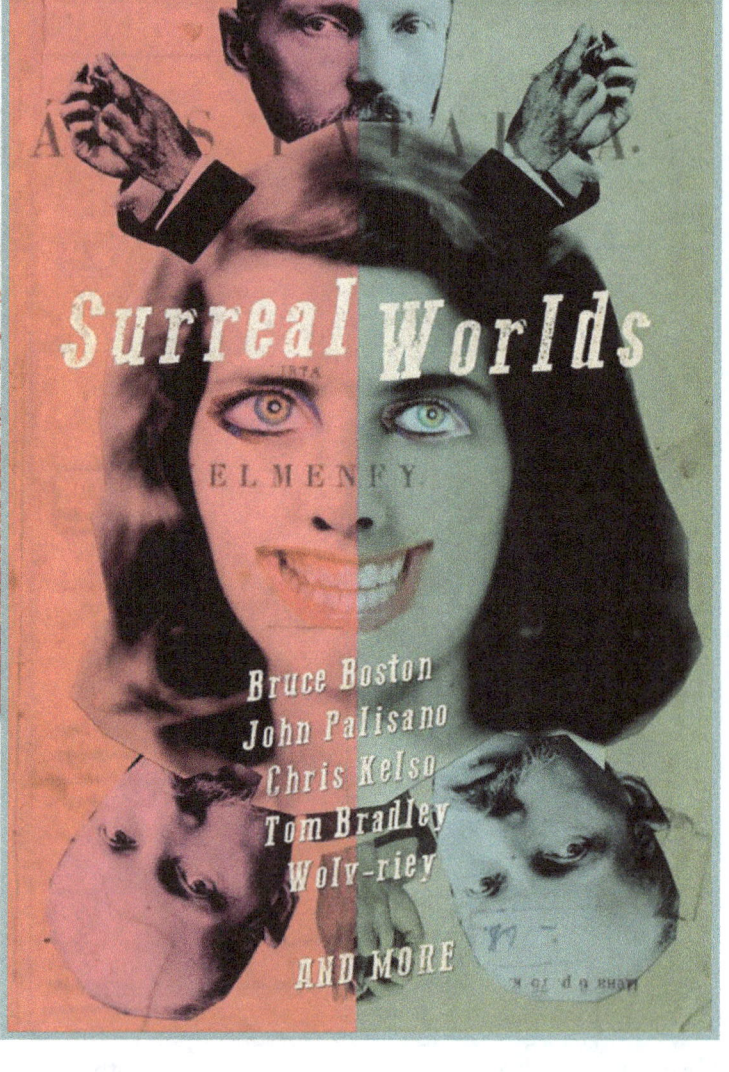

writer might seem, she/he is juggling a lot of everyday activities, including eating and sleeping. If not for the efforts of an awesome team, Bizarro Pulp Press simply wouldn't exist. Lori Michelle, the head formatter (and book formatter), is the pillar of our press. Editor Sean Leonard works extremely hard to make sure our words make sense. Chris Kelso, one of our authors, is also our "hype man," going out of his way to help promote projects and let people who use social media know that

make things up?

(It should be noted that Bizarro Pulp Press does not publish work that has been "made up," but rather, the press specializes in publishing non-fiction).

In 2015, the *Surreal Worlds* anthology will see the light of day. The collection features work from several award-winning authors, including (but not limited to): Bruce Boston, Steve Rasnic Tem, and Tom Bradley. This year's lineup also includes a dark comedy called *How to Successfully Kidnap Strangers* by Max Booth III, and a metafictional journey through the mind of Michael Allen Rose in *Boiled Americans.*

Our impressive lineup for 2015 will satisfy a diverse range of readers.

*The Boy Who Loved Death* by Hal Duncan
*Die Products* by Alan Spencer
*Sick Pack* by MP Johnson
*Great American Slasher* by David C. Hayes
*Rattled by the Rush* by Chris Kelso
*Beyond the Great, Bloody, Bruised, and Silent Veil of this World* by Jordan Krall
*The Bohemian Guide to Monogamy* by Andrew Armacost

We've tried to post tentative release dates in the past, but we anticipate delays. As pretentious as this

we exist. We also have amazing artists who create our covers, including Matthew Revert, Jim Agpalza, Justin Coons, and George Cotronis.

If anything, I hope you can take away one thing: Bizarro Pulp Press is made up of a group of folks who create interesting projects because we love to, and we believe in what we do. JournalStone Publishing has been amazingly, and not surprisingly, supportive of our endeavor, and we couldn't be happier to work with a professional group of creators, designers, writers, editors, and artists.

While we will never seek to define a genre or venture to suggest that we know what we're doing, we're going to continue to push the limits of literature and find out where the edge of the creative horizon is.

**P**aul Di Filippo is many things, including a prolific writer of novels and short stories, a comic book writer, reviewer and essayist. He hand-decorates postal envelopes and has an impressive selection of his envelope art on his website. He's an outgoing, affable sort, and when approached about an interview by a perfect stranger, he insisted on buying me a cup of tea at a café near his Providence, RI home and getting to know one another for a while. It was an easy, free-ranging conversation about writing, careers, and computer programming, and then we retired to his apartment to meet his wife and dog, view his enormous library of books, and talk about the transhumanist movement in literature and society. At his dining room table, surrounded by mountains of yarn, we shared ideas about the physical and psychological future of the human species.

**KHV**: You've been writing about the transformation of human beings in different ways for years and years. What interests you about transhumanism and possible changes to what we are as a species going forward?

**PD**: Well, you know, for the entire history of *Homo sapiens,* our genome has been fixed. It hasn't been subject to alteration and, nowadays, the prospect that that will no longer be true seems quite imminent. In the headlines, recently, we saw that actual scientific organizations are arguing for a moratorium on tampering with the human genome, so it's that real that people are actually worried that it's going to be imminent, so they are trying to put it off until we have a better grasp of what it means. So, the immanency of it makes it more interesting.

# A CONVERSATION WITH PAUL DI FILIPPO

## BY K. H. VAUGHAN

Photo courtesy of Paul di Filippo

In science fiction in the past, it was always Darwinian evolution that was seen as a factor. You had those great stories about ten million years in the future, people will have evolved into giant brains with little atrophied legs and so on, and so that was kind of the transhumanism of past science fiction: that it would happen over immense millennia, and it would happen kind of Darwinically. But, the fact that we now seem able to take it into our own hands makes it a much more urgent topic.

So, having seen that, even several decades ago, it seemed to me that, in science fiction, if our remit is to examine all of the potential pitfalls ahead of us and the potential glories ahead of us, then this is something that was right on the radar and right on the horizon. It needed some kind of fictional extrapolation and that's kind of what motivated me. Plus, it's very interesting. There's a lot of drama, there's a lot of sheer narrative potential in having alterations to the human species.

**KHV**: It seems to me that a lot of the stuff I read, and the stuff that seems very popular right now, tends to be on the darker side. Apocalyptic. Dystopias are very big right now. Why are people so concerned about what might happen? Are there rational grounds versus irrational grounds for this concern?

**PD**: Well, the whole issue of positive science fiction versus negative science fiction extends across every subgenre in a way. It's not just transhumanism or bioengineering where this crops up, and science fiction used to have a much more positive outlook. There were always dystopias going back as far as H. G. Wells or Aldous Huxley. There were always dystopian visions, but there were matching or equivalent positive visions of how technology could improve the human condition, and the balance seems to be skewed, as you say, more towards the dystopian these days.

Neal Stephenson, a very good science fiction writer, has made public pronouncements about how skewed this balance is and how he's hoping to restore it to a more even balance and produce some more positive visions that will guide society. He recently founded Project Hieroglyph, they did an anthology of kind of uplifting optimistic fiction that he felt was needed to balance this dystopian urge. So, I don't know, I think the literature can only reflect what is out there in society in general, and a lot of our problems seem huge or insurmountable and the social systems dealing with them seem inadequate, so a lot of that is driving the dystopian attitudes that people have. The old solutions don't seem to work, and the new ones haven't yet been formulated, so I think it just becomes easy to take the dystopian line towards things.

KHV: That's a little ironic, because if you look at where we are, at least in the U.S. and other industrialized countries, most people in human history would probably feel tremendously privileged to live here and now, but our outlook is in a lot of ways bleak.

PD: There is a kind of willful…not denialism, but kind of a willful pessimism in a way, and someone who has spoken out against this is the scientist Stephen Pinker. He just had a fascinating essay buttressed with a lot of statistics and reports where his thesis is that so many major trends are upward. He's most famous for the recent book *The Better Angels of Our Nature*, in which he argues that violence in human interactions is at an all-time low, and that warfare… there has never been as little warfare, even though our headlines seem to be full of it. He argues that there has never been as little consequential violence as there is now, and his essay that supplements this larger book looks at

health rates and education rates and rates of societal freedom, and he sees everything trending upward in a positive manner but being ignored by media and consequently by the populace at large who get their interpretation of things from the media. So, if you follow his argument and subscribe to it, it's like why aren't you writing stories that reflect this? It becomes kind of a conundrum about why more science fiction writers aren't doing this.

KHV: Yeah, we do seem to have a…I don't know what you'd call it…but there's an anxiety or tension. I don't know if this is about the shift in how global stability feels a little in flux or if it's more of a vague paranoia that seems to be infiltrating our consciousness, but it does seem to be out of proportion to the facts of our existence these days.

PD: Some of it is, I think, down to our individual over-connected lifestyle. I mean, not to say that ignorance is bliss, but I think that if you are fed a constant stream of seemingly bad news it's bound to distort your actual vision of how things are.

KHV: Right. There's a filtering process. There are people that are drawn to every tragedy, every horrible news story. There's an infinite amount out there if you want to look for it but it doesn't reflect the actual risks that we experience.

PD: And when global communications first took off with the advent of satellites that allowed real-time transmissions from around the globe, you had live transmissions. So now a typhoon in Japan could be seen and you could see live pictures of the destruction, but it was in the moment and it wasn't infinitely replayable. Now, if you want, you can watch the tidal wave that struck Japan on an infinite loop and just never forget about it. I think a lot of it is the fact that everything is in your face forever. That's part of it.

KHV: Looking at some of your work, I noticed a lot of references to singularities and panopticism and issues related to surveillance that are obviously very current and in our awareness for a lot of reasons. How do you think that's influencing where we are as a culture? In some cases I could see in your work in *Wikiworld*, where aspects of surveillance end up having a positive effect—someone keeping an eye on your apartment when you are out, but others that seemed to be less positive. Do you have some ambivalence about that or do you have a stronger view one way or the other?

Stories & Visions for a Better Future

EDITED BY
Ed Finn and Kathryn Cramer

FOREWORD BY
Lawrence M. Krauss

*Hieroglyph*

PREFACE BY
Neal Stephenson

Elizabeth Bear • Cory Doctorow • Karl Schroeder • Neal Stephenson • Bruce Sterling • and more . . .

**PD**: I try to investigate in different stories different aspects of it, from the upbeat to the downbeat. There's a brand new anthology out called *Watchlist*, and it's all about the surveillance society. I have a story in that which looks at some of the downbeat aspects of the surveillance society. I think the fact that we're all basically on a public stage now can have a debilitating effect. You look at internet scandals now and how somebody can go from being an innocuous unknown citizen to being the object of derision for millions of people. That has a debilitating effect on your psyche I think: to know that that could happen to you. It kind of ties in to that movement in Europe "right to privacy" where they've gotten Google to alter their search results if the courts determine that certain information should be removed. That ability to move innocuously through society and not feel like someone is always looking over your shoulder or looking at you and pointing a finger, that has been taken away from us to a large degree and I think that's bound to have an effect on our psyches.

**KHV**: There's a definite intrusiveness to it.

**PD**: Yeah. But you know, somebody like David Brin, who has a book called *The Transparent Society*, he tries to see the positive aspects of it, and Isaac Asimov way back in the sixties, before any of this became overwhelming—I mean there wasn't even the digital environment that we subsist in now—Isaac Asimov argued that a transparent society would protect people and have some positive benefits. And Brin argues the same in his book, and maybe we're heading toward that but we're just in the teething stage now.

**KHV**: I think the transparency is the issue, that if you think of Bentham and the panopticon, you've got to be able to inspect the inspectors as well. That's the key.

**PD**: Right.

**KHV**: I just saw an article, I believe it was in Los Angeles, where they have more police with body cams and they have found that it's producing a reduction in complaints of excessive force because, on the one hand it makes police behave better because they know they are being filmed but, on the other hand, people are less likely to file false complaints, so it potentially has a protective aspect for everyone. But I think it's difficult for people to get over that insecurity of being constantly watched or potentially surveilled all the time.

**PD**: There's a couple of great science fiction works, one is a short story and one is a novel, and the short story came first. It was by Damon Knight, the great SF writer, and it was called *I See You*, and it was all about the invention of a time-space viewer. The same trope was handled by Stephen Baxter and Arthur C. Clarke in a novel—I think it was called *The Light of Other Days*—but in both cases, the invention of an omnipotent time-space viewer was projected to be the effective end of human civilization. Because when you think about it, if you had a screen and you could look at all of time and space without constraint, so you could zoom in on Obama's bedroom when he was talking with Michelle or you could zoom in on Putin when he was conducting the Politburo meetings.

**KHV**: Or missing for ten days.

**PD**: Yeah, yeah. Access to that level of information, the ultimate in transparency, would effectively destroy civilization. So, that's like the upper bounds of the transparent society and it's pretty bad, so maybe we need something between total secrecy and that level of access to all information. There's probably things we're better off not knowing. And that kind of ties in with the famous quote from H. P. Lovecraft, I think it's in *The Call of Cthulhu*, where he says the worst thing that could ever happen is if the human brain was to be able to make all the connections between all the events in the universe that there are, you would go insane, and I think there's something to that, there's levels of information that we're not capable of processing.

**KHV**: Absolutely! One of things that I teach, I teach a course on genocide, and one of things you talk about when you start talking with students about the worst of human behavior is that they all come knowing a little bit, they've seen *Schindler's List*, they know about the Holocaust. Maybe, in this part of the country they know about the Armenian genocide, maybe a few other incidents here and there, but when you give them the *Big Golden Book of Atrocity* and have them start to thumb through that, you really have to tell them, look, there's always something worse that you can find out if you go and look for it. Part of the key to approaching this literature is to find out how much you can handle and not to flood yourself with even more and more and more, to know your limits.

**PD**: Well, I remember as a kid, growing up before the internet you'd go in the library if you were someone who liked reading and when the librarian wasn't looking you'd wander into the adult shelves, and maybe, if you had a friendly librarian, they'd even let you take out some adult books. So I remember I was probably in, like, fifth grade, I had discovered a book, it was called simply *Treblinka*—and it was by a Frenchman, I think, and I had never looked it up after, I should—and I took it out and that was my first awareness of the Holocaust. It was like your mind was blown! And you went through an immense period of mental adjustment dealing with this aspect of human history and human behavior. I would have been about ten years old. Ten, eleven, twelve.

**KHV**: That's a lot to absorb at that age. Even when you are older and have a better sense of your place in the world and some defense mechanisms that's a lot to approach that stuff. This may be an awkward *segue*, but you've got a lot of humor, and sense of playfulness in your work, even though you are often dealing with issues that are serious.

**PD**: Well, I'm basically an optimistic, playful person, so I like to try and incorporate that into the fiction. If I write a downer, tragic story it doesn't feel false, but it feels limited. Like, I think tragicomedy, some kind of Shakespearean… you've got this awful tragedy going on, but then you have these gatekeepers making fools of themselves in the middle for comic relief, and that always struck me as more organic or realistic and conformed to my view of what existence is all about. Life is too important to be taken seriously—isn't that Oscar Wilde or some other wit who said that? And I try, I think humor in fiction is always a plus in my book, and if you've got a message to get across, the humor can help convey it. It's more fun to read somehow.

**KHV**: And those little bright moments can get you through the darker parts as well. I mean, *The Road* by McCarthy, it's a grind. It's beautifully written, it's powerful but it can be a struggle to march through that because it is so unremittingly dark. And it wouldn't be his style to lighten things up. That's kind of who he is and what he writes, except maybe for some elements of more grotesque absurdity you might find here and there.

**PD**: Now, if you compare *The Road* to one of my favorites—I don't know if you would call it a post-apocalypse novel, maybe a post-change novel—it's John Crowley's *Engine Summer* in which civilization as we know it anyhow is effectively over and people are living in these remnant niches and yet that book is so—and I won't reveal the actual fate or condition of the protagonist at the end, it's not a happy fate—and yet that whole book is so bright

and life-affirming that it's an example of how you can do that: deal with some real, serious consequences in a light-hearted or light-handed way.

**KHV**: Coming back to the mind and the body and where we're going, going ahead, what do you see on the horizon? What are the changes that you see happening soonest, are there ones in particular that you have concerns about or that you think might be potentially dangerous?

**PD**: It seems to me that the first thing that they're going to engineer is repairing defects, because that is acceptable. You have a genetic defect or condition, or even an organic condition like cancer, to get you back to the baseline of health, that seems very arguable and not problematical. I mean everybody deserves the best health they can have, and if we can do it by tinkering with our genes, who's gonna object to that? So, that's the first step on the slippery slope if you want to look at it that way, and I think that's where the first advances are going to come. You've got sickle cell anemia or your child has it and we can cure it and who's going to argue against that? Nobody.

Next is going to come the so-called "improvements." Now you want photosynthetic skin or something like that, and it's like, "O.K., we can do that for you, and it's not part of the inheritance of Homo sapiens, but we can do that." And once you start approving the first improvements in the human condition, however small, that's where you end up in the Bruce Sterling *Schismatrix* universe where everybody is virtually their own species, you know, because they've had so many things tinkered with. So that I think is the progression from little non-problematical fixes up to drafting a new organism from scratch.

**KHV**: And then you get into some of the more technological modifications that are increasingly coming on board. Everybody thinks it's amazing when an amputee gets an artificial limb that is neurologically connected, but I saw an article where it was reported that someone was able to produce a temporary night vision with injections into their eyes.

**PD**: Yes, that was all in the headlines this week. We've been talking more about the organic side of things, but the whole cybernetic—turning people into cyborgs—and, you know, we all know somebody with artificial knees or hips or pacemakers inserted, so we're well on the path toward cyborg organisms. Getting away from the bioengineering side of it, that's another whole realm. We've already seen many advances in that. And you know, somehow, the squishy side of things always has a certain instinctive level of repulsiveness…like a lot of the body modification people, you see people with implanted horns and a lot of piercings and that turns some people off because it's somehow tampering with the squishy elements of the body, whereas a pacemaker just seems more like a new kind of wristwatch or something. It doesn't seem like a body horror kind of thing that a lot of horror fiction engages in. So who knows? We might see cyborg people before we see bioengineered people.

KHV: There's something about that that makes people very uncomfortable, you look at the Borg in *Star Trek*, there's an aspect that disturbs some people.

PD: And that's one, you bring up *Star Trek*, and here's a future a thousand years in advance of ours, but there's no real genetic engineering that we can see. I mean, Kirk is still Homo sapiens—he hasn't been tampered with. There are aliens and hybrid aliens, and human hybrids like Spock, but that future has no genetic engineering at all, and that was because at the time it was created, it just wasn't so much on the horizon.

KHV: Or theoretically, there might have been the period when they did that, sorted it all out and we've passed over it.

PD: And the future is not linear or unidirectional, and you get some SF that acknowledges that like Frank Herbert's *Dune*. He had to explain why there were no artificial intelligences and computers and it was because there had been the so called Butlerian Jihad where artificial intelligences were too powerful and they were eventually exterminated and there were laws passed that there would never be any such thing allowed. So there can be all sorts of setbacks and zigzags in the course of human progress.

KHV: The *Battlestar Galactic* reboot had that idea that we had to get everything back to analog and hardwired communication and get computers out of the loop. William Gibson in *Neuromancer* talks about having that electromagnetic shotgun pointed at every AI's 'head' to make sure that they behave.

PD: Right. In terms of what humanity will accept, look at the furry subculture. If there was technology that allowed people to become real-life organic furries, there would be a subset of humanity that would jump on that instantly.

KHV: Oh, absolutely. I mean it's almost certain to happen, right? Once you've got an idea out there and a technology, somebody's going to implement it. You wonder what we're going to look like in a hundred years.

PD: In my *Ribofunk* stories, I've got the animal hybrid underclass of "splices," and that was taken directly from Cordwainer Smith, I acknowledged that fully. He did such great work with that in his *Instrumentality* stories that I felt I wanted to take the idea and push it a little further if I could. But that whole notion of blending the genome, it's not just improving the human one but taking components of other species and mixing them in. That's a very potent kind of trope that science fiction can play with.

KHV: And there is that issue of the divide in social class today that is really kind of an extension of that, with scary implications.

PD: A British writer that I really admire, Adam Roberts, his newest novel is called *Bête*, the French word for "beast," and it's not strictly transhuman, but transbestial, I guess, where it's all about a future where this organic software chip is developed that allows any kind of animal to achieve sentience and it's a fascinating novel. I think I may have just invented a new word, transbestial, but if it's a new word, it's not a new concept because David Brin, again, has his whole *Uplift* series in which humans conceive of this notion that one of their ethical roles is to uplift animal creation and distribute sentience among as many species as possible.

KHV: But you couldn't assume that those sentiences would resemble human sentience or share our concerns, which is the issue with AIs that troubles some people, that AIs would have cognitive capacity that goes far beyond what humans individually possess, but be profoundly alien and not necessarily have our interests in mind.

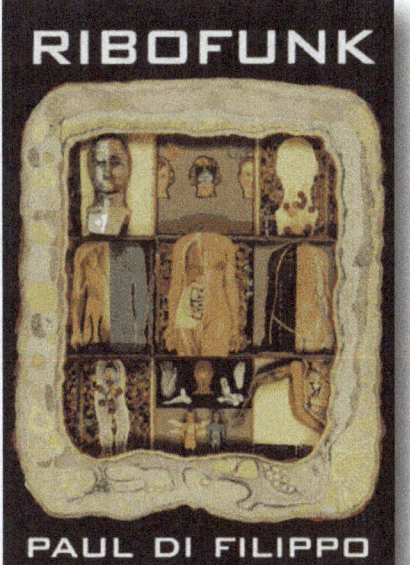

PD: Sure, and are we being egocentric or humancentric? Is it a gift to bestow sentience on other creatures? Sometimes you wonder. I mean, Adam Roberts deals a lot with that in *Bête*, a lot of the animals resent being uplifted.

KHV: It would make sense. Even with human beings, there is a basic trope again, that knowledge is not necessarily a good thing. It doesn't make us happy, per se. Some level of not knowing…

PD: That's the Edenic condition.

KHV: So what kind of things are you working on now? What's coming up?

PD: I mentioned that I've had to push back the new novel because I have some nonfiction writing that must be done, but the new novel…it doesn't have a title, it's a little nebulous, but it's going to be set in the future which is science fiction in its core but kind of reads like fantasy. So it's kind of like Gene Wolfe's *The Shadow of the Torturer* where it was literally a future environment, but reads like a fantasy one. So, it's going to be in that vein. I shouldn't reveal too much of it but it's going to be about a way in which the actual physical laws have changed, so that's going to give it the fantasy element.

That's the novel project. I'm still thrashing out a lot of it. I do know that it's going to be kind of like a *bildungsroman*. It's going to take a character from his youth to his elderly years, following all the changes through it, which I've never done in a book before, so I'm looking forward to it and I've admired other instances. In fact, Lucius Shepard, a very good writer who passed away a couple of years ago, his last book (*Beautiful Blood*) was inspirational because it followed that arc, took a character from his youth right up to his old age.

KHV: Circling back to the overall theme of transhumanism and how people are going to different, and maybe radically different going forward, obviously *Ribofunk* is a great collection for those kind of stories…

PD: Thanks.

KHV: And some of the stories in *Wikiworld* also touch on those ideas. Is there other writing of yours that people might look to if they are drawn to those themes?

PD: Well, scattered stories here and there in my other collections. I probably should put them all together in some kind of big transhumanist volume. I've never dealt with it in a novel before, which is territory I probably should investigate, dealing with it in novel length. There is my story collection called *Harsh Oases*, the title story really belongs in the *Ribofunk* sequence I think, but it was written after that collection so that's another collection people might track down. There's one or two there besides the title one. I do have a story called *The Singularity Needs Women*, so that's one that might appeal to people interested in transhumanism. What interests *me* about transhumanism is that it is not just a literary trope any more, there are actually transhumanist

organizations and people in the scientific community and lay community that are devoted to this as kind of a program, or a manifesto, or as a way of living. It's actually seeping out from the literature and there's a feedback cycle where the movement influences the literature and vice versa.

KHV: The acceleration of technological change is just extraordinary, and things we thought were impossible keep coming faster and faster. The changes we'll see in the human body in the next twenty years will probably be staggering.

PD: One of my favorite headlines from last week was "A Germ Clad in Graphene Functions as a Living Sensor," and I'm saying, "you take a germ and you give it an artificial skin and now it's a sensing device?" And I'm saying, "where am I?" [Laughs] I'm pretty much living in the transhuman *Ribofunk* future at this point, I think. We're at the cusp anyway.

\*\*\*

You can learn more about Paul's writing and art at http://paul-di-filippo.com/.

K. H. Vaughan's long-standing interest in transhumanism is on display in *The Future Embodied: Evolution of the Human Body* from Simian Publishing.

# THE HERPLE IS A HAPPY BEAST, OR, "NEIGHBORS ARE DELICIOUS!"

By Paul Di Filippo

I never wanted to become a herple herder. Very, very low on my bucket list—actually, right off the edge and into the abyss. But, you know, shit happens.

I did not spend my childhood dreaming of tending flocks of synthetic meat creatures, all the while building romantic castles in the air which featured me riding the range on my PintoPard. My teenage years did not find my bedroom adorned with e-ink posters of high-tech herphands and mega-rich herple barons, but rather those of the typical taqwacore pop stars of that era. I did not major during my college years in livestock or agriculture or transgenic splice optimization. In fact, I majored in quantitative analysis and statistics and operations research at Dartmouth's Tuck School of Business. Graduating in the top percentile of my class, feeling quite proud of myself, I landed my totally pliant first job right out of school with Mahon China Investment Management Ltd.

I loved Beijing and my high-flying consumption patterns. Wine, women and song. Or rather, *shaojiu*, *ernai* and augie-karaoke, right? Perhaps I craved the lush life a little too much. When I had a chance to substantially increment my income—to a life-changing degree—I leaped at the opportunity, despite the highly unorthodox, "off-label" scheme involving certain, shall we say, less-than-ethical and quantifiably illegal actions on my part.

Well, the venture was life-changing all right, just not along a positive vector. I and my co-conspirators were caught, thanks to being ratted out by a low-level AI we thought we had solidly suborned. (And those illicit computational cycles on a photonic machine we juiced the silico-sape with did not come cheap.) Languishing in a Chinese jail (*congee*, rats and flea-counting had replaced the aforementioned w, w & s), I faced possible execution—just because I and my fellow rogue quants had skimmed a few points off the global economy. I spent all my savings (squirreled away in unconfiscated Swiss accounts) on the best lawyer possible and, through him, the dispensation of much *guanxi* to the proper officials. I got off with a sentence of twenty years of stink.

The Chinese biofab boys tweaked my metabolism until I exhibited full-blown trimethylaminuria, more commonly known as "fish malodor syndrome." I exuded a permanent hardwired stench that had been known to make veteran fatberg hunters from the sewers of London retch. The hack was interlinked with fatal cardiac consequences attendant upon tampering. But the Chinese would happily reverse it all upon due completion of my term of punishment. This mod installed, I was deported back to the USA.

As you might well imagine, my job prospects—even my residential options—were narrowed down to an extremely small range.

I could not live in any kind of communal apartment building, or even in any spacious suburban setting with widely distributed homes. In the former case, my accumulated stench would eventually fill a substantial building. In the latter scenario, my mere presence lowered property values in the entire town that hosted me.

Likewise, I could not work in any kind of factory or office space where fellow humans congregated. And I could not live a hermit's rural existence and support myself by virtual employment. I had been banned from the digital commons for the same period of time as my stink, out of fear that I would find some way to cause any number of small countries to tank with some subsequent fiscal shennanigans. Okay, so Moldavia was just now emerging from the interregnum of food riots and fortified keeps that I and my pals had plunged it into. I had made a long and very sincere apology in front of the judge and jury and reporters, and it was all archived on VimmyTube. That should have covered things well enough, I thought. And finally, moneywise, my crimes had plucked me straight out of even the social welfare net.

No, my only option to keep body and soul together was to find a loner's physical job out in some pastoral wilderness, where I wouldn't have to thrust my obnoxious self in anyone's face.

Thus, viz, and QED: herple herding.

My current home and place of employment was the Coyote Creek Ranch, some three thousand acres of native rangeland with scattered pockets of timber, one of the many ranches in the region owned by ConAgra. Coyote Creek itself cut across the ranch for about two miles, carving out a lush riparian zone rich with wildlife. You could find me by geepsing the coordinates for Grant, Montana, at the western edge of the Horse Prairie Valley in Beaverhead County. I lived all by myself in a beautiful log home, featuring three bedrooms and four baths. The fieldstone fireplace alone merited inclusion in many home-dec tumblrs. I amused myself by alternately stinking up the three bedrooms in random fashion.

Human companionship, I had none. I never ventured into the town of Grant. Drones from Butte or Bozeman or Missoula delivered all my supplies. Several non-sape utility bots helped out. My Boston Dynamics PintoPard, whom I had named "Topper," provided transportation through the wilderness and a modicum of low-turingosity conversation.

And then, for company, there were the herples.

Thousands and thousands of herples.

You lucky and oblivious consumers never stop to think about living herples in their everyday environment when you're at the grocery store or supermarket or restaurant or food truck or kitchen fridge. So long as you are supplied with your vari-flavored herple meat—be it chicken herple or beef herple, pork herple or salmon herple, or a dozen other alternatives—you are content to regard the source of the synthetic foodstuff as an unacknowledged mystery, unworthy of thought or concern.

As well you should. For herple meat, that miracle synthetic protein that solved the world's food problems with complete ethical probity—nay, ethical sanctity—is indeed a done deal, a given, a foundational mainstay of civilization which requires no particular attention—except from those such as your modest narrator, Herpherder Langdon Goliad, and all the others tasked with the mild and pleasant job of raising the herple to maturity. You might as well bother to parse your breaths minute by minute, as ponder the herple.

Consequently, most consumers probably have no real conception of the herple's origin or shape or lifestyle. So allow me to explain.

This verbal portrait, of course, depicts the mature herple, not the tiny nymphs that emerge from the hatcheries and the slightly larger ones from the feedlot that are delivered to me also by drones.

First, assuming you're an ingenious sartor at work in your lab, you take a simple marine starfish or echinoderm, and blow it up to the size of a swimming-pool floatation mattress, in all its five-armed glory. Next, take the functional innards and meat of your common scallop, after discarding the heavy and useless bivalve shell, and scale those up as big as the rubber tire on a large industrial backhoe. Cover the tender scallop with the borrowed protective carapace of a shrimp. Mate the vertical scallop organically and seamlessly to the horizontal starfish. Endow the composite organism with lungs and some very rudimentary senses. No brain, of course, as the scallop's ganglia suffice for its simple range of behaviors. Splice in whatever genes from baseline beasts you need to achieve the desired taste.

Now, place what looks rather like a giant upright rose-tinted pulsing cinnamon bun with protruding yellow ventral fingers on a pasture. The free-range herple—so named for its absolute brainlessness—will now trundle slowly in a random walk, starfish mouth pressed to the nutritious grass, getting bigger and bigger and more delicious and meatier, squirting out the occasional almost odorless liquid pasture-replenishing excrement, until it is harvested and slaughtered.

Nearly a hundred years ago, the famous bioethicist Peter Singer opined that scallops and their cousins were the highest form of organism that a self-respecting human being could or should eat, given that their nervous systems and consciousnesses were too rudimentary to experience suffering.

Even earlier, a cartoonist named Al Capp had conceived of a creature named the Shmoo, infinitely bountiful and tasty and amenable to being eaten.

The herple claimed these two great thinkers as its spiritual parents.

My job minding the herples was simplicity itself. They were enrobed with smart dust so I could track and monitor them. An app on my otherwise dumb phone alerted me whenever one threatened to stray outside the boundaries of Coyote Creek Ranch. Then I would ride Topper out to the stray and redirect it back onto our property. Sometimes a herple got trapped in a thicket or fell into a ditch it could not emerge from on its own. I effected a rescue. Otherwise, I had no urgent tasks. I passed most of my copious free time reading actual paper books and watching antique DVDs. (I wasn't even allowed any smart AV media devices, lest I hack them.) I became intimate with a thousand gradations of Montana weather and climate. I tried writing my autobiography, but got no further than fourth grade. I taught Topper to play Scrabble, and he frequently won.

I often thought of the joke about the factory operated by unfailing robot workers and otherwise staffed only by one human and one dog. The human's only assignment was to feed the dog. The dog was present to bite the human if he tried to interfere with the robots. A cautious and monitory Topper played the dog's part here.

Several years of this bland existence, and I could feel my anger, guilt and impatience mellowing to a kind of bland zen acceptance. My frequent appeals for early release continued to come back denied. I foresaw that by the end of my time here, my brain and ambitions would approach that of a herple.

And then something began eating my flock.

\* \* \*

Walter Scarrow, the ConAgra executive responsible for Coyote Creek Ranch's bottom-line performance, was not happy with me. I had only his vocal tenor to go by, my dumbphone lacking any visual functions, but that was plenty. I could picture a young, slick, ambitious fellow disinclined to let the ineptitude of some subordinate mess up his own annual bonus. In short, someone rather like what I myself had been at Mahon China Investment Management Ltd.

"Tell me again how many herples have gone missing," Scarrow demanded.

"Exactly one hundred and fifteen during the past nine days. And they haven't gone missing, precisely."

"What do you mean?"

"Well, their carcasses are still present. Or were, until I buried them. As far as I could tell, forensically speaking, each herple had just one bite taken out of it before being mauled and savaged."

"Rendering them totally unfit for processing, of course."

"Of course. Unless you'd like to introduce possible pathogens from the mauler into the food chain. You do remember past ConAgra debacles, I believe, such as—"

"That's quite enough, Goliad. I don't need any lessons in corporate responsibility from a fishboy fuckup like you." Scarrow paused. "You say you captured video from the attacks?"

The smartdust with which the herples were cloaked featured an omnidirectional array of low-res nanocams. "Yes. But all the attacks have been at night, and the nanocams don't deal so well with that low level of ambient light."

"What could you see?"

"Not a pack. Just one attacker. Something about the size of a human—maybe a little bigger—moving really, really fast. No weapons deployed that I could spot. Just the lone creature."

"What kind of predators do you have down there?"

"My god, what don't we have? Montana is like a freaking zoo! We've got bears, big cats, wolves, eagles— you name it. And that's just the baseline stuff. But here's the thing. Every single specimen of all those species are tagged with smartdust too. I get regular updates from the US Fish and Wildlife Service whenever any critter gets close to the ranch. Then I herd the herples out of danger. But there's been no report like that in weeks."

"So we're talking about some weird animal that's off the grid. Maybe escaped from some black clinic."

"I guess."

Scarrow pondered the marching orders he was about to deliver, but I could easily anticipate them. And he did not disappoint me.

"You do realize that each of those herples has a market value of about twelve hundred dollars. So your negligence has cost the company"—I did the math in my head faster than Scarrow—"one hundred and thirty-eight thousand dollars so far. You've got to intercept this killer and neutralize it."

I refrained from asking how my actions could possibly be deemed "negligence," simply because I had failed to anticipate the utterly unprecedented. "And how would you suggest I do that?"

"That's not my baliwick, that's yours. Otherwise, you will have to be replaced with someone more competent. Just take out this attacker, by any means at your disposal, if you want to keep your job. Goodbye, Goliad. I'll expect some results in the next few days."

After I finished swearing at the dead connection, I began to seriously angst about losing this pitiful niche. Finding this job had been arduous enough. I didn't feel like starting from scratch just to secure another humiliating prole sinecure.

From here, my emotions seesawed into anger at Scarrow and at myself for ever ending up in such a bind. Add in an unhealthy dollop of self-pity, and I was soon a totally non-pliant mess.

I went seeking advice from the only source possible: Topper, my mechanical steed.

Topper occupied a kind of porte-cochere structure with open sides in the warm months, one of which, August, now ruled the calendar. In the winter, smart walls with built-in heating elements snapped into place. Not that Topper needed much protection from the elements. But not having to shovel him out from under a snowdrift every time I wanted to use him made my life easier.

My presence roused Topper out of his rest mode. A seventh-generation product of Boston Dynamics, powered by feedstock-omnivorous fuel cells, he resembled his ancestors in looking like a headless sofa on stilty legs, except a thousand times sleeker, faster, more capable and more compact. And smarter too, natch.

Topper's pleasant voice, issuing from his midsection, always disconcerted me slightly.

"Langdon, I trust all is well. Do you need my services?"

"Yeah, listen to this."

After I had recounted my dilemma, Topper said, "Can you plot the coordinates of the one-hundred-and-fifteen attacks on a map and show it to me?"

"Sure."

"Please do so. Meanwhile, I shall order us some weapons and other gear."

Unlike me, Topper was totally connected to the infosphere. His ability to communicate with the outside world in modern mid-twenty-first-century fashion came in handy. I learned about his functionality that time I managed to gash my arm with an axe while chopping firewood, and the medevac entomopter arrived before I even finished tying off the makeshift bandage. Totally ungrateful, I had tried physically to hack into his communications module while he was offline. Believe me, you don't want to know what even a modulated kick in the gut from a seventh-generation PintoPard feels like. But of course, there were

no hard feelings afterwards—at least not on Topper's part.

Inside the house, I found the paper USGS map of the ranch. Laboriously, using the GPS data from the kills stored on my tracking app, I plotted the deaths with a pen. It took forever, and I cursed my lack of any iTools that would have made the task trivial. But the old-fashioned, concentration-requiring work by hand did have the effect of calming me down. I brought the finished research out to Topper, who scanned it with the forward-facing eyes in his "chest."

Suddenly I realized something. "Hey, you had all those GPS coordinates of the kills already. You didn't need me to plot them out on paper."

"This is true, Langdon. However, I judged that your emotional state required a distracting task in order to regain optimal levels. Was I wrong?"

"No...I guess not. All right, what have you learned?"

"I have stochastic forecasts of where the next strikes will occur, ranked in order of probability."

"What'll we do with that?"

"We will camp out each night until we encounter the creature, then subdue it."

"You planning to kick it to death?"

"To the contrary, you shall effect the capture, and thus gain the esteem of Mister Scarrow."

"How?"

As if in answer, the buzz of an approaching drone caught my ear. Soon, I had the delivery unpacked.

Among certain other items, one pistol represented an active-denial system weapon, or in common terms, a "pain ray." The other was a scattershot Taser shotgun with multiple XREP loads. Both guns would blanket a wide target area, requiring no expertise on my part.

"I think those should be sufficient for any eventuality," said Topper. "Now, if you'd care for a Scrabble rematch."

I sat on a wooden crate amidst the summer warmth and bird calls and pleasant scents (my own stink had been edited out of my sensorium, the highly ethical Chinese authorities feeling that a perpetual fishy assault on my own nose would constitute "cruel and unusual punishment"), took out my phone and booted the Scrabble app. Topper got to go first.

"I believe my initial play is worth fifty-nine points, Langdon."

Regarding my tiles, I sighed. "Is 'fubar' a word?"

"Not officially, no."

* * *

Midnight of our third night camping out. The ritual was getting really old. Cold beans and shivering under a blanket. We couldn't have a light or a fire, for fear of giving ourselves away to any attackers, and I was perched uncomfortably all night on a small folding stool set in an improvised blind made of poles and smart camouflage fabric. Daytimes were for sleeping.

Right now, trying to stay awake, I cradled both of my weapons across my lap. Topper, legs folded under him, bulked nearby, looking like a remarkably sleek boulder.

The passive happy idiot herples all around us, being diurnal creatures, had hunkered down in whatever passed for sleep in a mollusk-echinoderm chimera. I fantasized submarine snores, like something out of classic SpongeBob.

The night-vision glasses were giving me a headache, so I lifted them off my face. The lofty star-spangled darkness slammed back with renewed vigor, as if in eternal triumph over mankind's pitiful and short-lived technology. My mind wandering along these lines, I mused on how science continually succeeded in reifying the most outrageous fantasy objects born of primitive dreams. The herples, for instance, resembled scaled-up versions of the Kaldanes of Mars, those heads with vestigial spider legs that I had seen once in the fifth *John Carter* film.

My thoughts began to evanesce into less intelligible conceits, and I wondered if I should pop my first stay-awake pill of the shift. How many nights would I have to be out here—

"You can hide from my eyes," came the soft feral feminine breathy whisper just millimeters from my cheek, "but you still smell so delicious, for miles and miles around."

I landed on the ground about twelve feet from where I had been sitting, the apparatus of the blind entangled around me like a bony straitjacket. I thrashed and yelped. "Topper, Topper, wake up!" But all the noise I made failed to drown out a mad ecstatic predator's laughter.

While I struggled, I heard next the unmistakable wet smacking sound of herple meat being chomped and rended. Voiceless, the poor herples gave no alarms or screams. Insanely, I began to salivate, recalling the wonderful taste of roasted turkey herple at Christmas.

Freed from the tangle, I found myself still clutching the Taser shotgun. I swiveled around frantically, unsure where to discharge it.

The whole scene suddenly flooded with light, nearly blinding me. Topper had activated his onboard LEDs.

With more sensitive vision, the attacker reacted even more intensely to the glare than I had, letting out a yowl of pure rage.

I brought the gun around to where a photo-negative silhouette loomed in my patchy vision, and let both barrels fly.

Several of the XREP projectiles connected, each discharging its incapacitating amperage into the target, which convulsed and dropped to the ground.

Very cautiously I approached the still recumbent form.

Alongside me, Topper dimmed his lights, allowing me to see more clearly.

"Holy shit, it's some kind of catwoman!"

"More woman than cat, I would estimate, with apparently just a twenty-three percent transgenic component, plus or minus three percent."

I suddenly realized the catwoman was totally naked save for a lovely rust-colored pelt, that I had not seen a naked woman for several years, and that she had said I smelled delicious.

\* \* \*

Luckily the Coyote Creek Ranch barns offered enough leftover building material to construct a sturdy outdoor cage to hold my conquest. No way was I going to share the house at night with something that could turn a five-hundred-pound herple into so much raw chum. The more and thicker walls between me and her, the better.

The day after we brought the bound unconscious catwoman back home, draped across Topper's withers, I still had not decided how to deal with her and her transgressions. And her obstinate, obdurate and obstreperous behavior was not making my decision any easier.

This morning I had erected my camp stool right outside her cage—out of reach of her incredibly fast clawing—and sat regarding her ruminatively. Placid for the moment, finishing her requested breakfast of raw, thawed trout— did I mention how great the fishing was in Montana?— the catwoman lifted her eyes from time to time to regard me with enigmatic intent. Their nonhuman aspect, along with her fangs and her lustrous fur and angrily switching tail, left me feeling as if I had stepped into some Qingdao Studios fantasy epic: *Man-Kzin Wars XXII*, maybe. Humans with this degree of transgenic alteration were still a small louche minority, not generally encountered in respectable levels of society.

Beside me, Topper too regarded our captive. When I said nothing, the PintoPard spoke.

"Miss, perhaps you would care to share your name with us now?"

"*Rowr!*" The plastic breakfast bowl bounced off Topper's body. "Let me out of here! I'll turn you all to pink jelly and shredded circuit boards!"

Topper calmly replied, "Contrarily, that would seem the very inducement not to free you."

The catwoman's anger stoked my own. "You listen to me, you rotten selfish furry bitch! Your fun and games among my cattle almost cost me my job. It might yet, unless I turn you in to the authorities. At first, I admit, I was a little intrigued by your case. You seem to be some kind of antisocial loner, like me. But now I'm rapidly getting turned off by your lousy selfish attitude. Show me something that would make me be on your side."

The catwoman slumped down in one corner of the cage and started to sniffle miserably. "Chee Lan," she said. "My name is Chee Lan."

"That is the cognomen of a fictional catwoman," said Topper.

Chee Lan jumped up. "It's my name now! I made it my own! Through all the pain of being reborn!"

"But before then?" I prompted.

Chee Lan's expression grew distant. "Before then, it seems like a dream…"

Thalia Cress had been an administrative assistant at the San Francisco Public Utilities Commission, in the department that regulated waste-to-power companies. Her duties, pay and prestige had been minimal but sufficient for her modest nature. She lived alone in a micro-apartment of some two hundred square feet, with no steady romantic involvement or cultural passions. All her life, from nursery school on, she had been trained to be a good docile member of society: unquestioning, obedient, hard-working. Respect for authority figures was ingrained in her.

Which was why she blindly obeyed her boss's orders

to conceal his bribe-taking, without even profiting a penny from it herself. And of course, when he eventually went down, so did she.

Thalia lost her job, but got off with a suspended sentence and some community service. A criminal! Her parents wept and wept. Her old girlfriends shunned her.

A lifetime's worth of some received moral probity inside her snapped. She took her not inconsiderable working-girl savings to a black clinic in Los Gatos, and emerged as Chee Lan.

Chee Lan's backwoods hegira eastward across the broad West, ending here in Montana, had taken nearly a year.

"A year of being chased and shot at and feared. Of cold nights and hunger and total aloneness. Of sore paws and fleas. Of looking at lighted windows from outside in the rain and snow. And you know what? It's been the best fucking year of my whole goddamn life! What a boring little wimp Thalia Cress was! Chee Lan would have chewed her up and spit her out! *Rowr*! And when I found your herples, I was in heaven! Such delicious neighbors!"

"But why did you kill more than you needed to eat?"

Chee Lan looked somewhat chagrined. "I couldn't help myself. Once I bit into those tasty, tasty herples, a kind of madness came over me, a blood lust. It was their sheer inviting defenselessness that did it. I just had to kill until I was satisfied. They begged me to die."

I thought then about my own lust for more money than I had ever really needed, and found little difference between us.

So I told Chee Lan my life story in return.

She listened with apparent appreciation. "Wow. So that's why you smell like you do."

"You, uh—you said I smelled delicious."

Chee Lan ran a raspy tongue over her sharp incisors. "Oh, you do, you do. I could just lick and lick and lick your sweat all day."

"But no biting?"

"Not fatal, no."

I moved to the cage and unlocked it.

"Langdon," said Topper, "do you think this is wise?"

But I was already undressed and rolling on the soft ground with a wiry and erotically static-charged Chee Lan, and could not really fashion a coherent reassurance to Topper's question.

* * *

I had never been this far north of the Coyote Creek Ranch before, but the landscape was still familiar: rolling green hills, plenty of watercourses, a mix of deciduous and evergreen trees, some larger isolated rock formations. The rare almost untraveled paved road, across which we cut, avoiding people at all costs. God's country. Riding with the metronome gait of Topper, Chee Lan jogging on all fours beside me like a blown orange autumn leaf (those sartors had done some ingenious work on gimbaling her joints), I felt happy and completely at peace.

Three days back at the ranch had passed in a veritable two-person orgy. Chee Lan had gone without sex almost as long as I had. But eventually, we detumesced long enough

to ponder our future—even without Topper's annoyingly avuncular prodding.

Reluctantly, like adults, we soon came to the conclusion that we had to part. Our brief affair had to end. I could not survive without civilization and a job, and indeed was looking forward someday to regaining my place in society. But in her new being, Chee Lan could not stand to be bound to any one place anymore. Indoors equaled cages.

"But I can't just let you go free," I said, having donned a mask of corporate sensibility over my personal sadness. "I can't take the chance that you'll attack my herples again."

"You won't simply accept my word?"

The shallow claw furrows on my back still ached, even under the topical anesthetic antibiotic cream. "Not when all your instincts demand otherwise."

"All right then. I'll go to Canada."

"How will that solve anything?"

"The USA-Canadian border," said Topper, "is relatively permeable south to north. The Canadians are lax. But north to south, it's lethal."

"I see… Okay, it's a deal. But I'll have to come with you, to make sure you cross over."

"That would be fine. I'd enjoy your company."

"Me too."

And so I phoned Scarrow and fed him a story that approximated the truth.

"I neutralized the predator," I said. "Some kind of weird chimera. One of those escapees you hear about."

"Fantastic! You'll be Jack the lad again before you know it. I'll certainly put in a good word with the parole board at your next hearing. Meanwhile, what kind of bonus can I send you? How about some vintage DVD porn?"

While Scarrow and I conversed, Chee Lan was sitting on my lap and licking from my collarbone up to my ear. Her tongue felt like a wet warm flexible emery board.

"Uh, yeah, sure, we'll talk soon!"

I put the utility robots in charge of the herples. They could do a halfway decent job for a week or so, although their default response was to cluster the herples tighter than the beasts preferred, causing a lack of meat-toning exercise. I packed clothes and kit and set out with Chee Lan.

Now, here we were, in the middle of a relatively short journey of some three hundred miles across a beautiful territory, with no responsibilities other than to enjoy the trip and ourselves.

It was an idyll. I never wanted it to end. We saw wonders. A giant herd of megatheriums, shuffling like landships across the grasslands. Endless acres of remediative sunflowers growing on former fracking fields: not only did their powerful roots repair the geology, they also concentrated hydrocarbons within themselves for harvest. And then there came the endless aerial river of passenger pigeons, each modded bird carrying out, almost literally, cloud computations. And the nights—I won't embarrass you with the details.

Then came the day we would reach the border. We made a noontime camp amidst a small clearing in what seemed a primeval forest where shafts of sunlight formed a golden cathedral. We both lingered, reluctant to say farewell.

"Won't you come back to the ranch to live with me?"

"Won't you go dingo, and roam with me?"

The hopeless requests were *pro forma*. We both knew how irreconcilable our needs were.

We started to have sex one last time.

Luckily we were both low to the ground when Topper flew over us at waist level, a silver missile.

I had never seen a grizzly bear so big as the one that had invaded the clearing. Ragged, desperate, obviously a lab-born escapee. But even more appalling than its size—which had allowed it to bat away Topper as if the PintoPard were a mouse—was the ring of wriggling octopus-like tentacles emanating from around the bear's neck.

"Fire!" roared the beast. "Give fire! Bears need fire! Cook food!"

I scrambled for the Taser shotgun where I had offloaded it from Topper. The robot horse was struggling to right itself, like an overturned beetle. I grabbed the gun and blasted both barrels at the bear. The stings of electricity had no more effect on it than the same number of hornets.

Then Chee Lan launched herself through the air at the beast.

Her mouth fastened on the bear's neck, above the tentacles. The closest extrusions wrapped around her and tried to pull her off. Meanwhile her back claws dug into the bear's belly, while the bear's foreclaws raked at her lithely twisting form.

I hoisted the shotgun by its barrel and made to dash in and use it as a club. But before I could get in close, the bear toppled, a geyser of arterial blood spurting from its neck. It landed atop Chee Lan.

I never had any particular reason before to believe in hysterical strength. But somehow, using the shotgun, I levered a thousand pounds of grizzly off Chee Lan.

She wasn't conscious, but she was still breathing.

Topper labored over, one motor making a whining noise in a dragging leg. "I do not detect any single mortal wound, but cumulatively…."

"What can we do?"

"The medevac 'mopter is already en route. But your first-aid kit is right here."

Even after his beatdown, and with a busted leg, Topper had secured the kit and dragged it over with a hoof. That was friendship, that was grace under pressure. No ties of flesh even necessary. It dawned on me that my robot horse was a better man than I.

I sprayed and clamped and injected and bandaged as best I could, then I cradled Chee Lan's head in my lap. Her blood and the bear's was all over my nakedness.

I remembered what Chee Lan had said, about earning her new name through the pain of being reborn, and prayed she could do it again.

The EMTs who rushed from the 'mopter redid my paltry half-assed fixes and stabilized Chee Lan. Soon the two of us were riding in the 'mopter to a big hospital. The EMTs and pilot all wore pocket-sized rebreathers to tolerate my stink.

Topper had been left below, awaiting an overland salvage buggy.

If I had known then I would never see the PintoPard again, face to sensors, I would have made a more formal farewell, and told him how much he had done for me. As it was, I had to be content with sending him an e-card every Xmas and letting him beat me at Scrabble now and then from hundreds of miles away.

Much to my initial surprise, the 'mopter headed north, not south.

And that made all the difference in our future.

Turned out this ambulance and crew, the closest to our call, were Canadians, returning from delivering a recovering US patient home when they had gotten our distress signal.

Now we were flying into Medicine Hat, Alberta, their home base.

Once we got Chee Lan settled into intensive care under deft robotic ministry and saw that her prospects for full recovery looked bright, official attention turned to me and my status.

I got ready for a quick deportation back to Montana.

But I hadn't counted on being an instant social media sensation.

News of Chee Lan's heroic battle with the grizzly, featured in Topper's purloined, jittery, sometimes upside-down AV feed, had gone viral, with the naked butt and pixelated genitals of yours truly featuring prominently. Soon headlines everywhere—FLEEING CROSS-SPECIES LOVERS FACE DEATH BRAVELY TOGETHER—had us pegged as the Fishboy Romeo and Catgirl Juliet.

Chee Lan's new biofabbed identity was legally deemed distinct from that of her past human avatar, Thalia Cress, and she was given Canadian citizenship. I received legal immigrant status.

And then the Canadians got the Chinese to commute my sentence! The hero rewarded! Relations between Canada and China trumped those between the USA and the People's Republic. It didn't hurt that the Canadian Prime Minister's wife was named Xiayun Zhao.

I stood in the lobby of the Medicine Hat hospital to meet Chee Lan on the day of her release.

She wrinkled her sensitive nose. "You don't smell like dinner anymore."

"I've got a solution for that. Just listen…."

So now Chee Lan and I live in a cute little cabin just outside of town. One bedroom, one bath. At least, we share the house when she's not out prowling the Alberta wilderness, roaming under the wide-open skies in all kinds of weather, working for the government to spot dangerous escaped chimeras and tag them. I worry about her, of course, but she's a big girl.

As for me, I run Goliad's Fishing Tours. I take out anglers on the South Saskatchewan River, where we fish for super-sturgeons. Wrestling those one-ton fish into the boat with exo-skeletal assist usually leaves me liberally slimed and smelly.

And if I know Chee Lan will be home when I get back, I make sure never to wash up.

HAL BODNER SHOWS US BABY JANE'S EVEN DARKER SIDE. WE SEE GUNSLINGERS SHOOT IT OUT AT LOW MIDNIGHT. DR. CALIGARI'S LEGACY OF EVIL ISN'T OVER.

JG FAHERTY KNOWS ABOUT A CAMERA OF SPECIAL ATROCITY. AMY GRECH FINDS TOO MANY MEANINGS IN THE WORD "SHOT." JAMES DORR EXPLORES NEW TERRITORY FOR ZOMBIES. JAMES CHAMBERS PROJECTS HALLUCINATORY MONSTROSITIES. POETS KAREN HEAD AND CAROLINE SHRINER-WUNN BLEND THE EROTIC AND THE MACABRE. REEL DARK SMASHES REEL AGAINST REAL, AND IT DELIVERS A RANGE OF CHILLS AS VAST AS THE MOVIES.

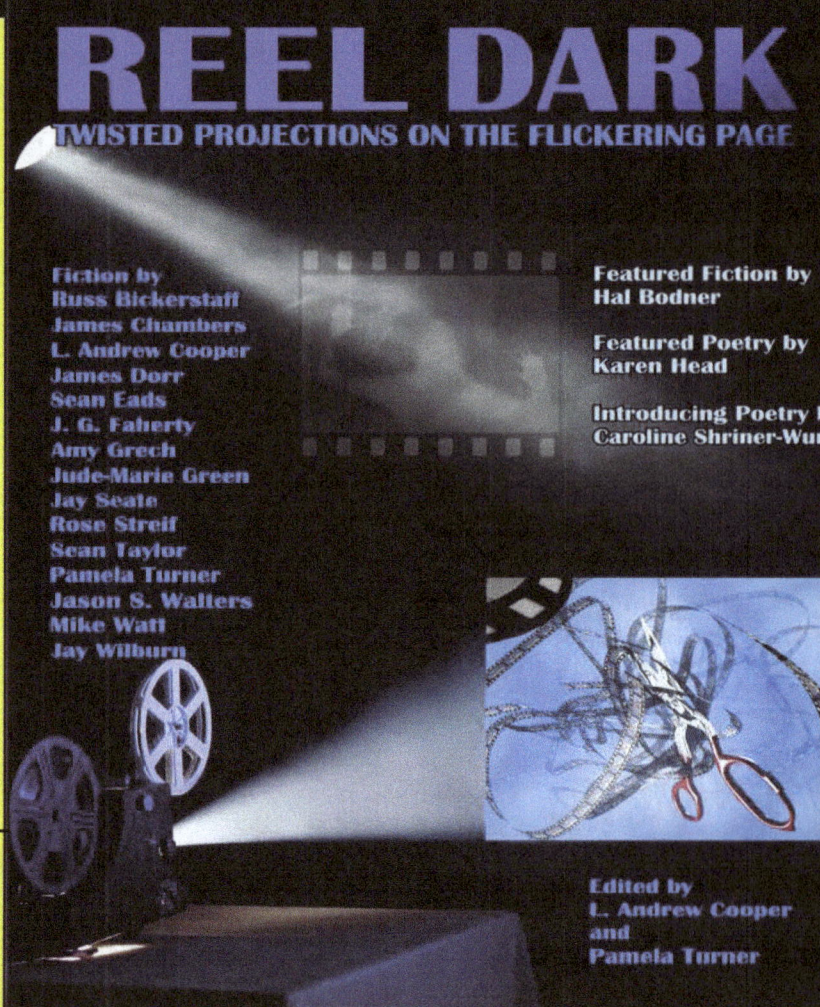

REEL DARK
TWISTED PROJECTIONS ON THE FLICKERING PAGE

Fiction by
Russ Bickerstaff
James Chambers
L. Andrew Cooper
James Dorr
Sean Eads
J. G. Faherty
Amy Grech
Jude-Marie Green
Jay Seate
Rose Streif
Sean Taylor
Pamela Turner
Jason S. Walters
Mike Watt
Jay Wilburn

Featured Fiction by
Hal Bodner

Featured Poetry by
Karen Head

Introducing Poetry by
Caroline Shriner-Wunn

Edited by
L. Andrew Cooper
and
Pamela Turner

BlackWyrm Publishing
www.blackwyrm.com

AND IF YOU DELIGHT IN THE DARKER SIDE OF THE REEL, TRY WHAT CRITICS HAVE CALLED EDITOR L. ANDREW COOPER'S "GRAND GUIGNOL" TERRORS (KIRKUS), OR SIMPLY "MODERN HORROR AT ITS BEST" (R.J. SULLIVAN, AUTHOR, THE GOD KILLERS).

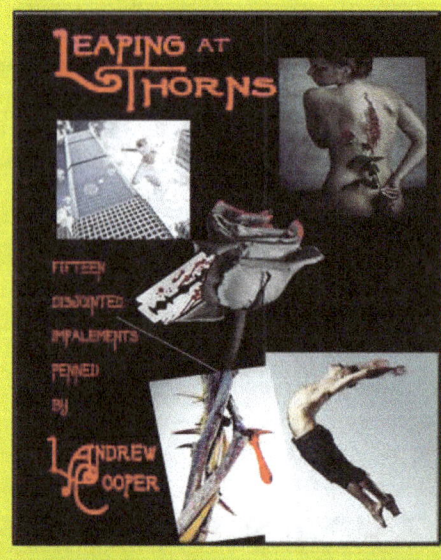

# Horror in a Hundred Stories

## Feelings
### By William Morgan

Mother lay in the kitchen, throat slashed. Father sat crumpled on the couch, his face barely recognizable from the blows of the baseball bat.

I felt nothing.

I always feel nothing. Dead inside. Empty. A wasteland of ruin.

My sister, Mary, comes home tonight. She's pregnant, due next month. I anticipate her arrival by clenching the butcher knife, and promising cesarean. My younger brother, Johnny, will be with her. Sullen, disrespectful, a walking raging hormone who thinks he's all that. I have a power drill and nail gun to prove him wrong.

One way or another, dammit, I'm gonna feel something….

## The Wolves
### By Rachel M. Martens

A howl echoes through the frozen air. I try to run faster, but the woods are dense and I trip over the brush.

I need to get home. I can't die tonight.

Another howl joins the first. And another. I can't count them all.

I need to get home to Lucy. She'll be angry that I'm late again. She won't understand this time. Just let me get home.

The howls overtake me. Suddenly, I am in a clearing, frozen, surrounded by them.

A white wolf rises before me, grinning, baring bloodied teeth.

She leaps. Her eyes are blue, like Lucy's.

## Mr. Brown
### By Jack Koebnig

It had been our initiation. Had been since the summer.

But it went horribly wrong and very quickly our smiles turned sour.

The test was simple: knock on Mr. Brown's door and run away. It had worked many times before. Except this time Mr. Brown must have been lurking behind the door and as soon as little Billy knocked, the door flew open and he was yanked inside.

We should have stayed to help but when we saw Mr. Brown through the downstairs window ripping Billy's arms from their sockets… we ran.

We ran for our lives.

# Paranormal & Urban Horror Audio

NOVEMBER 2014

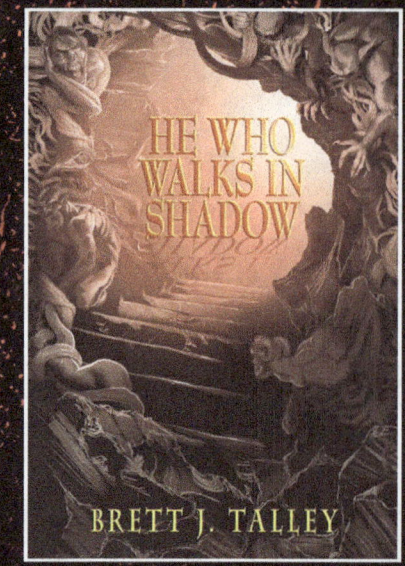

JULY 2015

OCTOBER 2014

## New from Audio Realms and Samhain Publishing

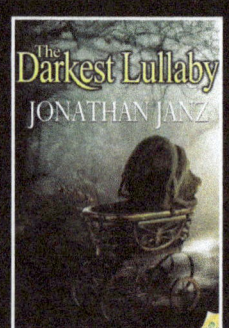

JUNE

JUNE

JUNE

JUNE

JUNE

JULY

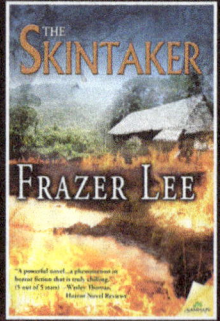

JUNE

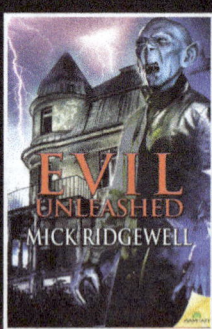

JUNE

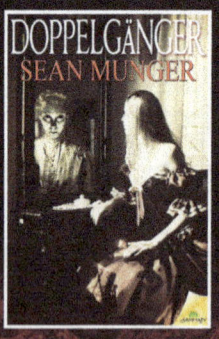

JUNE

JUNE

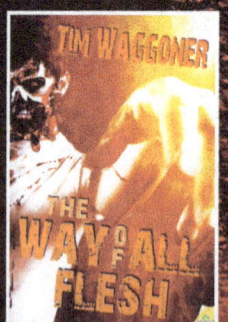

JULY

JUNE

JULY

JULY

Available at Audible.com
Amazon, iTunes, Overdrive &
audiorealms.com

Audio Realms
Publishing Company

JUNE

JULY

# The Magus of Silicon Valley:
## Ray Kurzweil's Transhumanism as Contemporary Esotericism

### BY EGIL ASPREM

(Originally presented at ESSWE4, University of Gothenburg, June 26-29, 2013)

The human species can, if it wishes, transcend itself—not just sporadically, an individual here in one way, an individual there in another way, but in its entirety, as humanity. We need a name for this new belief. Perhaps transhumanism will serve: man remaining man, but transcending himself, by realizing new possibilities of and for his human nature.

"I believe in transhumanism": once there are enough people who can truly say that, the human species will be on the threshold of a new kind of existence, as different from ours as ours is from that of Pekin man. It will at last be consciously fulfilling its real destiny.

Julian Huxley, "Transhumanism" (1957), 17.

## Introduction

The main protagonist of this paper does not appear on your list of usual suspects in discussions about Western esotericism. Raymond Kurzweil (b. 1948) is an American engineer, inventor, and entrepreneur who has founded a dozen companies and has about a fifty patents to his name.[1] His original claim to fame was as developer of the first text-to-speech reading machines for the blind, in the 1970s. Appropriate for the theme of this conference, Kurzweil is also in the health food business: the company "Ray and Terry's Longevity Products" specializes in food supplements that promise to increase lifespan. To those here who are musicians, Kurzweil is perhaps best known as the inventor of the Kurzweil synthesizer, which helped form the new sample-based sound of the 1980s.

But in recent years, Kurzweil has moved on to slightly more ambitious projects, such as how to live forever. In fact, Kurzweil believes we are on the verge of technological breakthroughs that will lead to the complete restructuring of the fabric of reality, transmuting the universe into a vast, thinking being. This event is referred to as "the Singularity." Kurzweil's extreme estimations about the future of technology have made him a prophet of the so-called transhumanist movement. In this paper,

[1] According to a Google patents search, 20 June 2013.

I will argue that Kurzweil's transhumanism contains a dimension of *transgressive and millenarian spirituality* that is best understood as an emerging form of contemporary esotericism.

Let me briefly outline the argument. When I consider transhumanism as a form of esotericism I do *not* mean that it is the contemporary heir to one of the many historical currents that have been lumped together under this rubric. I merely argue that transhumanism *shares* some key conceptual elements with so-called "esoteric currents." Thus, I argue for a *structural similarity* with esoteric discourse. The historical *background* for this similarity could occupy a long and fascinating discussion on its own, but in this paper I shall not go there.

The *second* part of my argument is that transhumanism, as a movement, is currently *merging with* and *mobilizing* parts of the occulture. Transhumanist milieus appear to be converging with the technophilian, science-oriented wing of what used to be the "New Age movement," and with fashionable "Eastern" religious systems. Thus, transhumanism adds a new set of discursive elements to what Kennet Granholm calls the "discursive complexes" that make up contemporary esotericism.[2] Most crucially, it provides a new eschatological scenario in the form of the Singularity, at a time when the previous big scenario has recently failed. I am, of course, referring to 2012.[3]

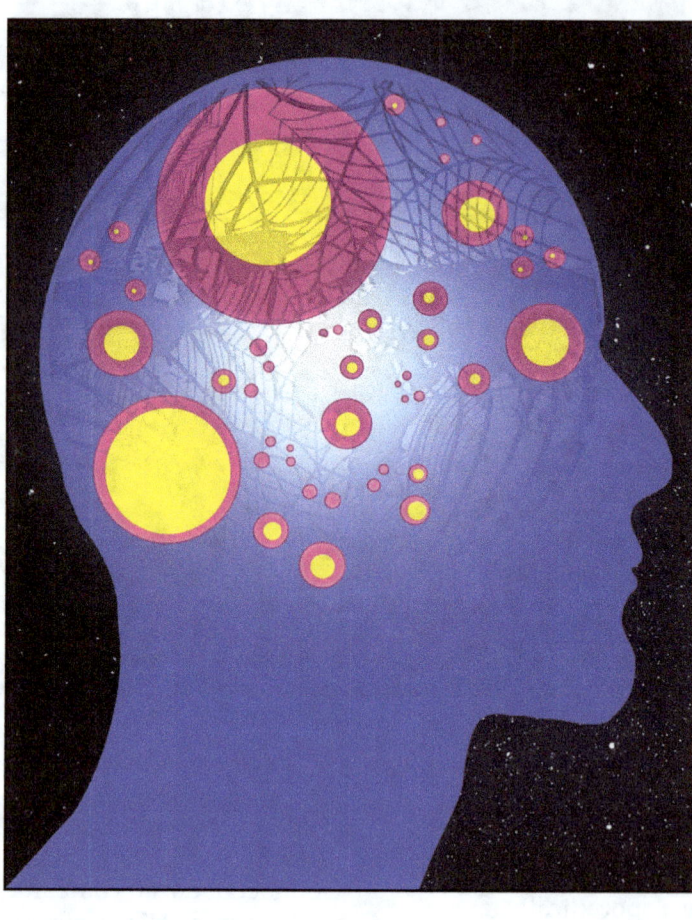

be mentioned,[4] transhumanism came to its own as a movement in the late 1980s.[5] And, while it has contributors and followers in a number of countries, the transhumanist movement's centre of gravity is undeniably located in Silicon Valley. In fact, the ideological, political, and spiritual ideals of transhumanism flourish at the core of the US tech industry. This is understandable, since the transhumanist literature typically imbues the technologies of Silicon Valley with messianic significance.

Ray Kurzweil stands as the centre of this milieu. In 2008 he co-founded the Silicon Valley-based "Singularity University" together with people such as Google CEO Larry Page. It is a private education institute based on Kurzweil's ideas, aiming to "educate, inspire and empower leaders to apply exponential technologies to address humanity's grand challenges." Last December, Kurzweil was made director of engineering at Google. To be clear: We are not talking about a figure at the fringes of Silicon Valley, but of an influential leader at the heart of one of our days' most powerful industries.

Kurzweil's grand visions of our imminent technological future have been presented in a number of books. The titles of three of these are revealing of the increasingly ambitious message. In 1990, Kurzweil published *The Age of Intelligent Machines*, arguing that we would soon see computing power explode so that machines would be able to compete and beat humans in an increasing number of cognitive tasks. Nine years later, he released *The Age of Spiritual Machines* (1999). At this point, the best human chess player had already been beaten by a machine, home computers had become commonplace, and the world wide web had fully emerged. The next frontier was to make machines more like humans, and eventually to *transform* humanity itself. By *merging* human and machine intelligence, Kurzweil argued, we will become a new species of supermen. This

### What is Transhumanism?

Transhumanism is a radically utopian movement, concerned with the development and application of human enhancement technologies. The baseline assumption is that humanity has the power to transcend its biological limitations, and that such transcendence is desirable, or even necessary for long-term survival. The tools for overcoming biology and reaching our true potential are found in the gamut of recent and emerging technologies, from biotechnology and medical research, to nanotechnology and artificial intelligence. The unbounded use of such technologies is considered the road to total freedom, promising to make us a species of immortal, omniscient, space-travelling demigods.

Although a number of historical precursors could

---

[2] Cf. Kennet Granholm, 'Esoteric Currents as Discursive Complexes'.
[3] On the 2012 millennarian predictions and the social movements that coalesced around it, see Sascha Defesche, *The 2012 Phenomenon*; Joseph Gelfer (ed.), *2012: Decoding the Countercultural Apocalypse*.

---

[4] Including, but not limited to, the Russian cosmist movement at the turn of the 19th century, and the more recent writings of some futurists and science fiction authors during the cold war. The term itself was coined by Julian Huxley in a 1957 essay.
[5] With such events as the foundation of the Foresight Institute (1986), *Extropy: The Journal of Transhumanist Thought* (est. 1988), and The Extropy Institute (1991). An international network continued to develop through the 1990s, with the establishment of The World Transhumanist Association (1998; now Humanity+), *Journal of Transhumanism* (1998; now *Journal of Evolution and Technology*), The Singularity Institute (2000), etc. Dozens of organizations, associations, journals and institutes now exist—there is even a Mormon Transhumanist Association (est. 2006).

far more ambitious project was continued in his 2005 book, *The Singularity Is Near*. In this book, transhumanism's millenarian dimensions become more explicit, as Kurzweil describes a coming event that will transform not only human life as we know it, but the entire universe: the "singularity."

### The Coming Singularity: Kurzweil's millennial predictions

So what is the singularity? To grasp this concept, we need to understand Kurzweil's view of history.[6] Transhumanists tend to share a "macrohistorical" vision[7] by which all of human *and* natural history, even the history of the universe itself, can be understood in terms of one single mathematical concept: the exponential function.

This "grand narrative" is unmistakably shaped by the experiences of the tech industry over the past half century. It may indeed be seen as a generalization of the famous "Moore's Law," originally formulated in 1965 by the co-founder of Intel, Gordon E. Moore. Moore's Law originally predicted that the number of transistors on integrated circuits increased exponentially, doubling every eighteen months. However, this trend was expected to flatten out when some physical boundary was met—which Moore thought would happen already by the mid-1970s.

Kurzweil defends a much more radical version of the exponential view, which he has dubbed the "Law of Accelerating Returns." It is more radical in three ways: First, it is *recursive*: the *results* of change accelerate the future *speed* at which change happens. This contrasts with Moore's Law, which has doubling-times fixed at 18 months.[8] Connected with this, exponential growth is seen as practically *unrestrained*. New technological abilities tend to find new and previously unforeseen ways to *sidestep* limitations. Reaching a "limit" only means that the exponential process starts over again on a higher level. Third, these *overlapping* exponential processes are *universalized*; exponential growth is *not* confined to computing power alone, but applies to *all* of technology, as well as to all of *evolution*—including non-biological evolution. The exponential function thus expresses the *telos* of the entire universe—from the big bang to the end of times.

The concept of the *singularity* results quite naturally from understanding historical and cosmological development as an exponential function. It delineates the final exponential turning-point, where change will accelerate so fast as to practically transform everything in the blink of an eye.

In Kurzweil's view, the singularity will be triggered in the near future, when artificial intelligence first outmatch the human brain, and continue to expand exponentially *beyond* human capacity. This "explosion of intelligence" will be the exponential tipping-point, and Kurzweil dates it to 2045. But the super-intelligent AI will not be some lonely computer, like HAL9000, locked away in the deep vaults of a secret research facility. It will be created in a distributed network of intelligent nanorobots, that will be *infused in* the human organism, and connect our individual brains with everyone and everything else. The intelligence explosion will not happen separate from us—it will *be* us, radically transformed and fully merged with our machines and with each other. We will not only have telepathic abilities, but the ability to completely merge our personalities and memories with each other if we so wish.

Once this happens, we will change the world forever. Kurzweil imagines that this conscious cloud of machines that we will now have become will set out to transform and rearrange the matter that makes up our planet. Eventually, all the matter and energy of the solar system will be made part of the expanding network of intelligence. We will transform our surroundings into a massive brain. Matter

---

[6] Again, the ideas expressed by Kurzweil are not all original with him. The mathematician, computer scientist and science fiction author Vernon Vinge appears to have been the first to conceptualize and name the technological singularity, more or less in the sense presently understood by singularitarian transhumanists. This happened in essays in the mid-1980s, first in an opinion piece in the futurist journal *Omni*, in January 1983. See Vernor Vinge, "First Word," *Omni* 1 (1983): 10.

[7] Cf. Garry Trompf, "Macrohistory."

[8] For a discussion and modelling of the mathematics involved, see Hermann Brunner, "Modelling Moore's Law: Two Models of Faster Than Exponential Growth."

will become intelligent and conscious; "infused with spirit," as Kurzweil puts it. Expanding exponentially, this process will eventually ripple through the galaxy until, quote, "the universe wakes up." Intelligence and consciousness is the destiny of the universe—and humanity's role is to bring its release.

### Structural similarities: Transhumanism as esoteric discourse

It is not hard to draw analogies between transhumanist thought and concepts that are familiar from the study of esotericism. We can, for example, discern an "alchemical" ideal, concerning the transmutation of the body, the soul, and the world itself, and the attainment of immortality as a stage towards spiritual perfection. We find a concern with "higher knowledge"—a vast extension of reason beyond present limitations, requiring the complete transformation of our minds. Combined with both these is an ambition of *apotheosis*—of becoming divine, eternal, perfect beings. There is even a notion of "living nature," although expressed through an *eschatological* event where the "dead" universe comes alive and wakes up at the end of history.

In fact, this apocalyptic vision, and the combined views on history, evolution, and human potential, is perhaps the most intriguing aspect for our purposes. At first sight, it may look like the transhumanists are simply yet another group attempting to "immanentize the eschaton," in the sense of Eric Voegelin. They seek a "transcendental fulfilment" *within* history.[9] But this reading does not carry all the way: the Singularity is imagined to lead to genuinely transcendent eschatological event. In fact, it combines *eschatology* and *theology* in ways that resonate with premillennialism and dispansationalism—apocalyptic theologies that have been strongly influential also on modern esotericism, from Theosophy and Thelema to the New Age. I suggest that Singularitarian transhumanism belongs to this same theological neighbourhood.

Moreover, the macrohistorical outlook of transhumanist spirituality implies an evolutionary "theology of emergence."[10] This is neatly illustrated in one of the many dialogue-sections of *The Singularity Is Near*, where Kurzweil has himself discussing religion with his good friend, Bill Gates. After discussing the need for a new, essentially leaderless religion that can come to grips with the concept of the singularity, Gates asks: "So is there a God in this religion?" To which Kurzweil answers:

> Not yet, but there will be. Once we saturate the matter and energy in the universe with intelligence, it will "wake up," be conscious, and sublimely intelligent. That's about as close to God as I can imagine.[11]

The divine *emerges* from matter. There is no Creator god,

existing independently of the world; instead, a divine intelligence is created *by* and *inside of* the universe, in a sort of emergent pantheism. Essentially, Kurzweil has the monotheistic creation story in reverse. Not only that: since it is *humans* who will create god, Kurzweil's version will also come across as the ultimate idolatry. This is Kurzweil as the "hermetic," god-making magus.

### Converging milieus: Dmitry Itskov and the *Russia 2045* initiative

Kurzweil defines a "Singularitarian" as "someone who understands the Singularity and has reflected on its meaning for his or her life."[12] One person who has most certainly done this is the young Russian multimillionaire and online media tycoon, Dmitry Itskov (b. 1980). Itskov has realized that the singularity is coming in 2045, and has decided to take a proactive approach by investing his fortune in a project for physical immortality through Avatars. The first prototypes will be remote-controlled via brain-computer interface, but later, brain transplantation and even consciousness upload will be available. By the time of the singularity, the avatars will have become "holographic"—a code word for bodies made up of polymorphing nanobots. Irrespective of whether or not this is a feasible science project, there is little doubt about Mr Itskov's favourite movie.

But Itskov's vision is a lot broader than this. He believes that the coming Singularity forces us to reform our spiritual and political outlook. To this end he has established the *Russia 2045* initiative, aimed to facilitate a transhumanist revolution in the five spheres of technology, politics, culture, ethics, and spirituality. What is interesting with the *2045* initiative is that it takes concrete steps towards *synthesising* transhumanist ideology with spirituality. In practice, this means lobbying the support of established spiritual positions. Itskov has for example been able to gather the support of the Dalai Lama. The *2045* initiative has held two big international conferences. The first one in Moscow in 2012 featured an "interfaith dialogue" panel. Besides a Russian Hindu monk, a Tibetan Buddhist, and the Orthodox archbishop of Ottawa, it featured Alan Francis, an American Gurdjieff follower and 4th Way guru, active in California and Russia. Their transhumanist wisdom can be viewed freely on YouTube.

The second conference of the 2045 initiative transpired just a few weeks ago, in New York City. Again, the list of speakers is intriguing, because it brings together transhumanist ideologues such as Kurzweil, with engineers and scientists working practically with robotics, neuroengineering and artificial intelligence, and a number of household names of "New Age science." Amit Goswami of *The Self-Aware Universe* is there, as are the two main theoreticians of "quantum consciousness," Roger Penrose and Stuart Hameroff. The scholar and Tibetan Buddhist spokesperson Robert Thurman is also there, speaking about the "merging of our cybernetic and subtle bodies."

### Transhumanist spirituality and the future

---

[9] Voegelin, *The New Science of Politics*, 120.
[10] For this concept, cf. Asprem, *The Problem of Disenchantment*, 232-247. This outlook is in line with concepts from Teilhard de Chardin, Alfred North Whitehead, and Samuel Alexander.
[11] Kurzweil, *The Singularity Is Near*, 375.
[12] Kurzweil, *The Singularity Is Near*, 370.

The *Russia 2045* movement is only a recent and high-profile example of a trend that I think is much more pervasive:

the transhumanist gospel is merging with parts of Western "alternative spirituality." I think we should expect to see this trend become much more visible in the years ahead.

There are particularly two reasons why further convergence seems likely to me. One concerns the *persuasiveness* of transhumanist spirituality in a world that is, after all, really becoming more deeply infused with new technologies. Considering that those who create (and profit from) the new technologies and those who develop transhumanist ideology are sometimes *the exact same people*, we should only expect this rhetorical force to intensify. On

social class that is becoming increasingly powerful. If their cultural influence continues to increase, it means that tech-savvy esotericists who are able to tap into the symbolic capital of Silicon Valley are going to be more successful.

The second aspect has to do with what Michael Barkun has termed "improvisational millennialism":[13] With the singularity now starting to become fixed at the date 2045, singularitarian transhumanism can supply a new eschatological scenario for post-2012 millennialists. The 2012 phenomenon connected the psychedelic prophesies of Terence McKenna with Maya calendar speculations, UFO-logy, conspiracy theory, and much besides. Now that Itskov's movement is targeting the 2045 Singularity directly at Western spiritual communities, we should not be surprised to see this date become the next big candidate for the final "transformation of consciousness." This time it is not meditation or psychoactive substances alone that are going to expand our minds and transform the world, but rather the infusion of nanobots in our brains. The rest, as usual, will be the end of history.

**Selected sources:**

Barkun, Michael. *A Culture of Conspiracy: Apocalyptic Visions in Contemporary America*. Berkeley and Los Angeles: University of California Press, 2003.

a slightly Marxist perspective, transhumanist spirituality can already be seen as the religious "superstructure" of a

Brunner, Hermann. "Modelling Moore's Law: Two Models

[13] Michael Barkun, *A Culture of Conspiracy*, 18-24.

of Faster Than Exponential Growth." http://hoelder1in.org/Modeling_Moores_Law.html (accessed 19.06.2013).

Diamandis, Peter H. *Abundance: The Future Is Better than You Think*. Free Press, 2012.

Ettinger, Robert. *Man into Superman: The Startling Potential of Human Evolution—And How to Be Part of It*. Ria University Press, 2005 [1st ed. 1972].

FM-2030 [F. M. Esfandiary]. *Are You a Transhuman? Monitoring and Stimulating Your Personal Rate of Growth in a Rapidly Changing World*. Warner Books, 1989.

Fukuyama, Francis. 'Transhumanism'. *Foreign Policy*, September 1, 2004. Online: http://www.foreignpolicy.com/articles/2004/09/01/transhumanism.

Kurzweil, Raymond. *The Age of Spiritual Machines*. Viking Press, 1999.

Kurzweil, Raymond. *The Singularity Is Near*. Viking Press, 2005.

Kurzweil, Raymond. *How to Create a Mind: The Secret of Human Thought Revealed*. Viking Press, 2012.

Vinge, Vernon. "First Word." *Omni* 1 (1983): 10.

Vinge, Vernon, "The Coming Technological Singularity: How to Survive in the Post-Human Era," 1993.

Voegelin, Eric. *The New Science of Politics*. Chicago, IL: University of Chicago Press, 1987. http://www-rohan.sdsu.edu/faculty/vinge/misc/singularity.html

**Filmography:**

Ptolemy, David (director). *Transcendent Man: The Life and Ideas of Ray Kurzweil*. Ptolemaic Productions / Therapy Studios, 2009.

Waller, Anthony, Toshi Hoo, and Raymond Kurzweil (directors). *The Singularity Is Near*. Fighting Ants Productions / Cometstone Pictures / Exponential Films, 2010.

THE ART OF STEVE SANTIAGO

WWW.ILLUSTRATOR-STEVE.COM

CARRION HOUSE

ILLUSTRATION/FINE ART/DESIGN
www.carrionhouse.com

# Spark

## BY R.B. PAYNE

The Aggressor GT materialized from the darkness to cut me off. Swerving, I hit the brakes and fishtailed into a four-wheel slide across the Pomona freeway.

"Motherfucking Dali."

Of course, he couldn't hear me screaming at him and even if he could, he wouldn't give a shit. Already, his taillights were fading in the moonless night.

Adrenaline jetted and my ears hissed. *Stay calm*. At a hundred forty mif you let the car do the work. The gyro had detected the slide and the safety harness squeezed the breath out of me as it ratcheted tighter.

The car threatened to roll but the stabilizers held. The tires bellowed smoke as I skidded into the piles of trash that littered the freeway shoulder. In the back seat, the Lam sisters squealed as the autosteer barely missed the concrete wall that separated us from oncoming traffic.

Releasing the brakes, I took control back from the computer. For a splitsec we rode roughshod over garbage, the spreader on the bumper flinging debris left and right.

In the passenger seat, Robbie howled with pleasure. I knew he was high on *flash* and this seemed a disneyride. The Lam sisters were laughing so hard they were almost crying.

"That was fun, Dinsky. Let's..." said Ting.

"...do it again!" finished Daiyu.

I maneuvered the car back onto the highway. We surged forward, the slice n' dice programming loading in a hypersec. The monitor blinked coordinates as the autofind GPS'd onto the Dali car.

We accelerated.

One sixty.

I heard the reassuring hum of the rear wing elevating.

One seventy.

Traffic was thin. Shooting past teenage gawkers and an armored food convoy, I redlined at one eighty. The dual Commodore Sloat electrical engines whined and I knew if I pushed harder I might fry them.

And us too.

I pressed the car anyway and the speedometer crept upward. Jesus, I hate the fucking Salvador Dalis. With their frazzled hair and waxed moustaches, they swagger around Los Angeles with their capes, surrealistic cars, and tattooed eyebrows. But the pisswads have got racers. Daytime commuters fear them and unless you got protection, you shouldn't nightride.

"Fucker's fast," I said, finally spotting his taillights.

Robbie, his head lolling, pumped shells into his twelve gauge. Gunplay would be a violation of the accord but you never knew how straightup these Dali jokers were. As Robbie opened his window, hot night air filled the car. Ever since the collapse the freeways were unlit and Robbie squinted into the darkness. Pulling on goggles and switching off my lamps, I went stealth. The Dali looked like he'd forgotten about us.

That was his mistake.

A mile later on a wide curve, I edged into his slipstream. If he were smart, he'd feel the drag and know I was there. But he wasn't smart. Otherwise, he would have known better than to mess with a Dinsky in the first place.

"Hurry up and..." yelled Daiyu over the high-pitched whine of the engine.

"...ram his ass," said Ting.

Not yet. Soon, we'd be at the Arcata interchange and he'd have to slow, maybe even drop below one fifty.

But before we got to the cloverleaf, the Dali got wise. Maybe it was the drag, maybe it was the dark shadow hanging too close to his tail. His brake lights flashed, but I was ready. We smashed his rear end, crushing it. Metal and a twisted piece of rubber bounced off my windshield. One of his tires was shredding. Still, he didn't slow.

Daiyu looked up from her cyclo.

"I posted the declaration..." she said.

"...and we're recording," said Ting, as she aimed her cyclo out the windshield.

Clicking on the aftermarket flare, aux current flowed to the electric engine and we strained past one eighty.

One eighty-five.

For a splitsec the Dali pulled away. An alarm screamed *danger* as my battery readout overshot the red and the electric engine shuddered.

"You're gonna kill us!" panicked Robbie as I slipped into the adjacent lane. The controls bucked for release. As we came alongside, the driver's face was illuminated from his instrument panel. It was a Dali, all right.

Finger up, he gave me the universal *fuck you*.

Maybe he was too young to die.

I couldn't care less.

Like some Ben Hur or Mad Max, I smashed his side panel, crumpling the Dali clock that tagged their cars. The Dali flashed a shooter. Robbie blew out his windows with a loud blast and fragments of glass clattered on our car like a hard rain.

Heavy grinding and the acrid odor of grease and friction told me that my gearbox was failing. I rammed the other car one more time, and finally his damaged tire gave. The Dali car swerved violently, flipped, and skidded across the freeway on its roof, a trail of sparks spewing from metal on asphalt. Still moving at a hundred mif, the car slammed into the concrete divider, the electric batteries erupting in a phosphorus blue and green explosion.

Fifty yards up the freeway we coasted to a stop. The Dali, covered in electro-fueled fire, scrambled over the hood of his car. He crawled for a few yards and collapsed, his body turning to wispy ash from the intense heat and battery spray.

One less Dali in the world.

Good fucking riddance.

The Lam sisters clapped and Robbie smiled. "For the good of the gang," he said, sliding the shotgun back into its mount.

"For the good of the gang," the rest of us echoed.

An occasional car cruised by as we waited for our battery to reset. A police helicopter arrived and its spotlight illuminated the burning wreck.

"Jesus, they're gonna land," said Robbie, squirming to get out of his safety harness.

"Sit tight. They're just curious."

Robbie relaxed as the 'copter swiveled and headed downtown. There, the few remaining skyscrapers shined like a cluster of lighthouses surrounded by a dark dangerous sea.

I stepped out to survey the damage.

Fucking totaled.

Later, with a half-charged battery and fried gearbox, I headed home. Robbie had succumbed to the *flash*, his head rattled against the window and drool ran down his chin. In the back seat, the Lam sisters whispered in Chinese and giggled like an old kung fu movie.

\*\*\*

Grandfather Hector scraped his fingers across his chin. Four days of stubble. That's how long he'd had my car in his garage.

He circled the wreck like a vulture over a carcass.

"You jammed it good," he said.

"Yeah, I know. How much, Hector?"

Hector was a master mechanic. Left over from the old days, his garage was filled with greasy tools, parts, and machinery of unknown purpose. Word on the street said he could even repair a gasoline car. Not that any of us had ever seen a working gasoline car. Most had rusted out and were stacked on the heaps that made the San Bernardino Wall.

For the record, he wasn't anyone's grandfather. Just an

old man that could make fast cars.

"Ten megawatts," he finally said, kicking a tire that had gone flat.

Ten megawatts was steep. "I don't fucking own Bike Town, you know."

"Not my problem, son. You want wheels?"

He had a point.

***

Bike Town was once the Fashion District. Wide streets for heavy trucks and gray warehouses covered block after block. Before the Big One, every building was a sweatshop full of illegals.

Now, sewing machines had been replaced with thousands and thousands of stationary bicycles equipped with dynohubs. Each bike had a meter and the riders got paid based on the watts they generated. When they grew tired, or died, there was always someone waiting to take their seat.

Cars need electricity.

Coming off the 101, we cruised into Bike Town. Above us, the streets were crisscrossed with cable runs of thick wire. Where those wires connected to the power aggregator, well, that was one of the best-kept secrets in L.A.

Robbie pulled to the door of a faceless building. Inside, two bulletheads patted me down.

"Tatossian," I said.

One of them nodded to a stairway. I took it two steps at a time. No need to knock, Tatossian already knew I was here. And why. I pushed through the door.

Inside the office, a glass window overlooked the bikers on the floor below. Packed like fishcans, the riders pedaled furiously. On a vidscreen, a road meandered through mountains while loud music thumped a bass line. The riders were gaunt and sweaty and grim as they strained. I almost felt sorry for them, but after the collapse, there were still too many people and not enough amps. I watched as children maneuvered through the narrow aisles passing out sniffs.

A hand touched my shoulder. "Dinsky," said Tatossian, a fat man sweaty for no good reason. "Street say you ran trouble on 60."

"Trouble? What trouble?"

He grinned. "Always tight lipped, eh?"

I didn't trust Tatossian. Maybe he hated the Dalis. Maybe he didn't. For all I knew he hated the Dinskys. Still, here I was to make a trade.

"Six for ten?" I said.

Tatossian nodded. "Where you want delivered?"

"Grandfather Hector."

A trickle of a smile crept across Tatossian's face. "Of course."

He tapped a button on his desk. I knew the signal had been given and downstairs Robbie was handing over the six bricks of vacuum-wrapped cocaine to the two bulletheads.

***

I hate daytime runs but my package had arrived and I was

anxious. I could have had it delivered, but I'd fetched my rebuild from Grandfather Hector so a test roll to Tijuana wasn't a bad thing.

Robbie and I picked up the Lam sisters at the Caheunga Mall. Over the last twenty years, the crumbling building had become a maze of cardboard apartments. They said twelve thousand people lived inside. All I know is that you could smell cooking and sewage and garbage for miles around.

Waiting at the entrance, the Lams were ready to daytrip. In utero, they had been twins co-joined at the jawbone. Pre-natal DNA therapy had separated them before birth. Now, they spent time at JPL where scientists studied their ESP abilities.

I'd asked them once, "Are you psychic? I mean, for real?"

"Of course, Dinsky, we know..." said Daiyu, winking at me.

"...everything you think," said Ting.

"The fuck you do," I thought, and the two of them laughed so hard I dropped the subject.

As the Lam sisters settled into the back seat, I realized I couldn't tell them apart except by their separation scars. Daiyu's ribboned down her left cheek, and Ting's was on the right.

Armed with sliver-guns, I trusted the Lam sisters to watch my back. And, both were an easy lay. No matter which one you slept with, you had the sensation you were fucking them both.

Out on the freeway, it was daytime traffic stop-and-go. You'd think that with the local pop decreasing by eleven million that L.A. would be a ghost town.

It's wasn't.

Angelenos gave up a lot after the Big One. No grocery chains. No pro ball, Lakers, or movie studios. But they wouldn't give up their cars. Most cars were converted gashogs—running on amps but looking like shit.

We finally cleared the jam (five cars in a pile up and three stiffs) and rocketed down the interstate. Bypassing San Diego, we zipped through the abandoned Mexico border crossing at one sixty.

In Mexi, people weren't artists like the Dinskys and the Dalis. That's just the L.A. scene. South of the Old Border, it's a war, and TJ was the turf of the Zapatas, a bunch of ambitious procurers and delivery-men. After consolidating the drug cartels and chasing off the Mexican army, the Zapatas expanded north. When I was a kid, there were FEDEX and UPS trucks everywhere. Of course, that was right after the collapse and before the wall sealed us off from the rest of the country.

Downshifting, I rumbled onto the gravel parking lot for the Zapata Taqueria. I cranked up the car's sound system; these are not people you want to surprise. I stopped far away from the peasants at the *Las Órdenes* window.

The smell of fresh tacos blew in as I slid the window down.

Enrique sashayed out of the taqueria, a yellow plastic basket in one hand. He eyeballed Robbie sleeping in the passenger seat and scoped out the Lam sisters with a toothy smile. Satisfied, he popped me a gang-slam handshake, and handed me the basket of tacos. I wish he hadn't. Still, I took a courtesy bite. The corn tortilla was fresh and the seasoning seemed spicy enough. I spit out a piece of bone and passed the basket to the Lam sisters. They dug in, hungrily.

Enrique sniffed. "You bring my payment, *Chivato*?"

"In the trunk. You got my package?"

"*Si*, overnight from Brazil, like we promised."

He signaled the restaurant and a dark-skinned girl ran to his side lugging something like an ice chest. In the heat of the afternoon, a wispy breath of steam rose from the seal of the lid, and I knew its contents were kept cool by liquid nitrogen.

I popped the trunk.

Enrique pulled out the bound body of a gang-switcher and slammed him to the ground. At one time, this piece of crap had been a dayrunner for the Zapatas but had sold them out to the Dalis. His name was Luis. With the sharp toe of a cowboy boot, Enrique kicked him into unconsciousness.

It had taken effort to snag Luis. A freelancer nicknamed Ratso worked inside the Dali gang and we paid him by the infoscore. Enrique wanted the pleasure vibe of dealing with Luis himself so we hauled Luis down to TJ.

A trio of Zapatas moseyed to the front of the taqueria and leaned against the adobe wall.

"Hey boys," called Enrique, still kicking the unconscious Luis. "I'm tenderizing the fresh meat."

Deep-throated laughter came from the Zapatas and I knew it was time to get moving. The Mexican girl loaded the container into the trunk and slammed it shut.

"Don't you want to check your package?" asked Enrique.

One of the Lam sisters shoved the empty basket forward, and I handed it out the window.

"Nah. If I can't trust you, who can I trust?"

Enrique cleared his throat and spit something onto the gravel. "If you hurry, *Chivato*, you can make the border before dark." His hand slammed the roof of the car with a thud signaling we were done. I knew he'd send a crew to intercept me after I was gone. It's nothing personal. He's just curious what's in the container but delivery-man ethics kept him from looking. It's all part of the Zapata Xpress promise of confidentiality.

Unless, of course, he jacks me on the highway.

I gave Enrique a half-smile. Even though I got his respect I knew he'd kill me just to show his crew who was boss. Of course, I might do the same and he knew it. I rumbled out of the parking lot and hit the highway.

One forty. One fifty. One sixty.

That ought to be enough to keep us out of reach.

At the border a hovering gunship tracked us. I knew they were scanning, but we were clean. All I had was the cooler containing what appeared to be a piece of meat. They probably thought we were four kids out for a picnic. As they buzzed us and veered off, I laughed.

*If they only knew.*

***

The problem with electric engines is that everyone thinks electricity is fast. Actually, it isn't. Without the push of electrons, direct current is fucking slow, about 8.24 centimeters an hour. The initial spark of an electric current triggers the actual speed of free electrons in a carrier, such as the copper wire in a car's electrical harness. The phenomenon is called *drift velocity* and the faster the spark that fires, the faster the transference down the conductor.

You got to know this shit when you want to go fast. Everybody wants quicker drift velocity. Sure, we've got tricks—battery-juicing, zoron conductors, shortened electrical harnesses, electro-hydraulic transmissions, or even body panels with friction-reducing silicon carbide. Still, when everyone's got the same techno, you search for a faster spark.

Back in L.A., Robbie perched on a chair in my garage, while the Lam sisters watched over my shoulder. Carefully, I popped the lid off the chest, a cloud of ice-cold air rising from the nitrogen packs. With my hands in thick gloves, I unsnapped the safety seal and lifted the inner container free.

Suspended in a translucent box, in a pink gel, was a gray cauliflower with a dangling tail. Excited blue, yellow, and red sparks twinkled across its variegated surface. Hooked to the dangling tail were old school nerve harnesses. Six neural tubes ended in external connectors through one side of the container. The pink gel, made from some South American tree sap, kept the brain alive and firing a steady stream of cerebral sparks.

Could it make a car go faster?

Robbie cleared his throat of *flash* drainage. "Do you think it can hear us?"

Ting laughed. "Don't be stupid. It's got no ears. But..."

"...it senses us," said Daiyu. "Just look at the pattern—yellow, yellow, blue, red, yellow, blue. It's..."

"...thinking for sure," finished Ting.

We all stared silently at something that was both beautiful and repulsive. Once, it had been someone's cerebral cortex. Now it was going to spark my car. Capable of transmitting electrical impulses faster than any known power source, the science had something to do with migrating neurons but that was beyond me. We watched until it fired again.

Yellow, yellow, blue, red, yellow, blue.

Spark.

Robbie turned away. "Jesus, it's too fucking weird. Is it true what I heard..."

"Yep. Jacked from a living person."

Carrying the box to the car, I lowered it into the engine compartment, carefully connecting it to the car's processor. I'd bought the installation instructions from a guy in Koreatown. Hand drawn, I hoped he'd gotten it right.

I latched the box in securely and slammed down the hood.

"Anybody want to go for a test drive?"

***

At two hundred mif, the car shimmied a bit. I'd have to adjust the rear wing but other than that, the spark unit worked like a dream. As I pressed the accelerator, we jumped to two twenty. Looking at battery consumption, I did a rough calc. On a full charge, I could hit two forty.

Maybe even two fifty.

As we headed home, we crossed the old Sepulveda Pass. On the hillside above the freeway were the ruins of the Getty Museum. Like most richierich buildings, this one had never been rebuilt. After the quake, my father had been one of the first people to reach the Getty. Most everything had been destroyed or burned but there were still some undamaged treasures. Dad was proud of the painting he'd recovered.

*Transverse Line* by Wassily Kandinsky.

I hadn't even been born yet, but Dad loved to tell that story. For sure, it's a great painting. Dad's been dead for years, and the canvas had passed to me.

It's the herald of our gang.

As we headed into the flats of L.A. we grazed Dali turf. I'd spotted a Dali tracker some miles back, but he wasn't pushing his luck during daytime.

As the ruins of the Getty passed out of my rearview mirror, I couldn't help thinking about the looting at the museum after the Big One.

*The Persistence of Memory*.

That painting had also been at the Getty the day the quake hit. That's how the Dalis got started.

The Fucking Dalis, I should say.

\*\*\*

Over the next months, I picked off Dali drivers one by one. The Dali cars were no match for mine. We raced one on the Imperial Highway in Brea until his car died, and we made sure he did too. A fiery crash on the 110 eliminated a whole carload of Dalis. We even trapped a loner in Fullerton, and when we were done with him, we mailed him back to the Dalis in a bucket.

Thank God the Zapatas will ship anything.

\*\*\*

I awoke to pounding on the bedroom door. In my bed, Daiyu and Ting lay entwined beneath silk sheets.

"Message from Ratso," Robbie called through the door. "There's trouble."

Rubbing sleep from my eyes, I pulled on my pants and woke the girls. Twenty minutes later, across town, Robbie pushed open the door to Grandfather Hector's garage. Cautiously, he peered in.

"Jesus," said Robbie, raising his shotgun. Ting and Daiyu pushed closer, and standing on their tiptoes, strained to look.

"What the hell..."

"...happened here?"

Both girls stared wide-eyed and turned to vomit. I left the sound of them choking and gagging as I stepped past Robbie into Grandfather Hector's garage.

The floor was covered with a beige substance intermingled with thick streams of blood. In the center of the garage was a twisted shape that had been a man. Not that you could say it looked like a man now. Cut up body parts had been delicately organized and balanced.

Slipping in the muck, I moved closer, careful not to cause the object to fall.

Grandfather Hector's head was severed cleanly just below his collarbone and balanced on other body parts. His head flopped backwards, like a man about to scream at the sky.

Below the head, his amputated arms and legs interconnected to form a square shape with an opening in the middle. A twisted arm ended in a hand clutching what had to be one of his breasts. On the other side, a foot rested on a hipbone that rested on a foot. All of this rested on his torso which acted as a base.

"I don't like this," screamed Daiyu hysterically from the door.

"Let's get the hell out of here," called Ting.

It was the only time I ever heard them speak in full sentences.

"We'll wait..." said Ting.

"...in the fucking car," finished Daiyu.

The two of them took one last look and disappeared.

"What does it mean?" asked Robbie, unable to take his eyes off the pile of human flesh.

"Maybe the Dalis wanted to know about the spark unit."

"What do you think he told them?"

"I don't know. He didn't know a goddam thing about it."

Something was bothering me; I'd seen this before. I tapped my cyclo and flipped through a series of book covers until I found it.

*The Getty Guide to Salvador Dali*.

I skimmed through digiprints. No. No. Nope. There it was. 1936. A Dali painting.

*Soft Construction with Boiled Beans*.

I lifted my shoe out of the mess. Boiled fucking beans? But the painting was also known as *Premonition of Civil War*.

Well, if it was war the Dalis wanted, it was war I'd give them. Over the next three weeks, we retired a dozen more Dalis.

That had to hurt.

\*\*\*

By autumn, the Dalis had retaliated hard against the Dinskys, and I'd lost most of my best soldiers. I'd tried to secure more spark units to give us an edge, but I'd had no luck. In the end, we'd done so much damage to the Dalis, and they to us, that the Matisses of Santa Monica were making inroads.

The challenge was agreed upon three weeks later.

A single race. Five miles. Two cars. No weapons. Winner takes all.

According to the agreement, I had wrapped and stored *Transverse Line* in the trunk. Their driver would have *The Persistence of Memory*. When the race was over, there'd be but one gang.

As we headed down the Pomona freeway to the race, I was already envisioning L.A. ruled by Dinskys, and Dinskys alone. Once I'd won the race, I'd quietly get rid of the remaining Dalis.

I hate the fucking Dalis.

"Shit," said Robbie, staring at a message on his cyclo. He was flashstoned and I couldn't tell if it was bad news or he was just having trouble focusing. After a moment, he said, "It's Ratso."

"Let me see that," I said, grabbing his cyclo. The message was four words.

*Dalis have gasoline car.*

Of course, gasoline cars are legendary. No electric car has ever broken the speed record of a gasoline car. Where the fuck did the Dalis get a gasoline car?

I'd been suckered. I squeezed the speed control tightly. The spark unit kicked in, and we went faster and faster and faster.

I'd never taken the car to top speed, and I needed to know.

Two twenty. Two thirty.

At two forty the car hesitated. Was that all there was? I squeezed tighter, forcing all the juice from the battery through the spark unit.

The car screamed; an almost human scream, as we lost power and the gauges went dark. Swerving off the highway, we coasted to a stop in an old Rest Area filled with eucalyptus trees. Leaping out of the car, I threw open the hood. Although the gel was still pink, the spark unit had turned black.

Dead.

Fucking dead.

Then it hit me. The Dalis had tortured Grandfather Hector, not for the secret of the spark, but for the secret of gasoline.

Still, maybe a spark unit could win.

If only I had one.

\*\*\*

As Robbie peed on a nearby tree, I raised the trunk lid, lifted the painting, and rummaged in the toolbox. Pushing a few wrenches aside, I found a hunting knife and slipped it into my waistband. I watched as Robbie zipped up.

I knew what I had to do.

For the good of the gang, I had to try.

On the far side of the car, I could hear Daiyu whispering to Ting but their eyes watched me like two cats stalking a bird. Words formed in my mind; like someone calling from a distant mountaintop.

"We will..." said one voice.

"...help you, Dinsky," said the other.

The two girls giggled as they watched my face and knew the message had been received.

I found a hacksaw.

Robbie meandered back and leaned under the hood. Daiyu and Ting moved closer as I came forward.

"Well, what do we do now?" Robbie asked. As he looked up to face us, Ting grabbed one arm, and Daiyu latched onto the other.

"What..." said Robbie. Seeing the saw in my hands, he struggled like an insane man.

"Fuck," he said. "Fuck no."

I unsheathed the hunting knife.

Robbie was strong, and he pushed off the car's bumper with his feet. Daiyu and Ting hung on tightly and, in

seconds, they had pinned Robbie to the ground, face down. I put my knees in the small of his back, pulled his head by the hair, and pressed the knife to his neck.

Feeling the blade, he went limp, gulping air. "We can find somebody else. Please."

"Not at this..." said Ting.

"...time of night," concluded Daiyu.

His muscles tensed as he struggled one last time to rise. "Jesus Christ, I'm your goddamn brother," he pleaded to me.

It was true.

I plunged the blade to sever his jugular. Robbie gurgled as he tried to scream. In a splitsec, he slipped into unconsciousness.

He wasn't dead, at least, not yet.

"Hurry," I said. Ting spouted something in Chinese, but I had no time to figure it out.

I laid the knife aside and grabbed the hacksaw. It easily cut through his scalp but it wasn't good for work on bone.

The blade snapped.

"Damn," I cried. "Ting, find me something sharp." I looked to see if she'd heard me, but she'd read my mind and was already at the trunk sorting through the tools.

She returned with a handaxe.

Robbie's breath was shallow as I hefted the axe. I swung and a cracking sound split the night. Wiping goo from my face, I could see that the skull was cleaved. Colorless body fluids and sharp bone fragments had gone everywhere. Gently wedging the axe blade into the narrow crack, I twisted until the tension popped the skull open, just like a coconut.

Shoving the handaxe at Daiyu, and using the hunting knife, I severed his neck at the spinal cord, optical and ear nerves, and pulled the mass of brain tissue from the skull. I gently separated the nerve tissue at the top of the spinal column. Slicing them free, all I needed to do was to properly attach the connectors like the original spark unit.

Dropping the knife, I lifted the brain into the full light of the car's headlamps. Kneeling next to the dead body, realization struck me like a lightning bolt. Robbie's brain was fried. Ruined by *flash*, dark patches and shrunken tissue holes blotted its surface. His brain was useless and I dropped it into the dirt.

I needed another alternative.

I tried to shut the thought out but the second I had it, they *knew*. As I ripped a look over my shoulder, I felt the knife blade slice and the warm gush of blood flow onto my shoulders. I sagged forward, and watched helplessly as Ting lowered me to the ground. A glint caught my eye as the handaxe in Daiyu's raised fist refracted the headlights of the car.

"For the good..." said Daiyu.

"...of the gang," finished Ting.

\*\*\*

Yellow, yellow, blue, red, yellow, blue.

Spark.

Photo courtesy of Anthony Neste

# Trans-Beauty: An Interview with Nelli Kowalik

## By Leah Jung

There were two reasons I wanted Nelli Kowalik as our futuristic trans-human womanoid for the latest issue of *Dark Discoveries*. Foremost, her beauty is so flawless, I am certain that her DNA is technologically advanced, and her radiance is so polished that I suspect she's accented with chrome. Second, whenever I've fantasized about having a cyborg in the family, it always had a name spelled non-traditionally, specifically ending in the letter 'i'—I'll even argue that the biggest flaw in *The Jetsons* was the spelling of "Rosie." Lucky for us, Nelli received our electronic transmission, and thanks to her greater-than-human intelligence, she knew that working with *Dark Discoveries* would be a surreal experience.

LJ: I'm not just being cheeky when I say you have greater-than-human intelligence! I was impressed to hear that you've spent a lot of time in the lab perfecting your very own shelf-stable cream cheese. That sounds quite futuristic. However, the idea actually stemmed from your family's traditional Russian recipes, correct? What inspired you to turn a time-honored hobby into a flourishing business?

NK: Yes! Quite futuristic indeed. You would never think to try a cream cheese that you don't have to refrigerate, but it tastes pretty spot on! It's called *Nelli's Famous Blends* and it's based off my grandmother's euro-oriented recipes. She sure is proud of this one! Anyone can try a sample for themselves, on the website: www.nellisfamousblends.com

LJ: This is your third magazine cover, amidst a growing portfolio of other beautiful photos and videos! Is your modeling and acting career also something that you've been groomed for since you were little, or did you set out do this on your own?

Photo courtesy of Anthony Neste

**LJ**: Let's pretend for a moment that blurring the line between man and machine becomes a readily accessible modification option. Would you be willing to undergo surgery to make any of your abilities bionic? Legs that make you run faster than an Olympian, fingers that can strum a guitar with perfect accuracy, or eyes that can see through walls? What cheat would you desire?

**NK**: Hm, this is a tough one. I will definitely have to agree with you on the eyes. Not only see through the walls, but see through the future and try to prevent violence and bad breakups from happening, haha.

**LJ**: I always ask our *Dark Discoveries'* beauties about their favorite horror or science fiction movies during our shoot, but you and I were too busy chatting about our experiences in New York City! One of my favorite classics takes place in our city, *Ghostbusters*! Do you prefer a more family-friendly fright film like *Ghostbusters*, or are you going to surprise me and tell me you love obscure, grisly movies?

**NK**: I try to avoid family-friendly fright films and watch the horror and paranormal movies based off true stories! One of my favorites is *The Amityville Horror*. I'll take that over any romantic lovey-dovey film any day.

**NK**: Thank you! All on my own. From meeting one photographer and director, to hundreds, through connections. It's been an amazing experience. I will say this, my foreign family was very musical growing up, so that helped prepare me to perform in front of a larger audience. If you're wondering what I played, it was the mandolin.

**LJ**: Thank you so much, Nelli, for your beauty and your brains! Was *Poltergeist* based on a true story? If so, I'm taking you to see the remake when it comes out! An absolute pleasure to have you within the pages of *Dark Discoveries*. And thanks for all the cream cheese!

# WHAT THE HELL EVER HAPPENED TO... T. CHRIS MARTINDALE

## BY ROBERT MORRISH

Photo courtesy of T. Chris Martindale

The 1990s have proven to be a popular era from which to source candidates for this column, and this installment is no exception, as I've chosen to profile T. Chris Martindale, whose debut novel, *Nightblood*, was a finalist for the Horror Writers Association's 1990 Bram Stoker Award for First Novel (a prize that was ultimately awarded to Bentley Little's *The Revelation* that year). Martindale went on to write a total of four horror novels, two for Warner Books and two for Pocket books, before vanishing from the horror scene in the mid-1990s.

I managed to track down Chris in his life-long home state of Indiana (where three of his four books are set), and where he currently works as a computer support tech for a large insurance company—a job which, he explains, came about from writing, in a way, "...from all those computers I bought to write with, enough rubbed off for me to pursue it as a profession."

**DD**: Did you ever write or sell any short fiction? If so, where did it appear?

**TCM**: No, short fiction isn't part of my skill set. I guess I'm too wordy; I get caught up in the details and forget to move the story along. I admire those that can do it, I just don't have what it takes.

**DD**: How did you get involved with writing gamebooks for Endless Quest and Dungeons & Dragons?

**TCM**: Back in the long, long ago, I saw an ad in *The Writer* magazine that TSR (who owned the D&D franchise at the time) was looking for material for their choose-your-own-adventure line. I was a couple of years out of high school, hadn't really written much but I figured what the hell, so I sent them a proposal and they liked it well enough. I ended up writing one Endless Quest book and two for their Advanced Dungeons and Dragons line. It was a good learning experience, showed me that I could actually finish a project if I put my mind to it, and the money got me my first computer. Plus the second book had a cover by Tim Hildebrandt and interior art by Steve Fabian, which thrilled me completely 'cause I'm a nerd for genre art.

**DD**: What led you from there to writing horror novels?

Was the popularity of the genre at that time a factor, or were you simply writing about what interested you?

**TCM**: My brothers and I were always horror and sci-fi and fantasy buffs, had all the comics, *Famous Monsters of Filmland*, the whole shebang. When I was little, my mom didn't read kids' stories to me, she read John Carter of Mars or the Tarnsman of Gor (though I think she left out the bondage parts for the latter). I've got her to thank for most everything that came after. It was ingrained pretty early on.

character called "Chris Stiles, Ghost Breaker." That's about as far as we usually got, just a name on a page, maybe a sketch my other brother Kevin would do since he was the better artist. But years later I came across a few lines Ted had written, the start of a story where Stiles wakes to find his brother's ghost in the room with him, and something clicked. That became the opening for *Nightblood*. I guess the moral of the story is never throw anything away, not even a few extra sentences…

Nowadays action/horror is pretty standard stuff—you can't swing a dead cat without hitting someone trained or

**DD**: Your first novel, *Nightblood*, was published by Warner Books in late 1989. Was that the first novel that you'd written, or were there other, unpublished early novels? Did you wind up with Warner via an agent?

**TCM**: *Nightblood* came out in January of 1990, and it was the first thing I wrote after the TSR game books. The original idea came from my brother Ted actually; when we were young, we made up our own superheroes and comic characters. Marvel Comics was going through a supernatural phase at the time with *Tomb of Dracula, Werewolf By Night*, that sort of thing, so he created a

destined or preordained to fight monsters—but back then it was fairly new. I thought maybe I could turn it into a series for one of those men's adventure publishers like Gold Eagle, the people who put out the Mack Bolan books. But they weren't interested. So I sent it to an agent in New York, he liked it, took it to Warner Books and they liked it too. That got me a two-book contract, the other being *Where the Chill Waits*.

**DD**: The protagonist in *Nightblood* is described as a "born hunter," your second novel, *Where The Chill Waits*, centers on a hunting trip, and I saw a friend of yours describe you online as a "firearms enthusiast." Tying all that together…

Do the themes of those first two books reflect the fact that you're an avid hunter, or am I jumping to conclusions?

**TCM**: No, I've never been hunting. I don't have a problem with it, I've just never gone myself. Though with the price of meat these days, maybe I should start availing myself of the opportunity...

**DD**: After your first two novels were published by Warner, your third novel, *Demon Dance*, came out from Pocket Books. How and why did you wind up switching

nonexistent, at least from my perspective. I could never seem to find them in stores. But that was okay, since I was almost embarrassed to tell people about them. True story: I offered a copy of *Demon Dance* to an acquaintance only to have them hem and haw and finally say, "That...doesn't look like something I'd be interested in...." Not that I could blame them.

**DD**: *Demon Dance* featured an old west setting... what led you to write that book, with that setting?

publishers at that point?

**TCM**: My agent got me a second contract with Pocket Books to write under a pen name. But that's when Horror took a giant shit and the market seemed to vanish overnight. Warner jumped ship before my second book had even hit the shelves. That meant I was free to publish my next two books—*Demon Dance* and *The Voice in the Basement*—under my real name; unfortunately they would be coming from Pocket Books. The few people I dealt with there were very nice but in the end, it seemed like they had a vendetta against their own titles. They saddled them with the worst covers they could find, and the distribution was almost

**TCM**: When I was growing up, the only books I ever saw my dad read were Westerns. He died of lung cancer when I was seventeen, long before I actually published anything. I think he would've read my first two books out of obligation, but I don't know if he would've enjoyed them. But a horror WESTERN, that's something else. I think he could've gotten into that. Plus I love westerns myself— *True Grit, Jeremiah Johnson, Outlaw Josey Wales, Open Range, The Shootist*. Some of my favorite movies. And that was probably the most enjoyable of the books to write. Which made it all the more disappointing the way it finally came out.

**DD**: After your first three novels appeared in a less-than-two-year span, it was another two-plus years before your fourth novel, *The Voice in the Basement*, appeared. Did it take you longer to write that fourth book, or did Pocket "sit" on it for a while?

**TCM**: They sat on it for a while. Who knows why—nothing they did makes sense to me.

**DD**: What happened after *The Voice in the Basement?* To put it another way, why haven't we seen any additional books from you? Have you written additional, unpublished novels?

**TCM**: After *Voice,* I was sorta disgusted with the whole thing. I was working full-time and writing all night, and that's a helluva lot of effort for something that'll just get screwed up in the end. I couldn't make myself write anything after that, and it wouldn't have mattered anyway since there wasn't a market for it. There's that saying, "You're only as good as your last two books..." and mine were dead on arrival. It just don't get no plainer than that.

**DD**: I read that you had approached a publisher about republishing your books in either print or epub form. Is that true? If so, I take it they declined…?

**TCM**: I did contact a couple of paperback publishers, whoever was doing horror at the time, but they weren't interested. I couldn't blame 'em—too much new stuff available, why take a chance with material that wasn't read the first time around?

**DD**: Any chance that, at this point, readers will see more of your work published, or are you done writing fiction?

**TCM**: I don't know. If I were a betting man I'd say chances are slim—those muscles are probably atrophied by now. But you never know. I've been wanting to make the original titles into ebooks for a while now—the only sticking point was the covers, they had to be something I could be proud of this time. Just recently I found a very talented artist in Hong Kong who created all four covers for a price I could afford, so with that out of the way I hope to make them available very soon. And if they sell okay, maybe that'll be incentive to give it another go. If not...well, I hear it's never too late for trade school. ☺

**DD**: I believe you've written some online movie reviews over the last few years? Where have those appeared?

**TCM**: Oh, those reviews were written some years ago. My friend Dana Fredsti and I share a deep and abiding love for really bad movies, and those were the sort of "paeans to craptitude" that we would email back and forth. I posted a few of them online so other friends could see them, and like all the flotsam and jetsam of the Internet, they're still floating around out there to this day. You can find them if you Google "reviews by The Freshmaker." I think the last one I did was for *Bloodrayne* with Ben Kingsley, a particular favorite of mine. It wasn't posted with the others but I think Dana put it on her blog at some point, so it's out there somewhere.

**DD**: Have you dabbled at all in other forms of media—screenwriting, comics, etc.?

**TCM**: I tried screenwriting and enjoyed it quite a bit, moreso than novel writing in fact. It fit me to a tee—quicker to write, very visual, the potential payday is much better and yet for the most part you retain your anonymity. No having to promote your work incessantly, no convention going, no signings, none of that social stuff I'm so terrible at. It would've been my dream job. I wrote several scripts, two with my friend Dana, including an adaptation of *Where the Chill Waits* that got some interest and was optioned a time or two. The highpoint of all that was getting to talk to director Stuart Gordon, which was cool since I'm a big fan of his work. But the project ultimately fizzled and all other attempts were more frustrating than anything else. After that I returned to actively not writing while Dana went on to great success with her Plague series for Titan Books (*Plague Town/Plague Nation/Plague World*). Great fun and they make a wonderful gift, tell all your friends...

**DD**: Do you actively read in the horror genre? If so, any favorite works you can cite from recent years?

**TCM**: Back when I was writing I was always reading horror—King, McCammon, Garton, F. Paul Wilson, Matheson, Masterton, too many to mention really. But when I stopped writing, I stopped reading, too. Not sure why, I guess I was just doing other things. Over the years I've picked up titles here and there, Dana's zombie novels, Joe Landsdale's Hap and Leonard books, *Heart Shaped Box* by Joe Hill, Ronald Malfi's *Snow*, a few others but nowhere near the same volume as before. Maybe that'll change now that I've discovered audio books. I enjoyed Peter Clines' *14* and the *Junkie Quatrains*, have several Jonathan Maberry books queued up on the MP3 player, along with the *Horror Stories of Robert E. Howard*, some Lovecraft, *Eyes to See* by Joseph Nassise, a couple by Larry Correia...I'm looking forward to all of them.

SIDEBAR:
**T. Chris Martindale bibliography**

*Duel of the Masters* (TSR, 1984; Endless Quest gaming series #21)
*Curse of the Werewolf* (Wizards of the Coast, 1987; Advanced Dungeons & Dragons Gamebook)
*Prince of Thieves* (Wizards of the Coast, 1988; Advanced Dungeons & Dragons Gamebook)
*Nightblood* (Warner, 1989)
*Where the Chill Waits* (Warner, 1991)
*Demon Dance* (Pocket, 1991)
*The Voice in the Basement*, (Pocket, 1993)

# THE FUTURE EVENT OF GLOBAL TRANSCENDENCE

## BY AARON J. FRENCH

"We might stand to have a little bit extra pain if it helps us remember complex information better," claimed Swedish scientist, futurist, and transhumanist Anders Sandberg during his 2012 TEDx event. The statement was in reference to intelligence-enhancing neural implants that had been installed into the brains of laboratory mice, making them more intelligent, but at the same time subjecting them to constant physical pain. Sandberg was advocating we use the same brain-enhancing technology in humans. What is most interesting here is that Sandberg taps into a longstanding religious tradition of equating pain and suffering as a means to transcendence and mental elevation—i.e. Brahman asceticism, the Shia holy day of Ashoura, Buddhist scalp-burning rituals during ordination, Catholic mortification of the flesh, etc.

Over the course of the nineteenth and twentieth centuries, and into the twenty-first, humanity has sped into new regions of intellect, science, technology, and medicine, revolutionizing the world in which we find ourselves today. By means of computer programming, fiber-optic cables, satellites, cellphones, cutting-edge physics, nanotechnology, and an unprecedented knowledge of the human body and its constituents, modern-day human beings teeter on the brink of a world-shattering transcendence, a yawning abyss of what the future might become.

With evolution and development barreling ahead so quickly, it is natural that impulses to evolve at a similar rate find expression in human thinking. The technology and science of the future appears to be leaving the formally-known world behind it, and human societies and their inhabitants are being forced to do the same. A transcendence and metamorphosis of former earthly conditions seems inevitable, as well as unavoidable. Thus, the question arises as to what is the safest, most natural, and yet most effective approach to the oncoming event of human transcendence? Will it happen naturally or do we, as a species, need to facilitate and precipitate this event? Will science bring about its occurrence, or should we do as we have done in ages past: look to the promises of spirituality and religion?

In order to divine a satisfactory answer, much less plot a course of action, we must first deeply understand, compare, and evaluate the impulse to transcend that seems almost inherent to humankind, which, if such an impulse has not always been present, has unquestionably gained traction over the course of history. Where might this desire to transcend originate, and how does it relate to scientific, philosophical, and religious ambitions?

Taking the event of global transcendence as a possibility, it is interesting to trace the impulses and yearnings of human transcendence through significant cases in the history of philosophy and religion; this includes the Continental Philosophy of Hegel (as in his Calvary of Spirit or *geist*), Heidegger, Nietzsche, and even Rudolf Steiner, who offers a completely outlined plot for the spiritual transcendence of humanity along Christianized philosophical lines. Christianity, especially some Protestant forms of Christianity, offers unique counter-perspectives to scientifically-dependent models of human transcendence (to say nothing of Eastern models), owing to the fact that Christianity depicts the attainment of a "new body" (or resurrection body), which is connected to the horizontal plane (as opposed to the vertical) and grants its adherents freedom from suffering, escape from bodily nature, and immortality—but only under specific conditions. The Process Theology of Alfred North Whitehead and his "evolutionary becoming" can be viewed along these lines, as well as the theology of Pierre Teilhard de Chardin, who posited an Omega Point in the distant future whereat all humanity and all matter and energy converge into a single infinity.

On the other side of the spectrum, the posthumanist movement of transhumanism, with its reliance on machine-based technology (as opposed to spiritual-based), seeks to precipitate a global transcendence via nanotechnology, computer software, artificial intelligence, and genetic engineering. Ray Kurzweil, Anders Sandberg, Hans Moravec, Hugo de Garis, and these kinds of scientists offer a vision of a transcendent humanity that a) does not need to be patient and await the promises of religion and b) does not have to die in order to receive the transcendent qualities, but instead seeks to gain them in the materiel world, thus prolonging the earthly ego indefinitely (in other words to "immanentize the eschaton"—a phrase first introduced into modern usage by Eric Voegelin).

The term transhumanism was originally coined in 1957 by Julian Huxley, who was the grandson of Thomas Huxley. Julian Huxley wrote about what he called "Evolutionary Humanism," which advocated eugenics as a path for the betterment of the human condition. He said science must play a part in the future evolution of humankind, and furthermore that human beings were charged with taking control of their evolution by utilizing brain-level performance enhancements, eugenics, and other technological and scientific means. In *Evolutionary Humanism* in 1952, he wrote: "Utilize all available knowledge in giving guidance and encouragement for the continuing adventure of human development."

In 1970, Moore's Law was established, named after Gordon Moore, co-founder of the Intel Corporation. (As of January 2015, Gordon Moore's net worth is $6.7 billion.) In layman's terms, Moore's Law is a computing expression that states that processor speeds, or overall processing power for computers, will double every two years. This means that the number of transistors in a dense integrated circuit board has doubled approximately every two years. And this is why every few years, we must all buy new smartphones and laptops in order to keep up with the exponential acceleration.

The phenomenon of Moore's Law led to the recent popular hypothesis of futurist Ray Kurzweil, director of engineering at Google, which he calls the technological singularity (the term, however, originated with Vernor Vinge). Kurzweil predicts the singularity to occur around 2045, and his prediction was recently featured in *Time Magazine* in an article by Lev Grossman.

Kurzweil's hypothesis is essentially this: that the exponential progress of technologies will result in a runaway effect in which artificial intelligence will exceed human intellectual capacity and management and radically alter human civilization. In his book *The Singularity Is Near* in 2005, he wrote: "[By 2045] the pace of [technological] change will be so astonishingly quick

that we won't be able to keep up, unless we enhance our own intelligence by merging with the intelligent machines we are creating." Kurzweil also claims that 25 years from now we will have billions of blood-cell sized nanobots in our bodies fighting off cancerous diseases, improving our memory and cognitive abilities. Eventually, these technologies will result in artificial intelligence, which will merge with the human organism and bring about a kind of bodily immortality.

However, there are those among the techies who are speaking out and employing religious language to do so. Elon Musk, CEO and chief product architect of Tesla Motors and cofounder of PayPal, was recently quoted as saying: "With artificial intelligence we are summoning the demon." Also, Stephen Hawking, beloved theoretical physicist, claimed in a recent BBC interview that "artificial intelligence could spell the end of the human race."

What's interesting about posthuman world-scenarios—the spiritual and the scientific—is that they can been seen not just from an ethical standpoint, or from a strictly dogmatic religious standpoint, or from a scientific materialistic standpoint, but from a more liberated "spiritual" standpoint, such as includes the esoteric thought of Rudolf Steiner. Viewing it this way determines a balance/compromise, in which we do not lose our spiritual Self *or* the benefits of the increasing technology as we move toward the inevitable global event of human transcendence, which transhumanists, of course, refer to as the so-called technological singularity (ca. 2045). However, spiritual thinkers have long classified this event under a different identifier, namely the spiritualization of the archetypal human form.

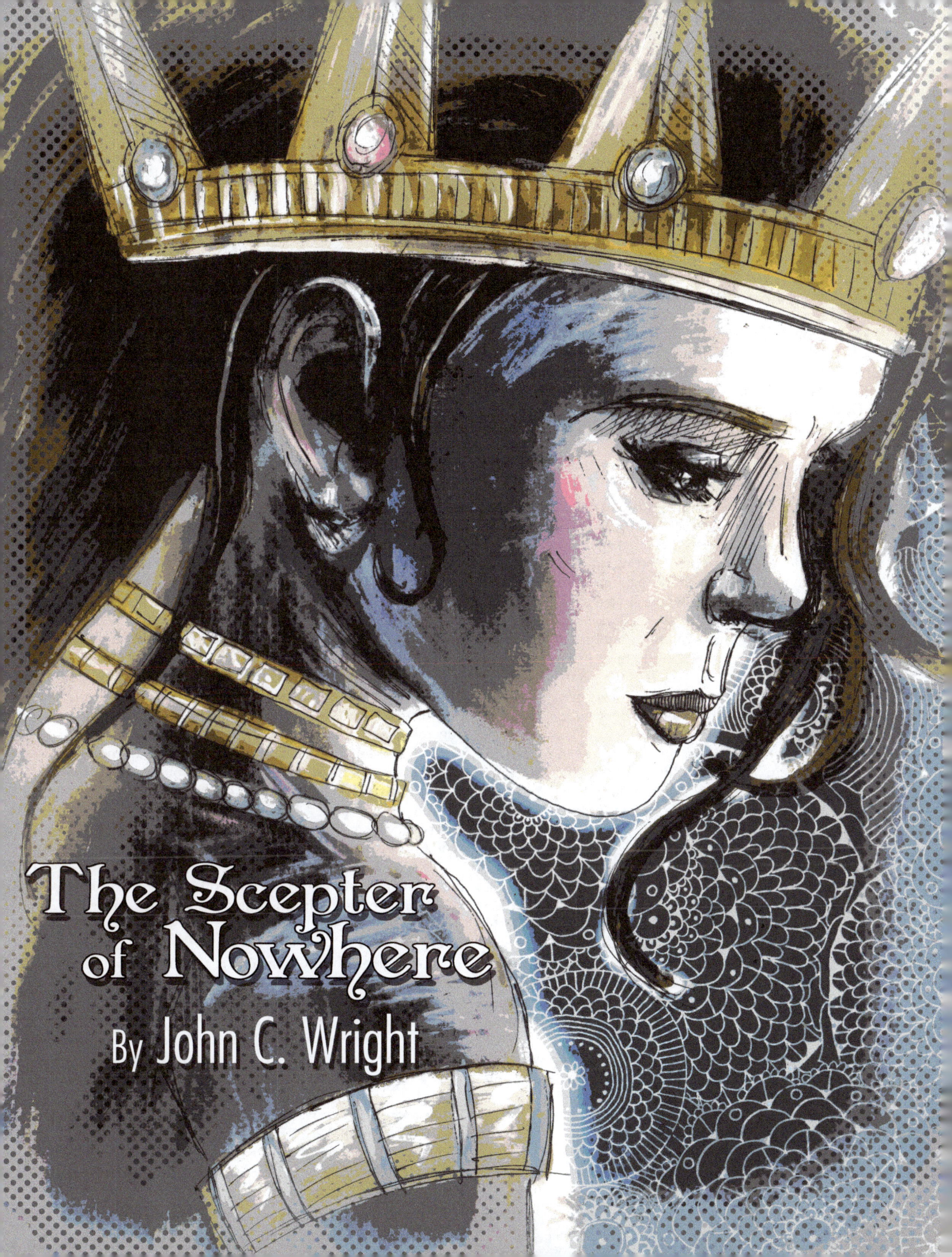

# The Scepter of Nowhere

## By John C. Wright

## 1

It happened so quickly. We used to be human beings. When I heard the bomb go off, I ran to the door at the end of the corridor. It had two narrow slits for windows, one in each leaf of the door.

Outside was an alley leading to a chainlink fence. Beyond the fence was a rubbish yard. At the other end of the alley two cars were parked, bumper to bumper. The wall opposite was pierced with countless dark windows, and the roof was crenellated with chimneys and utility boxes.

The alley was a killing ground. The cars were a choke-point. Snipers would have perfect concealment and a clear shot at anyone trapped in the alley, or trying to climb the fence.

What about the other way? I turned, but it was too late. The doors at the far end were flung open, revealing the stairwell beyond. A crowd from upstairs was pushing, panicking, rushing, screaming, clawing, falling down the stairway. Clouds followed them.

It was mostly schoolgirls and grannies. One had blood on her face. One was missing an eye, but was holding her eyeball to her cheek as if to push it back into place. One had half her hair burned away, and half her choir robe. One was holding to her friend's hand and had not noticed that her friend was headless, merely being held upright and moved along by the pressure of the crowd. One jumped down from the upper stairway landing, and fell onto the heads of women in choir robes, knocking them down, no doubt breaking bones. Those who fell were trampled.

Of the older women, the blind, the sick, who had come to the prayer meeting that evening, gray-haired and bent of spine, hobbling on canes or walkers or in wheelchairs, there was no sign. They had been left behind to burn.

The doors into the basement rooms were always locked this time of night. The only unlocked door led out into the deathtrap of the alleyway.

Spending years in missions in dark places in the world gives you certain instincts. Mine told me the attackers should have planted a second bomb, timed to go off just as the targets attempting to escape descended the flight of stairs. And the only place to put it—

I ran to the cabinet where the fire extinguisher was kept. The first place anyone trapped in a burning building would go, of course. I am sure what I had in mind. Maybe I meant to stop anyone else from opening it; or maybe I thought I could find and yank out a conveniently labeled red wire before—

Whatever I had in mind does not matter. I put up my arms, knowing that I could not shield the women behind me even if my body had been superhuman, made of something stronger than frail flesh and blood. But I was merely human, then.

Light and fire shattered the universe, starting with my face and moving inward, and the tiny burnt ember of my consciousness was flung into infinite night.

## 2

I woke up in hell. Neither the darkness nor the pain ended, but other sensations crowded in. My body felt like it was on fire.

I could not see. Lifting my hand to my head, I could feel the burnt and cracked edges of my flesh, the singed hair, and the crack in my skull. I was unwilling to put my fingers deep into the crack, not knowing what I would touch. I put my hand to my face. At first I could not find it. Some muddy and wrinkled substance, that I thought was burnt paper, was in the way. Someone put a phonebook on my face while I was sleeping, and crinkled it, and coated it with wet goo. Then I realized that was my face. There was no nose. The two gaping pits for eyes I could feel with my fingers, but there was no sensation of pain. Below the messy hole where my nose once had been, I felt another hole. There were some teeth left, and part of my tongue. Whether I had lips or not, I could not tell.

I could not feel nor move my legs. My hands encountered nothing when I reached. Had my leg been amputated? Both of my legs? Or, more likely, blown clean off?

The smell of burnt flesh choked me. Was I lying on the floor in the downstairs hall? Perhaps it had only been a second or two.

But no, I seemed to be lying on a bed. I could smell disinfectants. I could smell the unmistakable scent of corpses, an odor not soon forgotten. I could hear someone moving about the room. I heard voices.

"Is this our John Smith?" Male voice, English accent, perhaps Oxfordian.

"Yes, Doctor, it is he." Female, Middle Eastern accent.

"No identification, eh? No fingerprints on those hands. Good God! There is still debris in his head wound! I can see glass shards and metal splinters. Why wasn't he prepped? Why wasn't he operated on right away? Or given morphine?"

"We are overwhelmed. It is against health and safety regulations to give morphine to a dying man. He might develop a habit. Besides, he is brain-dead already. A vegetable. See? Look at him."

I said, "I am alive! I am alive!" but I did not make any noise. Instead, I heard something that sounded like a sick gobbling sound—wet, sticky, and grotesque.

The doctor said, "Shave his head and prep him for emergency surgery. I think I can fit him in to Dr. Omar's schedule."

The nurse said, "I cannot take the risk. Our hospital has not been attacked. We should do nothing provocative."

"Nonetheless..." But the doctor was afraid. I heard it.

"And we have no budget for charity cases. Health and safety forbids it."

"We can put him down on the research budget as an experimental test subject. A volunteer. Try out one of those new *Descheneaux* techniques, involving artificial brain tissue. They are calling it *programmable matter*. Since he won't survive anyway...." The doctor's voice sounded more cheerful, but it was fading, moving away.

## 3

I don't know if it was the same hour or even the same day. By the smell, I could tell I was in a room of the dead. The nurse was changing my bandages. She tugged and cut at the bandages in a deliberately painful manner, and laughed when I screamed.

She whispered in my ear, "This is the judgment of God against you."

And the nurse yanked the bandages in my groin hard enough to pull away the flesh.

## 4

I woke up in paradise. I opened my eyes, overwhelmed with a sense of joy.

The ceiling was diamond, but sculpted to look like wood, complete with grain, knotholes, and even a little twig with a diamond leaf protruding. I stared in fascination at the multicolored shadow, a shadow of light and not of darkness, which the sunlight passing through the diamond leaf made upon the ceiling.

I was ravenously hungry, but afraid to move: if I blinked, surely the sight would turn out to be delirium, and unending darkness would return.

Eventually I turned my head. I was lying, naked, in a bright chamber larger than a ballroom.

I stretched out my arms and legs, amazed to find all four limbs unhurt and full of vim. I lay on a pale circle of some yielding substance softer than mist.

The floor was a dark material I did not know, not metal, stone, nor ceramic. A floral pattern of gold threads ran through it. The walls were alternating panels of light and dark. Trickles ran beneath the lambent surface of the lighter sections, a thousand tiny waterfalls, making a restful sound. The fluid never reached the floor, but where it went, I could not see.

The dark sections were gilded with a climbing pattern of pollywogs beneath frogs beneath what seemed like feathery-winged frogs; above them were birds, fiery birds, and then shooting stars.

Scattered about the chamber were the large square ornaments held at various heights above the floor by an unseen force, adorned in arabesques. So handsome were these objects that a minute passed before I recognized them to be the seat cushions and chair arms and table surfaces of some futuristic, legless, levitating furniture.

I sat, I stood, I looked back. The circular couch was also upheld by nothing.

The entire wall before me was transparent. Beyond was a rolling landscape of brilliant green interrupted with black outcroppings. The grass was so vibrant a hue it seemed to explode into the eye. Low fogs walked like giants through the clefts and vales. High above marched a massy roof of magnificent clouds of white, pigeon-gray, and gunmetal-gray, twisted in knots and convolutions as complex as a human brain.

Oddly, a perfectly circular vortex, fringed with white swirls, was open in the heavy clouds like a bright blue eye, allowing the vast shaft of sunlight to slant down and strike this place that held me, mansion or madhouse.

No shepherd, no sheep, no crow, was visible in the whole vista of immense landscape. To the horizon, all was empty.

The rumble in my stomach reminded me that I was famished.

## 5

A soft noise made me turn. A buxom brunette was entering through one of the panels. She was naked as a jay, but bejeweled from head to toe, but with a face and form of unnatural perfection, and graceful in motion to match.

The panel did not slide aside; instead the surface-seeming surface rippled like a quicksilver pond, curving around her curves, parting before her bare body.

I watched, eyes wide and mind blank, as she glided toward me, a sonnet of motion. Her hair was a dark cloud and fell past her rounded hips, clinging in curls like twining vines. Her face was oval, reaching from a firm but small chin to a smooth, wide brow. Her lips were red as blood, and she never closed them fully. Her nose was small and her eyes were large, as green as the eyes of a cat, and she never opened them fully.

Despite this overabundant wealth of female beauty, she unnerved me. I was reminded of those composite pictures of perfect faces composed by computer geeks with too much time on their hands, trying to discover hidden ratios in the proportions of face and figure.

In her hand was an instrument like a thin scepter of white metal, as long as a walking stick, and adorned with keys or stops like a flute. She wore a cap or coronet of lacy silver, many necklaces, armbands, bracelets, rings and toe-rings. Jeweled chains jingled at ankle, calf, and thigh. An opal at her perfect breasts pulsed as it rose and fell. A diamond at her navel winked. A belt of massy gold swayed with delightful motion low around her hips. Gemstones glittered in her pubic hair, but this I did not inspect too closely.

I remembered myself, and turned away. A gentle caress on my shoulder made me jump. She was behind me, dangerously close. Her scent was wine, her voice an oboe, her words were night music.

"In perfect command of our bodies and environment, we no longer have need of the nudity taboo."

"I have need of it," I said. I took her by her creamy shoulders and moved her half a step away, and tried to keep my eyes on the ceiling. But when she made the slightest possible purr in her throat, and made the smallest possible yielding motion under my hands, they pulled her roughly to me and my lips found her warm mouth.

My soul fought itself. I was alive and should be dead. Wonderfully alive! I was nowhere, in an impossible world, holding an impossible beauty, and all my old life and its rules were forgotten.

Almost forgotten. "I am sorry—"

"For what? You kiss well," she said with an arched brow and cryptic smile. "I shall play the nerve-memory many times again."

I stepped away, trembling. "Who are you?"

"We are the Men Beyond Man, the Utopians, the Perfected, the Posthumans."

Had there been drapes, rug, or coverlet in the chamber, I would have thrown it over her. "Could you find something to wear, please, Miss Utopian? If this is the future, you must have spacesuits or something?"

"There is no need. All nature responds to our command. Observe!"

She flourished the wand, and depressed keys and pulled stops as nimbly as a flutist, then tapped the transparent wall.

The wall rippled, bubbled outward, yawning like a mouth, forming a lacy arch, unrolling like a tongue, forming an elfin stair to the grass below. The outer air came in, loud and shockingly cold.

Softly as a nymph and as regally as a queen, the vision of beauty descended the diamond stair.

On the bottom step, she turned, glanced back over her naked shoulder. The wind caught her long tresses and whirled them like a black flag. She said, "Your flesh is as our flesh now; sensations obey thought."

It was true. It was not that I suddenly felt warm, but rather that the feeling of being cold was remote, not immediate, as if happening to someone else.

"A robe would still be nice."

She said, "Surrender to no fear nor shame. All these things are done away with. Will you break your fast? All men hunger when raised from the dead."

"*What—*?"

"Recall that Christ ate the morning he was raised, fish and honeycomb. Recall also that he told his disciples swiftly to feed the daughter of Jairus, when he raised her. If you would sup, then come, and see."

And she strode away across the rich, thick grass. I did not look behind, but followed the gorgeous nude through the cold.

### 6

Fast as I trotted, I somehow could not catch her. Dreamlike, she always was just out of reach, and in the blustery wind, just out of earshot. The grass of the swooping valleys were as sea waves, rippling and hypnotic, almost nauseating, and the flowing masses of her hair rose snapping in the gusts, exposing the peach of her rear to my ungoverned gaze, but the grass hid her calves.

The air of unreality grew. Even the pounding of my heart was odd. Or was it my heart? If my flesh was like hers, it was a posthuman heart, somehow invulnerable.

The name of Christ had introduced a false note into this dream-world; for that name reminded me of life. Even in a dream, rules still held. One could not commit adultery in a dream, but one could lust in one's heart, which is the same.

Perhaps I was still in the hospital, dying; or, more likely, on the floor of the church basement a moment after the blast, burning.

If this were a dream world crammed into one, last second of life: should I be a beast? Or a man?

### 7

We descended into a vale as deep and round as a cup, a maiden stepping as lightly as a white doe and a scowling man. The wind dropped, allowing me to speak.

"Where are we?"

"The Gobi," she said.

"The Gobi *desert*? In China?"

"No longer desert. No longer China. All nations are abolished; all races, one. What your primitive age dreamed *religion* would do, we have done: decreed the brotherhood of man, vanquished sorrow, and healed the sad rift between men and nature." I could hear the pride ringing in her words.

"You spoke of Christ."

"These myths are false, of course, but there are strange time-echoes in the racial subconscious that carry reflections of the future to the past. Your visionaries, groping so earnestly for authentic spirit, could sometimes hear them. Hence myth oft hides truth. Poets dreamed of us long ages ere our dawn, and named us apsara or amschaspand, elf or angel, and called this Eden, or Elysium."

### 8

She halted at a black rock. Her scepter elongated, growing, and revealed more stops and tabs and keys. She thrust its heel sharply against the black rock.

"This is anthracite, and I am redirecting the carbon atoms. Oxygen and carbon I take from air and soil. Naturally, I could reorganize the cellulose in the grass more quickly to the same result, but that would be too humble a demonstration."

"How does it work? Your, ah, flute?"

"Think of atomic vibration rates as notes in a scale from Hydrogen to Unbinilium. To control basic molecular architecture requires a phrase of vibrations, a song. Themes of crystals and cells are kept in these memory tabs."

Her fingers flew over the keys.

"Each range controls a different order of magnitude: first are primal forces; next, are leptons, bosons, and composites; tachyons and exotics; then atomic forces; electromagnetic; then molecular; then macroscopic. This is the medical range; that the architectural; and the final range controls environmental effects, weather and tides. This is the reduction key that breaks all chemical bonds; the dark red stop breaks all atomic bonds."

I made some comment about the dangerous nature of such a tool.

"In human hands, it could sink a continent, but in ours it is a scalpel. And should a continent be sunk, this thumb-ring is the reverse key. Even perfected beings can regret a hasty act, hence this undoes the last command from the system memory. The crown of the instrument absorbs all information of the surroundings down to the Planck level; the heel emits commands."

"Emits how?"

"By macronucleonics."

I frowned in recognition.

She misread my look. "You doubt? Look here."

She held up the opal resting between her breasts. "This is the transactinide element Ununseptium. It is forty times heavier than lead. In nature, it has a halflife of less than ten milliseconds. We have decreed it stable. It will never tarnish."

I picked up the bead, and held it as close as her necklace allowed. The play of light off its dull surface was eerie, showing depth, as if the thing were nested layers of gray glass about a dark core.

It felt strange under my fingers, tingly and slippery.

"By means of longrange nucleonic forces, artificial atoms can be made, lacking protons and neutrons. These hollow electron shells still interact with natural atoms according to all the rules of chemistry. Massless, the hollow matter can be collapsed, transmitted, replicated, and distended, all by simple vibrations."

"I am familiar with the principle," I said modestly,

letting the gem fall.

"Once the three basic forces of the universe, the electro-weak, the nucleonic, and gravity, were reduced to a single expression, the substitutions of their properties became possible. Longrange nucleonics opened a trove of wonder. The original mathematical analysis used was the work of a Jesuit scientist named Do-Chain-Now."

"*Descheneaux.*" I corrected her pronunciation automatically, but she did not hear me.

"At the moment of the Big Bang," she went on, "the trinity of forces existed in super-symmetry. When the universe expanded, the symmetry broke, producing the forces we know. However, other symmetries are possible, if the Big Bang, on a small scale, were recreated in a spherical supercollider, and broken along a different fracture line. The cosmogenic symmetry breaking sphere is too massive to rest on earth, but crystal instruments able to receive, store, and re-transmit the macronucleonic force can be formed at will." She held up her slender hand and the gems of her rings caught the light.

There was a flash and the smell of ozone. The black stone beneath her wand now held a smooth, glassy, bowl-shaped depression in which was a round loaf of sourdough bread, warm and issuing a delicious scent.

"Eat!" she said. "I have taken the liberty of programming pheromone neurotransmitters into the loaf, so that your brain will be programmed with the lore and habits of this our age."

"This bread will alter my brain?" My stomach rumbled, and my famine was as if I had a badger in there, clawing, but I did not reach for the loaf.

"Eat! It will make you wise."

I began wondering how accurate the time-echoes she earlier had mentioned might be.

I said, "And then what happens to me?"

"You become like unto us: a god."

"And if I like being mortal?"

"To be mortal is to die." And she was away, up the slope, her long hair wild in the wind.

I followed, with many a backward glance at the delicious, savory-scented, but dangerous bread.


### 9

At the hillcrest, for the first time, I saw the edifice where I woke. She saw the direction of my gaze and raised her scepter. The roof of cloud parted like the Red Sea.

Sunlight blazed on the work of titans. It was a spiral tower of black metal adorned with bronze and marble, mirror-bright. It was a mile wide at its base, twisted like the horn of a unicorn, rising and narrowing. Like an aqueduct, there reared arch after arch on course above course, holding gates from which an army to storm heaven could have emerged. In the triangular gnomons between the huge arches were postern gates or rose windows.

She said, "Of your original body made of natural matter, little remains. There is sufficient paratomic matter in your body that you can be carried rapidly where you would, without harm."

Again she raised her scepter. I saw her point the head at me, depress a blue key then a white, and point the heel at

the tower and release both keys. There was a blinding flash.


### 10

I opened my eyes. I was perched atop a narrow ledge, five thousand feet up or more. The cloud layer was below us. Here the sun was merciless, and the winds were breathless oven-air. The airstreams beating against the tower made distant howls.

The nude brunette was beside me, her head at my shoulder. There was no room here to move her away. Rather than stand with my left arm overhead, I placed it around her shoulder. My elbow was lost in the cloud mass of her hair.

The metal ledge had a woodgrain. "What is this made of? It looks organic."

"It is grown from an alloy of Darmstadtium, element 110, impregnated with negative mass particles to reduce weight."

"You *grow* rather than *build* your buildings?"

"The distinction is meaningless. And there is but one edifice. For convenience, the entire population is housed here, both incarnate and not, since matter transmission makes all points equidistant."

"How did you lose your…human nature?"

She mistook my meaning, because she smiled with pride. "It happened very quickly. Once the Do-Chain-Now process was perfected, soon we made our bodies out of programmable matter. Disease of brain or body is impossible. We cannot be harmed. Cast yourself to the ground!"

"*Descheneaux.* And, no, thank you."

"Your fears hinder you. You must have faith."

I released her shoulder and plucked her arm from my waist, fearing she might push me. "No."

She turned to face me, which displayed an indifference to height that was freakishly inhuman. Only her toes gripped the ledge; her heels were resting on nothing. A vastness of air was behind.

She said, "Do you not understand who you are? If I throw myself down and return again unharmed, will you foreswear your foolish hesitations?"

"No. Even if this is a jest, or a test, or a dream, some things are sacred. Life is sacred. I did not create myself; I have no right to destroy myself."

Now, her eyes flashed with a hot emotion. "You did create yourself! As have we all, following you! You are our Adam. Our primary!"

"You seem to have mistaken me for someone else…."

"You are the first to have artificial matter injected into your brain. It was done to stabilize a hemorrhage, nothing more. But even that small amount was enough to preserve you through decades of coma, then centuries. Your body failed, your heart ceased, but your brain did not die! The artificial matter replicated itself, replacing cell by cell, preserving what it encountered."

"And—you—copied this? Injected yourself?"

"Whether we started as a clan, or a cabal, corporation or cult is forgotten. We replaced the mortals, one by one by inviting the worthy to join us, using no violence, no fraud."

"And the unworthy?"

"One is wed forever with any to whom one grants

immortality. We were careful. Never did they suspect we moved unseen among them. We play-acted at their pointless battles and commercial ambitions, until there was but one land of mortals left, then but one city, one quarter, one household, one child. All lives in his life were but homunculi in a worldwide masquerade. He died one night in peace, surrounded by what he thought were friends, students, grandchildren. With him, man was extinct."

The image was dizzying. I murmured to myself, *"Who sups at the banquet of Phaedrus, may dip his hand in the dish with Typhon, all unknowing, or monster more malign…"*

"Then we gathered those trapped in the amber of imperfect ascension, or suspended animation. You are the last."

"Eh? Last what?"

"You are the last man, the last to be made posthuman! If you do not join us, all our world is vain!" She pushed her flute into my hand. "Forget your fear! Watch me! See, and grow brave!"

She smiled. Her face was perfectly tranquil, angelic.

It still took me by surprise. People fall much quicker than you think. You always imagine that if you saw someone leaping off a bridge, you could make some heroic grab in midair. In reality, if you see it, you are too late.

In one second, she was already sixteen feet below me, then sixty-four, and then one hundred forty-four, more than a ten story fall, all before I could react.

The sight of that last split-second was burned into me. As she stepped back, her serenity had departed, as if someone had yanked a mask off her face. I was looking right in her eyes when it happened. It was a different person with a different expression, now distorted with terror; her scream of shock followed her down until it mingled with the far noise of the winds striking the tower.

Her nude body bounced, leaving a long red smear on the black substance. Something like a mass of uncooked butcher's meat continued on.

I shoved against the wall behind me, trying to escape the brink, when it gave way, becoming liquid.

## 11

I fell into a long tunnel that penetrated to the core of the tower. Her flutelike scepter was still in my hand. I walked rapidly, my thoughts a torment.

In the center was a vast open space, paved with crystal. Underfoot was a ballroom. Here an endless congregation of nude figures, male and female, all of them perfect of physique, all adorned with gems, were dancing in a long and sinuous line. Their floor was also crystal. Below them was another ballroom of dancers, also writhing in celebration. An ache of loneliness pricked me for the first time.

Also, I saw that there was food, pyramids of fruit and bowls of wine, platters of many steaming meats, salmon and crab, pastries, prawn, lavish trenchers of salads and tumblers of soup. Oddly, the food was placed on the floor, and the partygoers ate without utensils, as if neither heat nor cold annoyed their fingers. They plucked morsels with kisses from each other's teeth, fearless of germs, as ignorant of privacy as puppies.

I heard the sound of silvery bells, and the slap of naked feet.

A redhead, thinner and more petite than the other woman, was swaying toward me across the crystal floor.

Like her twin, she was naked, crowned and beringed, braceleted, necklaced, and begirdled with bezants and ringing gems. She had the same walk, and stance, and gleam in her lidded eyes. The face was different, but somehow she had the same idealized features, oversized eyes, oversharp cheekbones, and overfull lips as before. She lacked the bony but stronger features typical of redheads. It made her face more clearly artificial.

"You are not the same person," I said.

"We are all the same person," she said. "When we replaced our flesh with new substance, we replaced our nerves as well. Our brains were made more efficient, and interlinked. Our thoughts flow freely, and we possess none, and share all. There are many of us, all one."

"She died. You killed her."

"I am she. Kiss me, and see."

I backed away. "Really? What was the last noise you made?"

"I told you to watch and believe."

"No. It was a scream."

"The unoccupied body contains animal reflexes of no particular importance."

"I saw you depart the body you were possessing. I saw her awareness return to her eyes as she died. Tell me your name?"

"We have no names. Names cause division. I am large; I contain multitudes; I am legion."

"A demon?"

"Do not flaunt your backwardness! Where your sages did but grope and bungle, we know! We have examined all the levels of the human mind, subconscious and superconscious and more. Our spiritual science discovered how to channel the vital force. We command the driving passions of evolution itself, the very blind and ever-changing principle which brought forth the universe! We serve the thrust of infinite potential, the psycho-cosmic energy called *life*, which reaches ever upward, ever onward, a flight above infinity!"

I laughed. "I think those time-echoes you mentioned told our primitive and bungling sages what waits in the future. A day of fire."

"All your religions could not provide true happiness, true pleasure. Below us is the celebration of life, raw life, the animal spirit, the joy that only immortals know. Do you not hunger and thirst? The women are lovely!"

I was parched and starving. Below, the line dance had devolved into an orgy, each dancer coupling with the one before. Many parts of the line of nudes were already rolling through the food, licking pastries from each other's flesh. All wore smiles of idiotic emptiness, or looks of narrow-eyed hunger indistinguishable from hatred.

"Would you prefer to be as you were?" she demanded, her eyes flashing, her bosom heaving. "That is your choice! Go down! Drown in pleasure, and live forever; or burn in pain, and die!"

That sounded ominous. I pointed the business end of the wand at her. "This is the stop that disintegrates things, is it not?"

"No physical hurt can touch us."

As she rose and approached, I retreated, helpless. If there was a real girl inside, it would be murder if I pulled the stop.

She put out her hand. "Give up the cannelure. It will not save you."

I halted, grinned, and proffered the scepter. The head was pointed at me, the heel at her.

Just before she closed her fingers on it, I let it slip aside, out of reach, pointing past her elbow. "Whoops!" I cried, and worked the blue and white keys as she had.

I was standing on the other side of the vast white floor. She turned, and walked slowly toward me, patient as a stalking lioness, patient as a deathless creature.

I pointed the wand straight up. All the floors above me, level after level, were made of a clear substance like crystal. I wondered what might happen. I worked the two keys.

### 12

I opened my eyes. I was standing on the white diamond roof of a tower above the edge of the stratosphere. In the same way I could, by an act of will, eliminate my sense of cold, I made the near-vacuum not disturb me.

I could see the grand curve of the Earth, and the air like a blue bright line following that horizon. The sun above was white and stark. It is supposed to be impossible, even in space, to see the sun and stars at the same time, because the human eye cannot adjust. My eyes were no longer human: the stars were bright and sharp as diamond points, and I saw countless millions more than I ever saw on Earth, even on the clearest night.

And I saw the moon to one side, white as a skull, covered with the ruins of empty cities.

And directly overhead, immense, I saw the golden sphere decorated with whorls and whirls of labyrinths. Something less like a spacestation cannot be imagined. But I saw the pattern in the swirls, and knew them, since I had drawn and redrawn them countless times on chalkboards, napkins, and computer screens. This was the supercollider. In its heart, the Big Bang was reenacted in miniature.

The redhead emerged from the solid rooftiles underfoot like a dolphin vaulting straight up out of a pool. Her fingers emerged at a position such that they were already encircling the wand, which seemed like cheating to me. There was a flash, and she stood four feet away, cannelure in hand. Like me, the vacuum did not harm her naked flesh.

She spoke, her words dim. "Do you not understand that all this has been a trial? We deny infinity to the unworthy."

She pressed a key and tapped the wand to the floor. The diamond substance at my feet parted, a small, bright item, no bigger than my hand, came up into view. Here was a crucifix of wood with silver trimmings, and a tiny ivory figure of the savior in agony.

She said, "All you need do is trample that object. As the first of the posthumans, you will be given a position of highest honor and be our king."

"Out of curiosity, why that? You don't believe…"

"But you do." She stepped forward, two feet away, one. She had a habit of standing too close. "This is the final test.

You must be human, worship nonsense, and die in pain; or else be posthuman, worship life, and live in unending orgies exploding with pleasure forever! Be our prince, and hold infinite power—hold the very scepter of utopia!"

There was nothing to say. It was absurd. An endless world of nothing is still simply nothing, and the prince of such a nowhere was no one. Who surrenders everything for nothing?

In my gaze was pity for one who had made that unwise bargain. She saw my eyes, knew my answer, grimaced, and twisted a key on the wand.

I fell. My eyes and lips and nose were gone, my hair, my earlobes, half my tongue and both my legs. The lack of air, the decompression, and the hard radiation from space were killing me, but that was not the worst. My whole body was my enemy. My skin was a mass of pain.

I could feel a hard, angular object under me as I fell, and instinctively, my fingers closed on it. Unlike everything else I had touched that day, it felt solid, real.

She was bending over me. "Ungrateful wretch! You forget all we have done for you! This is how we you found…"

I thrust the crucifix toward her voice, struck her face, and she screamed a nonhuman scream. It rose from a low moan of hate to a shriek of agony. She dropped the wand on top of me, and fell.

Blood was coming from my nose-hole, ears, leg stumps, and anus. With hands as dull and remote as empty gloves, I clutched at the wand, blindly. By touch I found and yanked out the thumb-ring, the reverse switch.

I stood up. The woman was kneeling in a heap, her head down. There was a burn mark running from her neck, across her face, and up into her hairline, and a second burn at right angles slashed across both cheeks.

She said in a low, trembling voice, "You are John Smith. The records say you bombed a church, and almost died in the attempt. We do not make mistakes. This is impossible."

"You were burned by the cross of Christ. All things are possible!" It had a nice silver chain, and I slung it around my neck. It felt warm above my heart.

"Superstitious fool. The matter in that object is programmed to damage us. Some members of your sect still linger."

"So I am not the last. You lied."

"They made that as a weapon. The only weapon in Eden! Are you proud of it?"

"Why not leave them alone? And me?"

"We cannot be content, until all are forced into perfection!"

"There are better weapons!" I pointed the wand at her suddenly terrified face, and gripped the dark red stop. "Whoops!" I cried, and yanked the heel up as I yanked up the stop, firing over her shoulder, striking nothing.

"Wait!" Another girl's voice issued from her throat. "In the name of God, don't shoot! I'm human!"

### 13

If you have ever seen an actress drop the voice and mannerisms of her onstage character the moment the curtain drops, all I can say is, this was nothing like that.

The eyes seemed a trifle smaller, the nose the tiniest bit

longer, the mouth a trifle too large and thin. The scar was gone.

I looked up, and aimed more carefully this time, picking which whorls in the design I deduced might be the electromagnetic accelerators. I fired again, and again. The unseen ray sliced neatly through the golden surface, and the release of energies were causing blue incandescence—maybe this was what fires looked like in zero gravity—to gush out into the vacuum. I pushed the dark red stop back in.

She said, "What is happening?"

"I am trying to prove that the time-echoes which the bungling sage who penned the Apocalypse detected were accurate. Do you have a name?"

"High Aieai Yray of Tycho Pressure."

"Beautiful name."

"Thank you. It is Lunarian. You are not the mad bomber whose brain could never die? For four hundred years, you were on display at the Smithsonian."

"Mistaken identity."

"Your name is not really Smith?"

"That is what the constables in the islands where I am from—"

She rolled her eyes. "I know what England is."

"—use for nameless men. Francis Earnest Everard Descheneaux. You may call me Doctor Descheneaux, but I prefer Father Frank. Pardon me for being naked."

She reached over and typed a command on the wand keys. Air solidified, took on hue and texture. A simple mantle now covered me. Aieai Yray wore a pleated white tunic.

"You remember what the demon knew?"

"The mental composite is not a—"

"We can discuss theological niceties later," I interrupted, "since the exotic material, including something called negative mass—which I am very pleased turned out to exist *just as* my theory predicted (ho ha!) and I hope Dr. Luttinger of Columbia was also resurrected so I can shake his hand—is about to evaporate into nothing, and all the hollow atoms of all the hollow people as well."

"Not immediately. The gems hold a reserve charge for about a day and a half."

"Show me how to unfold the wand. I don't need the periodic table; I need the bestiary of subatomic particles."

She did. The thing was simple to use. Well, simple for a physicist.

"What are you doing?" she asked.

I laughed. "One of the first things I discovered was how devilishly hard it was to keep a hollow atom hollow. The empty spot in the heart naturally attracts the correct numbers of protons and neutrons to fill it up. So I have to spray this tower (where all the peoples of Earth are conveniently gathered) with neutrons, which should proffer no difficulty. The hard part is the protonic energy, which will destroy everything if I am not careful. But I can make protons temporarily no-range on their interactions. It is actually the problem I solved first, before I solved how to extend nucleonic interaction range to macroscopic. I assume the demons—"

"The composite minds—"

"—let us just agree they are not human—will flee now

from all flesh, since they must expect all physical bodies to ignite into a huge mass of lightning. Where will they go?"

"If they expect all the substations to vanish, Wormwood is the only place."

"An interesting name for the symmetry breaking sphere! I suspect these time-echoes might prove really accurate."

Aieai Yray regarded me with puzzlement. "You were the only one left, the only unconverted human! They could have left you be. Why did they do all this?"

"You heard why. Hate."

She gestured at the burning globe, which I only realized then was much larger and much farther off than it seemed. Not a space station: a space city. "Why do you do this?"

"The last thing I remember, I went to a church to pray for my enemies, and I was blown in half by them by way of thanks. But I never surrendered my humanity, and I never surrendered to hate. This is my reward. Now watch! I have altered the composition of the outer hull to create the particle spray we need. When it explodes—Do you have any way to communicate with the world?"

She said, "I can talk to anyone holding a cannelure. Ah—What should I say?"

"In one day, they must concoct all the tools, clothing, houses, ships and livestock of civilization before the power vanishes. Disintegrate or bury any transuranics. Whatever they decide this day, they decide for life. They must wait for the space sphere to ignite, and then flee from the tower to another hemisphere! Warn them! When this thing falls, it will make a hole eleven miles long, and raise a bigger cloud than Krakatoa, or I am no judge." I laughed a jovial laugh at that thought.

Aieai Yray looked at me sharply. "But your flesh is not entirely converted: the hollow matter adheres to you by artificial bonds which your particle shower might not preserve. Your eyes and legs will fade away. All medical arts are long forgotten. What then?"

"Better a crippled human than a hale monster!" I grinned.

Her look softened to pity. "Are you sure you are a priest? You seem too—happy."

"If we live, I will explain the source of my joy." I handed her the wand. "Spread the word!"

"Tell me what to say…."

And I was repeating to her the words of the prayers of exorcism, which I heard echoing from countless lips down the whole length of the tower, when Wormwood turned silently into a vast, bright, star.

In the light of the new star, I could see countless people, clothed in white robes, streaming like gulls from every window of the endless tower, cloud on cloud. With my new eyes, I beheld that each had the face not perfect, not serene, but alive, and torn halfway between heavenly joy and hellish fears. Each was an individual face, infinitely precious.

And then the tower fell, and I stood on a cloud with the girl from the moon and watched the vast, vain, hideous stronghold collapsing, and its upper courses turned cherry red with reentry heat.

These were glorious sights to see on my last day of light. ◆

# The World of Neil Clarke

## By K. H. Vaughan

Photo courtesy of Neil Clarke

Neil Clarke is a Hugo and World Fantasy Award-winning editor and publisher. He is the owner of Wyrm Publishing and editor of *Clarkesworld Magazine* and *Forever Magazine*. In 2012, Neil suffered a near-fatal heart attack while attending Readercon in Burlington, MA. The damage sustained in this incident later required that he undergo surgery for the implantation of a defibrillator. These events inspired his 2014 cyborg anthology, *Upgraded*.

UPGRADED

MADELINE ASHBY
ELIZABETH BEAR
GREG EGAN
KEN LIU
ROBERT REED
PETER WATTS
E. LILY YU
& MORE

edited by
NEIL CLARKE

**KHV:** Can you tell us a little about what prompted you to launch the *Upgraded* anthology?

**NC:** Upgraded was a very personal project for me. In 2012, I had a near-fatal heart attack. After surveying the damage, my doctors strongly recommended that I get a defibrillator. As I recovered from the surgery that implanted the device in my chest, I started looking for cyborg stories and came to the realization that there weren't many recent anthologies that focused on them. Who better to edit a cyborg anthology than a cyborg editor?

**KHV:** Now that you've had some time since your own upgrade, how has it affected your thinking about the relationship between technology and the body?

**NC:** Prior to this, I think I was still very much in the enhancement as superpower camp. When I was born, the technology in my chest did not exist. As I've researched the topic, I've come to have a healthy appreciation for just how far we've come and how far we still have to go. I've also become painfully aware of the opportunities to abuse these new gifts. That said, I still think the quality of life issues currently outweigh the risks.

**KHV:** What areas of transhumanism interest you (e.g., specific technologies or systems, ethical or philosophical issues)?

**NC:** Aside from the obvious interest in medical applications (the opportunities with nanotech!), I find the security side of it fascinating. My day job is in technology and I have a lot of experience with those issues. As I was recovering in the hospital, I was reading articles on hacking defibrillators and talking with the techs about the truth behind the fiction the media was pushing at the time. We're right to be a bit paranoid about these technologies, but at the moment, there doesn't appear to be anything sinister. That could easily change by error or intention.

**KHV:** What human transformations are closest to realization? Are there transformations of the body and consciousness that you think are a science fiction pipe dream? If so, why?

**NC:** What I've been reading about more lately isn't an implanted technology, but the use of technology and stems cells to regrow or 3D print organs. Some fascinating stuff there that could become reality in my lifetime and replace the busted heart that I have. It's considerably less likely that I'll end up with the science fiction solution of an artificial heart like Jean-Luc Picard (Star Trek: The Next Generation). There aren't any advantages to doing so. That isn't to say someone won't invent one, just that science fiction often overlooks the less sexy solution for the sake of the story…and there's nothing wrong with that.

**KHV:** Some critics of the transhumanist movement describe it as a dangerous philosophy. Why do you think people are fearful of technological enhancement of the mind and body?

**NC:** It's the glass half-empty view. We need to have people on both sides of this issue so we can make sure it is done right. We very clearly need to be concerned about the privacy and security issues that will come into play with these technologies. What we need less of is the people who view the glass as either empty or full. In some ways, those are the most dangerous paths.

**KHV:** Does the future need us?

**NC:** Probably not. It will happen either way.

**KHV:** You read an incredible number of submissions. Are there transhumanism themes or ideas that you see too much of in the slush pile? What trends do you see? What would you like to see more of?

**NC:** Oddly enough, no. After reading all the submissions for *Upgraded*, I fully expected to be sick of the theme, but that never happened. I was also surprised that it didn't trigger an increase in that type of story in the *Clarkesworld* slush. On the flip side of this project, I can happily say that the theme is broad and deep enough to sustain a wide range of stories.

**KHV:** If you could pick another upgrade what would it be?

**NC:** Nothing currently on the shelf appeals to me. If I somehow landed in the distant future, some sort of nanobot-based health and repair system.

**KHV:** A number of well-respected spec fiction outlets have gone on hiatus or closed outright in the past year or two. Your publishing work continues to expand. What's been the difference, do you think?

**NC:** Actually, I think we're in a good time for genre magazines. I wouldn't have said that ten years ago. Readership was declining, most new publications paid authors practically nothing, and distribution systems were in shambles. We launched *Clarkesworld* at just the right time and were stubborn enough to stick with it. Digital has saved genre magazines and we were able to get in at the ground floor and keep up with the pace of change. A lot of the credit also has to do with the great work we continue to receive from authors. Their faith in us makes a huge difference.

**KHV:** What else do you have on the horizon?

**NC:** Aside from more issues of *Clarkesworld* and *Forever*, the next *Clarkesworld* anthology (*Clarkesworld: Year Eight*) should be out in July. I've also signed a two-book deal to edit *The Best Science Fiction of the Year* for Night Shade Books. The first volume should be out in 2016.

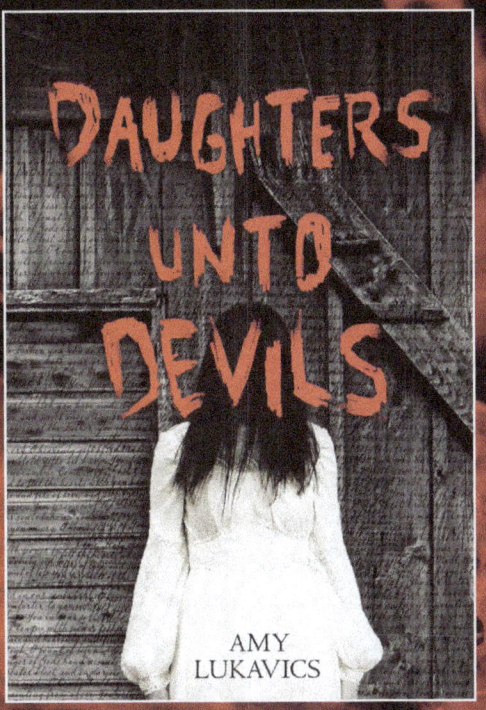

# WHAT MAKES NOT-SO-GOOD HORROR... NOT SO GOOD

## BY MICHAEL R. COLLINGS

Some years back, following my introduction to the magical darkness of Stephen King, I spent a summer binge-reading horror. Among the dozens I devoured, one comes readily to mind.

It was a first novel by a then-newcomer to the genre. I vividly remember working through it, reading the final page, staring at the mass-market paperback for a moment, then—in a fit of pique—ripping it in half along the spine and throwing it across the room. (Anyone who knows me and my respect for *all* books will understand how unlike me that would be.) And, immediately repenting both the pique and the tearing, going to the bookstore and buying a copy to keep on my shelf.

I did so for two reasons. First, to chastise myself for

mistreating a book. And second, to remind me what truly Not-So-Good horror looked like.

I mentioned the book occasionally over the years, during classes on creative writing and on con panels emphasizing writing skills, because the book, as I remembered it, represented an extreme in manipulative, exploitative content and inadequate characterizations, particularly for the many characters that were brought on stage only in order to be cruelly and violently slaughtered.

When I decided to write this essay, I took the book from my shelf and re-read it.

Yes, its content was still manipulative and exploitative; and, yes, its characters seemed flat and often unsympathetic. And, indeed, all but a few were introduced then, in a page or few, destroyed.

But what struck me this time through, after three decades of reading, teaching, writing, editing, and writing about horror, was that the book was, in addition to what I remembered, simply weakly written. With the advent and rise of indie authors and POD publication and the proliferation of small presses, a number of readers, writers, and reviewers have begun decrying the fact that many books—even books published by big-name presses— are at best workmanlike, at worst unreadable. Several have concentrated on first-time offerings, bemoaning the disappearance of potentially strong stories and characters under an overflow of basic mistakes.

Using my favorite Not-So-Good horror first-novel as a guide I would like to look at several of these…most within the first four pages.

A first-time novelist—indeed, *any* novelist, *any* writer— needs to start strongly. Readers may give a story only a few lines, at most a few pages, before deciding whether or not to continue. The writing should be controlled, paced, appropriate to the story, and focused on hooking readers and keeping them.

It should never be repetitive and boring.

Yet on the first two pages of this N-S-G novel, two sentences break both conventions.

The setting is a cellar, dank, dark, foreboding, and well-enough introduced, albeit a bit heavy-handedly. The creatures *de jour*, we are told, had "tired of hunting and concentrated, instead, on the raw meat which was tossed down into the rank, fetid darkness." The final clause is unnecessarily passive—"was thrown down"—particularly since the novel never quite explains *why* meat was tossed into the cellar; but more telling is the redundancy of *down*. A cellar is, by definition, 'down'; the sentence would be made more sprightly by deleting the unneeded preposition, leaving "raw meat thrown into the rank, fetid darkness." Or "tossed," "dropped," or any number of other verbs that would specify an action…always assuming that we are eventually told by whom and why.

This quibble over a passive and a preposition might seem little more than that, a quibble, except that shortly thereafter comes this: "Only a single shaft of weak light broke through the darkness, forcing its way in by way of a small hole in the cellar bulkhead." "Forcing its way in by way of" is repetitive and wordy, with *five* weak words in a row: two vague, repeated nouns—"way"—and three

prepositions. Replacing the three with *through* results in "forcing its way through a small hole," tightening the sentence.

Noticing that wobble, however, and concentrating on the sentence for a moment, suggests other, more subtle problems. "Only a single shaft" has two delimiters, *only* and *single*, and they mean essentially the same thing. In this case, both could be deleted and the remaining phrase—the already singular "a shaft"—would carry the necessary meaning.

Next, the light is "weak," is not in itself problematical but overtly contradicted by two subsequent verbals: *broke*, which implies a certain amount of strength; and the even more emphatic *forcing*. In attempting to build the sense of horror, the sentence undercuts its own beginning. The light enters through "a small hole in the cellar bulkhead." "Small hole" gives few explicit indications of kind or extent; perhaps *crack* would be more descriptive. And, given the setting, *bulkhead*, which normally refers to ships and aircraft, automatically defines the slanting exterior door leading into a cellar.

If one were to take all of this into account, the result might be: "A shaft of weak light penetrated the darkness through a crack in the bulkhead." No more is actually needed, and, taken in its context of simply establishing an eerie landscape, it would be more powerful.

On the next page, the world is described as "spinning round so fast." Same problem: redundancy. *To spin* is to 'revolve' or 'rotate'—that is, to move rapidly *around*. And, since things rarely spin slowly (most would fall if they tried to), "so fast" isn't needed. The world is spinning; in the established context of a drunk vomiting then leaning against a gatepost, that would be sufficient.

Six lines on, the character's "stomach continued to somersault." Two points. First, although he has vomited, there is no previous reference to somersaulting; thus the stomach cannot *continue* to do so. More directly, however, the sentence takes a nicely imagistic word, *somersault*, and replaces it with a flat, non-active verb, *continued*, which is about as useful as *is, are, was, were, seems*, and *becomes* in creating interest. The true sentence verb is hidden as a nominal phrase (a verb/infinitive functioning as an object). "His stomach somersaulted." Enough said.

A few words further in the same paragraph, the character "stumbled down the path towards the front of the house, stumbling once over one of the chipped granite slabs." Note the sequences of "preposition + *the*" following an otherwise fine verb; the short, rhythmical syntactic repetitions effectively defuse the aimless sense of *stumble*. Almost as if the author were aware of the inconsistence between verb and rhythm, he then repeats the verb as *stumbling*, followed immediately by the more overt repetition of *once* and *one*. Unless he stumbled twice over the same slab—which would indicate severe drunkenness—or once over two slabs, only one of the two words is needed, or, since *slab* is singular, both might be deleted. Stripped, the sentence might read, "He stumbled over a chipped granite slab leading to the house," with the option of adding other specific descriptors to make his inebriation more visual, if desired.

Two short sentences farther, he "fell forward" (a weak,

two-part verb that might as well be *fell, tripped,* or *tumbled*) and dropped a bottle of whiskey, which landed "in the thick grass on one side of the path" (note the parade of prepositions) and there "remained unbroken." Although Douglas Adams once wrote a similar phrase, he used it consciously and to comic effect. Here, the flatness of *remained* as a verb and *unbroken* as an adjective form of *break* seems unconscious, and the context speaks against comedy.

It would be unnecessary—and probably unseemly—to dissect the book page by page. But when this many wobbles occur in four pages, it makes it increasingly difficult to concentrate on the story, on the characters, the creatures, and the overriding sense of horror the author intends. But reading the novel cover to cover reveals that the problems never decrease; they continue throughout and include not only repetition, wordiness, weak substitute verbs, and prepositional strings, but also

- Frequent run-together sentences, that make readers stop midway through to determine which parts belong together;

- Cryptic, unnecessary adverbs, including "He smiled cryptically" and "She smiled inanely";

- Redundancies such as "small portable TV set," "at that precise minute in time," "collapsed in on itself," and "and also";

- Repetition of identical phrases, including "all manner of…," "obscene black monstrosities" (perhaps a dozen times); "sickle shaped teeth" (without the necessary hyphen to make them "sickle-shaped" rather than "shaped by sickles"—or better, *sickled,* which means shaped like a sickle)

- Syntactical oddities like "The three men got to their feet, a wave of pain so powerful that it staggered him, causing the rep to support himself against the wall for a second," in which *him* could refer to any of the three men and *rep* is ambiguous, since all three represent companies;

- Throw-away phrases such as "needless to say"; and

- Logical inconsistencies, including having a naked man "fumble for the key," while standing at the door—the text makes it clear that he knows that the key is elsewhere in the room.

Taken individually, none of the problems might seriously damage a strong story; taken in such numbers and such varieties, however, the story gradually becomes submerged beneath the weakness of the writing.

This essay is not intended to character-assassinate a particular story, certainly not to suggest that the writer did not polish and hone his craft through subsequent novels. It is, however, to argue that far too many horror novels—especially first novels—seem more intent on creating tone and atmosphere than on presenting a story clearly told and immediately accessible. Trying to create dark, eerie, threatening, and frightening landscapes and creatures, authors often concentrate on asserting words rather than creating structures, much as do would-be Lovecraftians who insist on using *eldritch, unutterable, gibbering,* or *rugose* in every other paragraph, deflating the effect of the words. In the case of this N-S-G horror novel, *hideous* and *monstrosities* occur more often than *eldritch* does in the entirety of Lovecraft's works.

I will keep the novel on my shelf. And I will probably refer to it from time to time. But at least now I understand more completely my reasons for ripping it in half after the first reading. Back then, at the beginning of my teaching career, I thought that what had distressed me most was the failure of content, substance. Re-reading it this time, I realized that the problem was more complex—and paradoxically much simpler—than that: at ground, it was the deficiency of the writing itself.

Photo courtesy of Cecile Grimm-Cabeen

# The 25th Annual Bram Stoker Awards® In Atlanta
## By John Palisano

You can't help but feel the tidal wave of energy when hundreds of creative minds gather in one place. The field of horror fiction is small in comparison to those of science fiction, fantasy, or romance. Those conventions get thousands and thousands of people. In contrast, the World Horror Convention is usually under a thousand guests. This makes for a very intimate and hands-on environment for those attending, which is one of the big selling points. We heard from none other than Charlaine Harris that she loved this aspect of the convention the best. It was wild seeing such a celebrity author hitting panels and readings without being mobbed or bothered. She was one of us.

The weekend began on Thursday night with the opening ceremonies panel where HWA President Lisa Morton introduced our Author Guests of Honor: Lisa Tuttle, John Farris, Charlaine Harris, Christopher Golden, Kami Garcia, presenter Dacre Stoker, toastmaster Jonathan Maberry, host Jeff Strand, and Lifetime Achievement winner Jack Ketchum. Artist Bob Eggleton was also on hand. Tom Piccirilli, Tanith Lee and editor Chris Ryall couldn't attend the weekend.

We were presented with goodie bags that included one of the most beautiful program books I've ever seen, featuring a full color wrap-around cover painted by Bob Eggleton, edited by Eric J. Guignard and laid out by Bailey Hunter. A stunning souvenir.

Thursday night was unusually packed with panels,

Photo courtesy of John Palisano

Lisa Tuttle

Lisa Morton

Photo courtesy of Cecile Grimm-Cabeen

readings, and films. There was Horror Open Mic Poetry, and some very popular panels whose topics included *Weird South*, *LGBT themes in horror fiction*, and *How to select Beta Readers*. There were short and feature length films throughout the weekend. I caught Lynne Hansen's award winning *Chomp!*, Greg Lamberson's *Give Up The Ghost* about a writer who loses his novel masterpiece in a computer crash, and the bizarro feature film *Jizzly Bear*, where the talented Allison Laakko and Josh Malerman delivered an unforgettable story of an awkward man and the serial killer bear he accidentally fathered while...well... you'll have to see it to believe it.

Friday morning kicked off with readings from Brad C. Hodson and Usman T. Malik. The day continued with more readings and panels. A few highlights included the

*Three Guys With Beards Talk Show* with Jonathan Maberry, Christopher Golden and James A. Moore. A true highlight of the convention was *Literary Estate Planning* held by Kelly Laymon, Ann Laymon and Les Klinger. An invaluable panel about what to do just in case. Friday also brought the first of many in-depth interviews with the Guests of Honor like Jack Ketchum. I caught Lisa Tuttle. At each, a souvenir bookmark was given out. You had to attend each to collect a full set. Horror trading cards! Later in the day, a very important panel took place discussing the problematic and troubling legacy of H.P. Lovecraft. It was an honest and thoughtful talk, addressing many of the controversies surrounding Lovecraft's peculiarities and xenophobia.

Friday also brought forth one of the largest mass author signings to date, numbering well over 200 authors, and stretching out through several large areas on the main convention floor. It was a true marvel to see so much talent shoulder to shoulder, newbies with veterans. The only problem with participating was: how does one meet all the authors and still meet those who want to see them? First world problems, as they say. Readings and panels continued until well past 11:00pm, but there were parties galore.

I found myself in a cramped hotel room with Sydney Leigh, Jeff Strand, Robert Payne Cabeen, Erik Williams, and John Skipp as Daniel Knauf introduced us all to freshly and expertly made absinthe, which kicked in just in time for a traveling carnival show of sword swallowers and circus freaks. That alone was worth the trip to Atlanta. You can't fake that stuff, especially five feet from your face. Absolutely riveting. The performers were great on and off stage. They were, most certainly, more of our people.

Photo courtesy of Cecile Grimm-Cabeen

Photo courtesy of Cecile Grimm-Cabeen

Photo courtesy of Cecile Grimm-Cabeen

On Saturday, tensions grew as the day would unfold into the Bram Stoker Awards ceremonies later that evening. Panel highlights included one on eBooks, Crowdfunding, Dacre Stoker's presentation on his lineage, Southern Gothic Literature, Skipp's Saturday Sinema film program, an interview with John Farris, Keeping Zombie Literature Fresh (featuring yours truly alongside Jonathan Maberry, Joe McKinney, Dana Fredsti, Mark Gunnels, and moderator Rachel Aukes) where we spoke about the past, present, and predictions for the future of the ol' rotters.

It's impossible to list everything without us just printing the program book. The biggest complaint I heard was that there was so much that people wanted to experience all happening at the same time. It was overwhelming in the best way. Kudos to Anya Martin for putting together a stellar programming schedule that left us all breathless.

The Bram Stoker Awards began with long time host Jeff Strand gently prodding the Hugos. He's always been great at moving things along and making us all crack up along the way. This night was no exception. A big highlight of the night came during Weston Ochse's near roast of Jack Ketchum for his Lifetime Achievement Award. Wes compared him to Rob Lowe several times—a running gag in the horror community.

A message from none other than Stephen King sank home just how much of a badass Jack Ketchum is to the horror community. Jack's acceptance speech was mercifully short and low on theatrics. In contrast, Maria Alexander had one of the longer acceptance speeches in Stoker history after she won best first novel for *Mr. Wicker.*

Photo courtesy of John Palisano

Photo courtesy of John Palisano

The scariest part of the convention had to be the jaw-dropping forty-seven-story tall elevator, which cascaded upward through a hollowed out hotel, which was reminiscent of being inside a giant whale, or a starship, or even the carcass of Great Cthulhu.

Crowd favorite William F. Nolan had everyone giving a standing ovation as he came to the stage, and left with everyone cracking up from his sharp wit. [see the list of winners at the end of the article]

With the stress of the awards over, it was time to party. Some headed to the Samhain party, while others made their way to the Gross Out Contest. Many made it to both, although there were a few casualties spotted here and again.

One of the biggest surprises was held for the Bram Stoker Awards ceremony, when President Lisa Morton revealed Rocky Wood's final project for the HWA he'd been working on when he passed away last year: StokerCon.

StokerCon means the HWA will be running its own convention next year instead of partnering with the World Horror Society. The inaugural year will take place at the Flamingo Hotel in Las Vegas on May 7-11, 2016, and is set to include R.L. Stine. The following year, in 2017, StokerCon will be held in Long Beach, California, with George R.R. Martin as our Guest of Honor. See you there!

## 2014 Bram Stoker Award® Nominees

### Superior Achievement in a Novel

Craig DiLouie—*Suffer the Children* (Gallery Books of Simon & Schuster)
Patrick Freivald—*Jade Sky* (JournalStone)
Chuck Palahniuk—*Beautiful You* (Jonathan Cape, Vintage/ Penguin Random House UK)
Christopher Rice—*The Vines* (47North)
Steve Rasnic Tem—*Blood Kin* (Solaris Books) **[winner]**

### Superior Achievement in a First Novel
Maria Alexander—*Mr. Wicker* (Raw Dog Screaming Press) **[winner]**
J.D. Barker—*Forsaken* (Hampton Creek Press)
David Cronenberg—*Consumed* (Scribner)
Michael Knost—*Return of the Mothman* (Woodland Press)
Josh Malerman—*Bird Box* (Harper Collins)

### Superior Achievement in a Young Adult Novel

Jake Bible—*Intentional Haunting* (Permuted Press)
John Dixon—*Phoenix Island* (Simon & Schuster/Gallery Books) **[winner]**
Kami Garcia—*Unmarked* (The Legion Series Book 2) (Little Brown Books for Young Readers)
Tonya Hurley—*Passionaries* (Simon & Schuster Books for Young Readers)
Peter Adam Salomon—*All Those Broken Angels* (Flux)

### Superior Achievement in a Graphic Novel
Emily Carroll—*Through the Woods* (Margaret K. McElderry Books)
Joe Hill—*Locke and Key, Vol. 6* (IDW Publishing)
Joe R. Lansdale and Daniele Serra—*I Tell You It's Love* (Short, Scary Tales Publications)
Jonathan Maberry—*Bad Blood* (Dark Horse Books) **[winner]**
Paul Tobin—*The Witcher* (Dark Horse Books)

### Superior Achievement in Long Fiction

Taylor Grant—"The Infected" (*Cemetery Dance* #71) (Cemetery Dance)
Eric J. Guignard—"Dreams of a Little Suicide" (*Hell Comes to Hollywood II: Twenty-Two More Tales of Tinseltown Terror* (Volume 2)) (Big Time Books)

Joe R. Lansdale—"Fishing for Dinosaurs" (*Limbus, Inc.,* Book II) (JournalStone) **[winner]**
Jonathan Maberry—"Three Guys Walk into a Bar" (*Limbus, Inc.,* Book II) (JournalStone)
Joe McKinney—"Lost and Found" (*Limbus, Inc.,* Book II) (JournalStone)

### Superior Achievement in Short Fiction

Hal Bodner—"Hot Tub" (*Hell Comes to Hollywood II: Twenty-Two More Tales of Tinseltown Terror* (Volume 2)) (Big Time Books)
Sydney Leigh—"Baby's Breath" (*Bugs: Tales That Slither, Creep, and Crawl*) (Great Old Ones Publishing)
Usman T. Malik—"The Vaporization Enthalpy of a Peculiar Pakistani Family" (*Qualia Nous*) (Written Backwards) **[winner]**
Rena Mason—"Ruminations" (*Qualia Nous*) (Written Backwards) **[winner]**
John Palisano—"Splinterette" (*Widowmakers: A Benefit Anthology of Dark Fiction*) (Widowmaker Press) Damien Angelica Walters—"The Floating Girls: A Documentary" (*Jamais Vu,* Issue Three) (Post Mortem Press)

### Superior Achievement in a Screenplay

Scott M. Gimple—*The Walking Dead*: "The Grove", episode 4:14 (AMC)
Jennifer Kent—*The Babadook* (Causeway Films) **[winner]**
John Logan—*Penny Dreadful*: "Séance" (Desert Wolf Productions/Neal Street Productions)
Steven Moffat—*Doctor Who*: "Listen" (British Broadcasting Corporation)
James Wong—*American Horror Story: Coven*: "The Magical Delights of Stevie Nicks" (FX Network)

### Superior Achievement in an Anthology

Michael Bailey—*Qualia Nous* (Written Backwards)
Jason V Brock—*A Darke Phantastique* (Cycatrix Press)
Ellen Datlow—*Fearful Symmetries* (ChiZine Publications) **[winner]**
Chuck Palahniuk, Richard Thomas, and Dennis Widmyer—*Burnt Tongues* (Medallion Press)
Brett J. Talley—*Limbus, Inc.,* Book II (JournalStone)

### Superior Achievement in a Fiction Collection

Stephen Graham Jones—*After the People Lights Have Gone Off* (Dark House Press)
John R. Little—*Little by Little* (Bad Moon Books)
Helen Marshall—*Gifts for the One Who Comes After* (ChiZine Publications)
Lucy Snyder—*Soft Apocalypses* (Raw Dog Screaming Press) **[winner]**
John F.D. Taff—*The End in All Beginnings* (Grey Matter Press)

**Superior Achievement in Non-Fiction**
Jason V Brock—*Disorders of Magnitude* (Rowman & Littlefield)
S.T. Joshi—*Lovecraft and a World in Transition* (Hippocampus Press)
Leslie S. Klinger—*The New Annotated H.P. Lovecraft* (Liveright Publishing Corp., a division of W.W. Norton & Co.)

Joe Mynhardt and Emma Audsley—*Horror 101: The Way Forward* (Crystal Lake Publishing)
Lucy Snyder—*Shooting Yourself in the Head For Fun and Profit: A Writer's Survival Guide* (Post Mortem Press) **[winner]**

**Superior Achievement in a Poetry Collection**

Robert Payne Cabeen—*Fearworms: Selected Poems* (Fanboy Comics)
Corrinne De Winter and Alessandro Manzetti—*Venus Intervention* (Kipple Officina Libraria)
Tom Piccirilli—*Forgiving Judas* (Crossroad Press) **[winner]**
Marge Simon and Mary Turzillo—*Sweet Poison* (Dark Renaissance Books)
Stephanie Wytovich—*Mourning Jewelry* (Raw Dog Screaming Press)

# DEUS EX
## HUMAN REVOLUTION™

BY RICHARD DANSKY

Transhumanism is something that largely gets dealt with in the AAA video game space in terms of character upgrades. The changes a player makes to their character are done in the interest of better stats, superior firepower, and the ability to generally kick more enemy ass. But a few titles have recognized that there is give as well as take in that relationship, and have played up the horrific aspects of becoming something beyond human. And the most prominent among them are not the usual suspects when one thinks "horror."

At first glance, numerous Japanese survival horrors would seem to fit neatly into this category, but titles such as *Parasite Eve* and the *Resident Evil* series were always more about becoming "other than human" rather than "more than human." As such, they fit more neatly into the body horror subgenre, rather than the transhuman.

shooter and left the transhuman horror of the original behind.

Another unlikely source of transhuman horror in games comes to us courtesy of Batman—or more accurately, the Joker. The end of the award-winning **Batman: Arkham Asylum** features the Dark Knight facing off against a monstrous, mutated Joker who has overdosed on Bane's teratogenic steroid equivalent, Titan. Batman, also drugged with the chemical, instead resists and gives himself an antidote, resulting in a showdown between the human and the more-than human. The entire plot of the game centers on the search for, use and abuse of Titan, with the barely human but still recognizable Joker reaching beyond human capability—and wanting to take Batman there with him in an ultimate test of wills.

Like **Far Cry**, **Batman: Arkham Asylum** ultimately rolls back its transhuman themes. But the bristling, musclebound Joker provides an indelible image, one that shows how far beyond mere human that character can go in body as well as mind.

But the *ne plus ultra* of transhumanism in games is the venerable **Deus Ex** series, with its most recent episode, **Deus Ex: Human Revolution**, being the most subtly horrific of the lot. On the surface, the *Deus Ex* games have always been sci-fi thrillers, with conspiracies, betrayals, and technological threats driving the action. And on

The original **Far Cry**, however, hid a real transhumanist cautionary tale underneath its protagonist's bright Hawaiian shirt. Best known for its stunning graphics and immense sightlines, *Far Cry* boasted a narrative that was about the perils of genetic experimentation unfettered by any moral boundaries. The protagonist, easy-going tour boat captain Jack Carver, was drawn into what could only be described as Dr. Moreau's worst nightmare, only instead of just encountering genetically modified creatures, he finds himself becoming one. The further he descends into the archipelago that houses the experiments, the more he changes, and the more powerful he becomes. But it quickly becomes clear that the obvious trade-off is the loss of his humanity, and there is visible evidence of the end of the road he's going down all around him.

Ultimately, the ending of the game suggests that Carver was "cured," reverting back to his "normal" self after he—and a volcano— have put an end to the experiments. Future installments in the series—now up to its 4th iteration—chose to focus instead on the moral complexities of the protagonist of a first person

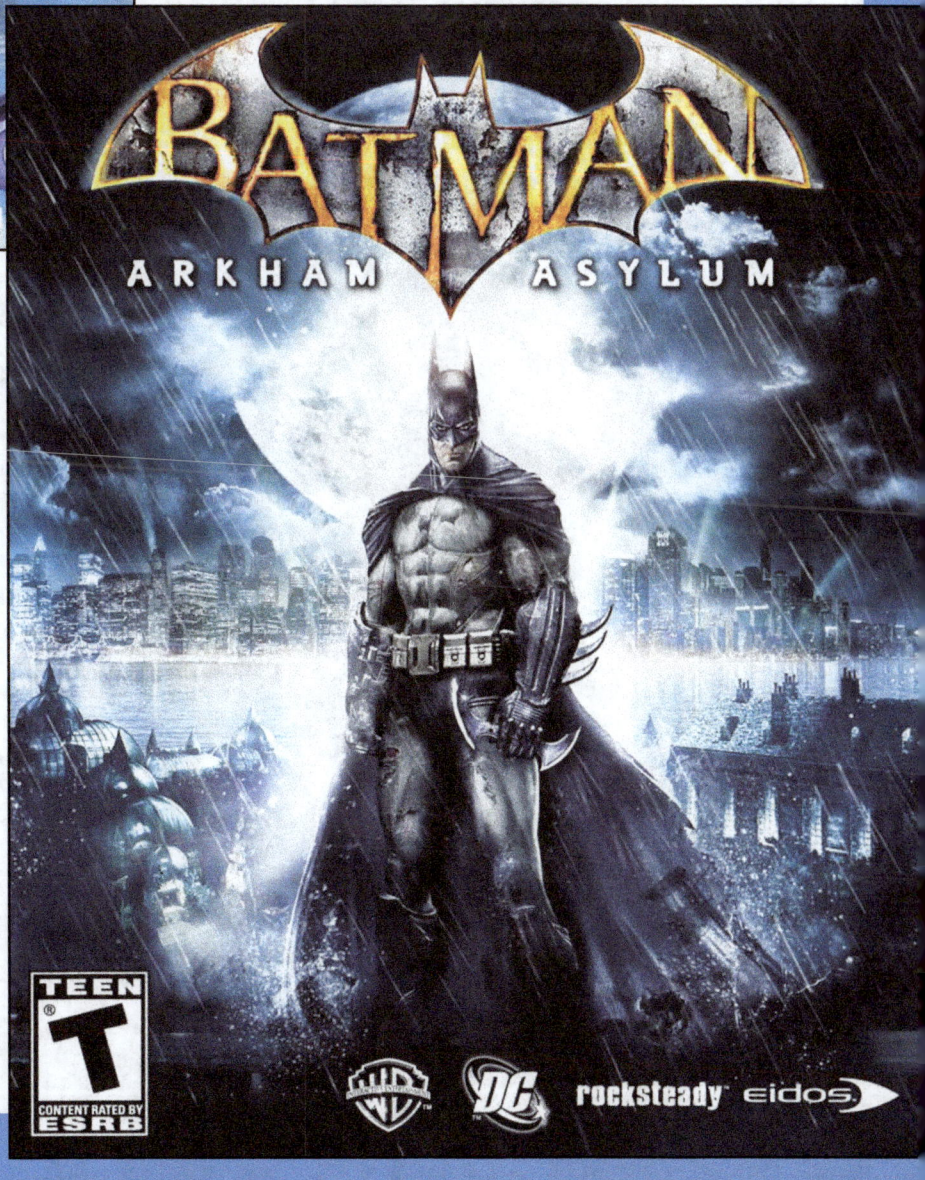

this level, **Human Revolution** is no different, with hero Adam Jensen waking up after a terrorist attack with a series of mechanical augmentations and the mandate to track down those behind the attack. What he discovers is a web of conspiracy surrounding the very notion of human augmentation—the replacement of human body parts with seemingly superior technology, which can be directed to a variety of uses. Set well before the original **Deus Ex** and its sequel, **Invisible War**, **Deus Ex: Human Revolution** is concerned with physical augmentation instead of nanotechnology, and the very real effects that technology would have on human society. The question of the benefits and risks of transhumanism is baked into the game's DNA as one of its central themes, with the gameplay benefits of Jensen's augmentations being visibly weighed on the carnage that is wreaked by and around him. While the benefits of transhumanism are obvious to the player from the get-go in the form of Jensen's increased capabilities, there is also a strong streak of implied horror as to the ultimate possibilities of the technology if misused—or used too well. The latitude the game gives the player in dealing with enhancements reinforces this theme; the player can engage—or not—at the level that makes them comfortable. The decision to upgrade is ultimately presented as a moral one as well as gameplay one.

**Deus Ex: Human Revolution** isn't technically a horror game, in that it's light on monsters, blood, zombies and other genre trappings. Where it finds its horror, however, is in the effects of transhumanism and the havoc that's wreaked in its name, both by its supporters and critics. The game's finale, set at an arctic outpost that's simultaneously stemming the effects of global warming and using modified human beings as living supercomputer processors as part of a plot to drive the world's augmented violently mad, embodies the dilemma and lays out the horror. There is good, there is bad, there is no hard and fast line between them and there will be damage done regardless. And at the end, the player must decide where they stand by defining what they'll do with the monstrous Hyron supercomputer that's left after the conspiracy is finally unraveled, and what they'll let the world know.

Ultimately, while horror games might be missing the boat on transhuman horror, games in general are not. From stealth to superheroes to FPS, the lurking horrors of transhumanism gone wrong are alive and well. And, with the sequel to *Human Revolution* announced in April, they're not going away any time soon.

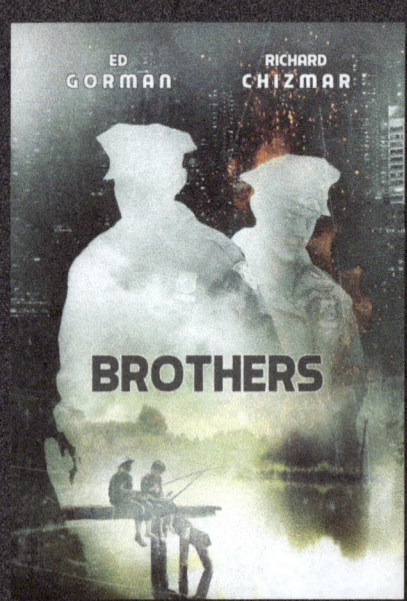

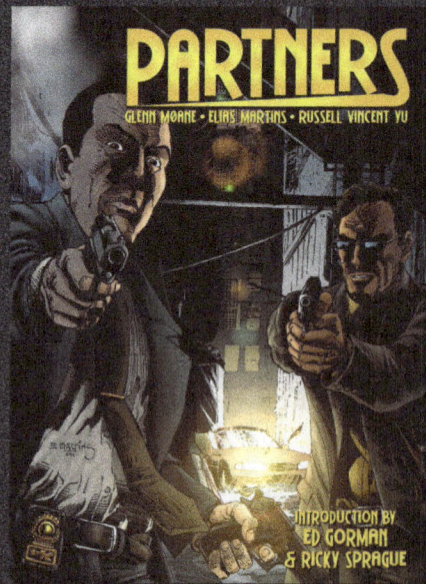

BUYZOMBIE
THE UNDEAD ARE ONLINE

HORROR WORLD

# HELLNOTES

Fiction, Movies, and Art
Dedicated to the Horror Genre

THE HORROR REVIEW

HORROR, SCIENCE FICTION & FANTASY REVIEWS

JOURNALSTONE
YOUR LINK TO ARTISTIC TALENT

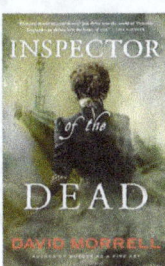

**Inspector of the Dead**
David Morrell
Mulholland Books/Little, Brown and Company
March 2015
Reviewed by Michael R. Collings

Recently, the Fall 2014 issue of *Dark Discoveries* concentrated much of its attention—in both fiction and non-fiction—on the possibilities inherent in secret societies in horror. It is a bit of a shame that I did not receive the ARC of David Morrell's newest thriller, *Inspector of the Dead*, sooner, since had I done so, my contribution to *DD* might have taken a distinctly different turn.

Not that *Inspector of the Dead* is explicitly linked to horror. Indeed, as might be expected from a sequel to Morrell's earlier *Murder as a Fine Art*, none of the traditional monsters of horror appear in this intricate tale of murder, madness, and revenge in mid-Victorian England. Darkness there is aplenty, and blood and gore, some tastefully insinuated, some described in intimate detail. But the story emphasizes the intellectual (and occasionally physical) exertions required for Thomas De Quincey, the notorious "Opium Eater"; his brilliant and resilient daughter, Emily; and their two stalwart detective friends from the London Police to solve a series of gruesome, upper-class murders that have a single point in common—clues left at each scene point to previous attempts to assassinate Queen Victoria and Prince Albert, suggesting a network of dangerous, unknown malcontents.

And the clues are moving irrevocably closer… presumably, to another attempt on the monarch's life.

As did the earlier story, *Inspector of the Dead* encapsulates history, sociology, psychology (both current and nineteenth-century understandings), criminology, and literature in a complex web leading to devastating discoveries and—as promised—a cataclysmic confrontation in the Throne Room of Buckingham Palace itself.

All of these elements are intriguing, of course, but what makes the novel of particular interest for me is that at its most fundamental levels, it *is* about monsters, the most devastating kind: human beings. There are allusions to other sorts, as when customers at a pub, having drunk doctored beer and gin, hallucinate creatures and break out into a deadly public brawl. But throughout, the story concentrates on what transforms humans into monsters.

For some, monstrousness is an almost unavoidable response to rigid Victorian morals, standards, and values. Churchgoers in the finer parts of town see nothing wrong with turning away starving children, often condemning the children to a lingering death by starvation…or worse. In their world, social status determines individual worth, and, in spite of twenty-first-century attitudes, many of Morrell's characters merely act the way they believe they are supposed to act. The main characters constantly confront this kind of unthinking evil as they move from the highest levels of society to the lowest and reveal to readers how tragically locked into assumption every stratum is.

Unfortunately, too many powerful and influential people turned their backs on a particularly egregious social injustice that resulted in the horrifying deaths of four Irish immigrants and set the surviving child on a course of revenge that would take dozens more lives in horrendous, meticulously planned murders.

Acting in the name of a secret society, "Young England," a criminal mastermind manipulates private and public confidence in the government, the nation, the monarchy itself nearly to the point of revolution, so convincingly that everything the police attempt to track down the villain results in strengthening the hold the society exerts.

The substrata of political and social commentary ultimately merge with the plotline to provide a single sentence, quoted from the historical De Quincey, that illuminates the entire volume: "The horrors that madden the grief that gnaws at the heart."

From such horrors come madness and desperation, obsessions with revenge and retribution…and human monsters.

Lest I have made *Inspector of the Dead* sound too much like a sociological treatise, readers can rest assured that Morrell provides not only opportunities for thought and consideration but also moments of high adventure, ranging from the battlefields of the Crimean War to the shadowed back streets of London's worst districts. The book is a brilliant amalgam of history and fiction, of reflection and speculation, of possibility and probability. And a thoroughly enjoyable read from beginning to end.

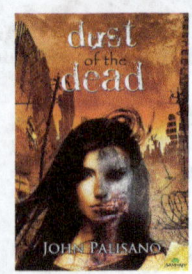

*Dust of the Dead*
**John Palisano**
**Samhain Publications**
**June 2, 2015**
**Reviewed by Marvin P. Vernon**

Mike Lane came to LA to be an actor but the zombie apocalypse got in the way. After a decade of walking dead, things are calming down. There are a few stragglers to take care of. However Los Angeles, as with the rest of the world, has returned to a slightly fragile form of normalcy. Mike, now working on the Los Angeles Reclamation Crew, is responsible for finding the straggling zombies and "reclaiming them," putting them at rest. But the last few are pretty rotted and dried up. The dust from their bodies seem to be affecting those who breathe it in and it just happens to be the season for Los Angeles' notorious Santa Ana winds. This new dust problem is especially affecting Mike's crew except for Mike himself who is left to wonder what is happening and is desperate to find out if there is anything he can do about it.

This is the beginning of John Palisano's refreshingly different zombie novel *Dust of the Dead*. With the glut of undead books and movies out there with mindless brain-eaters, Palisano gives us something a little different. The author's creatures aren't interested in brains and are not exactly mindless. They appear more disoriented and angry at first but, as the dust unsettles, they seem to be developing a speed and strength not inherent in the first zombies. The author goes over the first zombie apocalypse rather quickly giving us the background through Mike Lane's eyes. Mike is the center of this story and his first person narrative is dead on, letting us experience the carnage, sense the inevitable societal breakdown and know what we need to know in a nicely revealing and steady pace. The first zombie invasion, as Mike describes it, is treated rather casually. It is described as more of a major inconvenience. This is a good decision as it moves the tension and our expectations directly to what is to come. Without giving any spoilers, I will just say that zombie dust becomes a whole different matter and makes the protagonists a little nostalgic for the day of zap, bash and kill.

Even with all the surprises in store, the book mainly works because it is seen through the eyes of Mike Lane. Mike is pretty average. He is doing a job, has a girlfriend who he likes more than he lets on and develops a bond with his fellow colleagues. Mike has adapted to some hard times yet is seeing his world fall apart due to something that was previously unimaginable to him. It is that viewpoint that makes *Dust of the Dead* so interesting and worthwhile. It is brash, involving and full of thrills and scares but we also feel for our narrator and share his emotions as the world and his friends changes.

Mostly set in the San Fernando Valley, Palisano has a great sense of locale, taking us on a little tour of the Valley in Zombieland. The novel has a good regional feel and is especially entertaining for someone who loves Los Angeles yet enjoys reading it being destroyed, such as your fellow native Valley Dude reviewer. Novels with a good regional setting, even if you are not familiar with the locale, are always interesting when the area takes on its own character and meaning. Mike is a Valley Guy and feels like it. I appreciated that in the tale.

But even if you don't "feel" the environment, there is no getting around the fact that *Dust of the Dead* brings something new to the long-suffering and more than slightly-worn zombie legacy. It is good to see something new in this sub-genre. There is room for a sequel as the ending is intentionally open-ended. This is one of those rare times I would welcome a sequel.

*The Dark Servant*
**Matt Manochio**
**Samhain Publications, 2014**
**Trade paperback, 290 pp., $16.00**
**Reviewed by Michael R. Collings**

Matt Manochio's The Dark Servant surprised me. To be sure, it looked intriguing from the onset, with a nicely evocative cover by Scott Carpenter and a challenging title—there would be a formidable creature involved, that was certain, and it would be subordinate, presumably, to something even more terrifying.

The opening scene is nicely set: a high-school senior on his way to school, having an innuendo-laced cell-phone conversation with his girlfriend, only vaguely aware of a bad smell in the rural New Jersey air. Then, out of nowhere, hideous shrieks and an unsettling growl. And then….

A dangling modifier.

I couldn't help it. Even after nearly a decade of retirement, the English professor in me couldn't help but be jarred out of a narrative by an awkwardly constructed sentence. The boy, Travis Reardon, grabs an emergency flashlight from the glove box and shines it into the surrounding forest: "Eyes darting back and forth, the beam danced from here to there…"—and suddenly the flashlight beam has eyes. From that point, the book would have to prove itself for me.

Unfortunately, the next few pages contained additional wobbles, including awkward word choice (an "indecipherable" sun), repetitiousness, and the following, describing the police chief's discovery of anomalous hoof prints near the scene of a crime: "He let the hoof impressions ruminate before responding." My first response was something along the lines of "I didn't know hoof prints could ponder, let alone chew their cud."

Mostly because I don't like giving up on any book, however, I decided to continue.

Fortunately.

Imagine, if you will, one of the most fearsome creatures from European mythology, "older," as one character puts it, "than Christ." Imagine that it has come to a small New Jersey town and begun kidnapping, not children but high-school students on the cusp of adulthood, leaving no traces of its presence other than wrecked cars and damaged property. Imagine that it is eight feet tall, furred, horned, with terrifying claws, bearing a wooden crate on its back, into which it stuffs its victims. Imagine that its actions seem at best either sociopathic or psychotic—or perhaps both, since it cares nothing for human values and rules and revels in inflicting pain.

Oh, and that it speaks English fluently, although with a slight but detectable German accent (which is deftly handled throughout).

And that it begins its depredations on December 5th.

And that it is kidnapping its victims on the orders of its Master…who, we discover, is none other than "…Nicholas of Myra! Saint Nicholas! Santa Claus!"

To reveal that connection is not a spoiler, because in important ways—and most surprisingly effective ways—the novel is not about the monster, the Krampus, that serves as Saint Nicholas's "dark servant" in punishing evil and wicked children, although that seems, on the surface at least, the driving point of the narrative. No, what The Dark Servant concentrates on is the children themselves, adolescents at turning points in their young lives, making false choices and inadvertently setting themselves onto destructive paths. Sometimes the false choices are direct—physically bullying smaller, helpless children. Other times they are more damaging and potentially more lasting—for example, incessant cyber-bullying that can drive the victims to take appalling actions. And sometimes…but, no, that would be providing a spoiler.

Manochio tackles his tale with energy and verve (perhaps accounting for the occasional over-writing), blending brutal horror with moments of appropriate comedy, as when the rather myopic Krampus discovers that it has seriously misread the "Naughty List." Manochio takes what might in other hands have been a silly novel—really, Santa Claus!—and transforms it into a credible, highly modernized morality tale of guilt and punishment, of justice and retribution, of intent and responsibility. He seeds the narrative with carefully paced bits of information that make the revelation of the creature's identity inevitable but not intrusive, keying crucial bits of the story-telling to, of all things, school assignments, and by doing so making fantastic elements The Dark Servant more plausible. He incorporates recent technology into a mythic story in such a way as to make the conclusion satisfying. And he does so while maintaining interest in and focus on a handful of young people who are simultaneously unique and universal. By the end, the infelicities of writing are largely forgotten (except, obviously, by obsessive-compulsive English teachers, retired or not) and what remains is the resonant, final thematic statement: "You cannot kill evil—only its host."

I'm glad that The Dark Servant surprised me. I'm glad that I continued reading. It was well worth it.

◇◇◇◇◇◇◇◇◇◇◇◇◇◇◇◇◇◇◇◇◇◇◇◇◇◇◇◇◇◇◇◇◇◇◇◇

*Necrosaurus Rex*
**Nicholas Day**
**Bizarro Pulp Press, An Imprint of**
**JournalStone Publishing**
**December 12, 2014**
**Reviewed by Tim Potter**

Fourteen billion years in 64 pages. The history of everything that ever was, ever is and ever will be since before time. As told through the story of a stuttering janitor, a man conceived and transformed through acts of pure evil, a time-traveling anthropomorphised dinosaur that is the root of all matter and time.

*Necrosaurus Rex* is a story where every explosion of intimacy, no matter how small or large, is the universe trying to recapture the thrill of the Big Bang. It's as though the universe is a junky for creation and every physical act of love is its way of searching for a fix, one that will never recreate the high of that first time.

With all of the high-minded ideas it's easy to forget that this is also a pulp novel with great action and greater characters. When our protagonist, Martin, is presented with the idea of time travel he is immediately interested. He has lived most of his life in his own head, where Jurassic Park is the ideal world, and he wants to see the dinosaurs. He does and it doesn't go well. The reader learns never to mess with time travel and, maybe more importantly, never to mess with somebody with a time machine.

The amazing thing is that it's all there. All of time, history, creation, physics, everything, and it makes sense. The whole story is there, from the macro of the Big Bang to the micro of our protagonist's conception, and it really makes sense. There is not a misplaced word in all of the book, everything is working together to tell this story. As long as a reader goes in with an open mind and a tolerance for the absolutely disgusting and the absolutely beautiful, *Necrosaurus Rex* delivers. With more content and character than a thousand pages of your average book author Nicholas Day has achieved something amazing, something you have to experience to understand.

◇◇◇◇◇◇◇◇◇◇◇◇◇◇◇◇◇◇◇◇◇◇◇◇◇◇◇◇◇◇◇◇◇◇◇◇

*Aickman's Heirs*
**Edited by Simon Strantzas**
**Undertow Publications 2015**
**Reviewed by Mario Guslandi**

A seminal author of several collections of "strange stories," Robert Aickman is a cult writer worshipped by countless admirers (myself included) all over the world.

It was high time, therefore, to welcome the publication of an anthology of new stories inspired by the weird, inimitable atmospheres of Aickman's body of work. Mind you, however, as editor Simon Strantzas aptly observes, the scope of the volume was definitely NOT to assemble mere Aickmanesque pastiches but to show how his offbeat fiction has been able to influence and kindle the literary output of a new generation of writers.

In this respect the book is already a success, but the result, in terms of quality of the included material, is exceptionally good.

Among the fifteen stories featured in this anthology (all of which are accomplished and quite interesting), I will focus on those that I consider superlative (actually the majority).

Brian Evensong's "Seaside Town" is a truly

Aickmanesque story depicting the odd vacation in a French seaside village (where nothing appears to be as it should) of a strangely matched couple, while Richard Gavin's "Neithornor" is a subtly disturbing piece probing the secrets hidden behind bizarre, disquieting objects of arts, and DP Watt's "A Delicate Craft" is an unsettling, cautionary tale about witchcraft.

Lynda E. Rucker contributes the deeply atmospheric "The Dying Season," again featuring the crisis of a couple staying at a resort place, unfortunately off-season, when everything is empty, sad and a bit weird.

In the cruel, disquieting and puzzling "Underground Economy" by John Langan, a lap dancer's life gets changed forever by unexpected, unfathomable events and in the fascinating "The Book That Finds You," Lisa Tuttle admirably describes the efforts of a book lover pursuing the scarce (and somehow dangerous) work of an elusive writer.

Helen Marshall displays once again her great talent as a storyteller in "A Vault of Heaven," a splendid story portraying a man who, during a staying in Greece, learns the real meaning of beauty.

Daniel Mills provides "The Lake," a beautiful, insightful tale about the subtle melancholy of life and of childhood turning into adulthood, and about the terrors buried in the depth of the human soul.

Finally, Nina Allan, in her outstanding, bewildering novelette "A Change of Scene," describes the ambiguous friendship between two widows taking a vacation together in a village by the sea where some unpleasant truths lay hidden.

Other contributors to this superb, highly recommended anthology are John Howard, David Nickle, Nadia Bulkin, Michael Cisco, Michael Wehunt and Malcolm Devlin.

**It Waits Below**
**Eric Red**
**Samhain Publishing**
**2014**
**Reviewed by Michael R. Collings**

Over a century and a half ago, according to the narrative that forms Eric Red's *It Waits Below*, an unprecedented cosmic event occurred, a collision between the *Corona,* a Spanish warship laden with a golden treasure intended for the Emperor of Japan, and an interstellar wanderer, a comet forging a million-eons-long pathway through the stars until, in a one-in-a-billion chance it strikes and destroys the ship. And sends the treasure into the depths of the Mariana Trench, 30,000 feet down.

Now, in present day, the Enright brothers' salvage operation is determined to retrieve the gold. With a specially equipped support tender and a radically re-designed submersible, they intend to descend deeper than humans have ever gone and, in an equally radically designed suit, walk on the bottom of the Trench into the ruins of the *Corona*.

Everything is set. Every contingency has been accounted for. Nothing can go wrong.

Except, of course, everything does.

Through accident and oversight, the submersible falls into an uncharted crevasse, well below crush-depth for both the DSV and the suit. On the surface, a violent storm rages and, far worse, pirates attack on the theory that the Enrights have already retrieved the treasure; all they will have to do is take it from them. Enough elements of hazard for any action-adventure tale.

But *It Waits Below* has one additional complication for its characters. *Something* is alive within the comet, something that has lived for millions of years in the frigid vacuum of space, and now, with the comet lodged inside the sunken wreck of the *Corona*, it discovers the possibility of new, warm hosts to infest, to control…and to change.

Although the story is a bit slow in the beginning, as the various actors are introduced and the circumstances detailed, once Red sets things in motion, *It Waits Below* transforms into a non-stop thriller, with none of the characters given a moment's peace, a moment's rest from the various forces that have gathered. It gains steam as the creature metamorphoses, consuming more and more of the life-forms around it, until it finally emerges to battle against the steel-plated tender itself. The final, apocalyptic scenes are described with all of the special effects of the best visual creature-features; and, in keeping with its genre, readers are challenged to guess who—if anyone—will survive.

A relatively short novel (270 pages), it is a fast-paced read. Characters are clearly limned, their motivations believable throughout. The settings—both above and below sea level—contribute to the texture, in particular the absolute blackness of the depths and the characters' horror at being trapped there, helpless and unable to contact the outside world. The creature is grisly and horrific in all of its manifestations, some of which are shiveringly grotesque.

If there is anything about the novel that detracts from its effectiveness, it is the presence throughout of language problems—repetition of words, images, even clichés; long, awkwardly constructed sentences that require readers to stop and repeat to figure out how the pieces fit together; words misused or skewed that throw passages off balance; and abrupt shifts in diction from scientific-seeming to slang. The underlying story is sound; it would be well-served by a final, meticulous editorial sweep.

On the whole, however, there is much to appreciate, many tremors of horror to anticipate and endure, and the constant threat of destruction—of the divers, of the crew above, and indeed of humanity itself.

**The Sea of Blood**
**Reggie Oliver**
**Dark Renaissance Books**
**Reviewed by Michael R. Collings**

It is difficult to refer to a collection of weird tales as elegant without immediately calling to mind the admittedly dated, neo-eighteenth-century prose of H.P. Lovecraft. As remarkable as his stories are (and I find them enormously appealing) and as extensive as his influence has been in contemporary horror and dark fantasy, Lovecraft has one clear disadvantage for modern readers: his language—as structured, as self-consciously elevated, as effective as it might be to his fans—simply does not speak to all.

So when I refer to Reggie Oliver's retrospective edition of short fiction, *The Sea of Blood*, as elegant, I do so cautiously but meaningfully. It is tasteful—that is, every story is told in precisely the tone best suited to its effects, its themes, its purposes, and its characters. It is stylish—Oliver obviously enjoys the possibilities of prose and exploits (used as a good word) them to their fullest while never indulging in verbal effects for their own sakes. It is sophisticated—urbane, learned, even literary, but never at the expense of clarity or empathy. It is neither condescending nor snobbish—yes, there are stories about the upper-class and its affectations (particularly the serio-comic "The Blue Room"), but there are also gritty tales of starving actors and grubby (if haunted) theaters, of patronizing headmasters and students eager to learn, of ancient mysteries and modern terrors…and throughout runs a stream of elegance that makes each story inviting and enjoyable.

Most are reprints from earlier collections, although coming across them in their new context gives them an invigorating sense of freshness. I was familiar with "Baskerville's Midgets," for example, but in *The Sea of Blood*, surrounded by additional tales of actors and illusions, it took on an unexpected crispness. Others are new to this volume: "Absalom," "The Rooms are High," and "Trouble at Botathan," each contributing its particular strength.

I referred to the collection initially as weird fiction—a phrase I use rarely but that here seems far more appropriate than horror. Oliver's stories are odd, uncanny, eerie, and almost without exception end where more traditional horror might begin: with the assertion of a monster, of something inexplicable except as supernatural, of something unquestionably beyond possibilities in the world we assume is real. Instead, he tantalizes with hints and suggestions, with unusual moments and incongruous events that might lead to true horror…or might not. One step further, beyond the limits of the story, and he would have to acknowledge that, "Yes, it was all in the character's mind" or "No, such things can exist, even if every sense we possess denies them." Those final, piercing moments of ambiguity, of necessary ambivalence, cap the stories in ways that definitive conclusions could not, enhancing the sense of "the fantastic" in very much the way Tzvetan Todorov described it several decades ago. If Oliver knows of Todorov's then-groundbreaking study, he has learned his lesson well.

*The Sea of Blood* is fairly lengthy at nearly four-hundred pages, with twenty-three exceptional tales. It is not a collection to be skimmed but to be savored slowly, to be enjoyed as Oliver invites readers into unexceptional lives that turn out to be exceptional indeed…one way or the other.

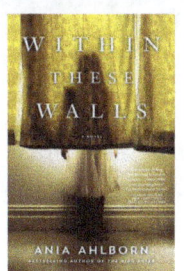

**Within These Walls**
**Ania Ahlborn**
**Gallery Books**
**April 21st, 2015**
**Reviewed by Marvin P. Vernon**

*Within These Walls* by Ania Ahlborn is an intriguing hybrid of psychological horror and haunted house tale. Both sub-genres are favorites of mine. What *Within These Walls* does so well is to bring them together in a novel that spans a thirty year period with complex characters and interactions. Most of the book takes place in a house where true crime author Lucas Graham and his 12-year-old daughter Virginia temporarily reside. Yet it is not so much the allegedly haunted house that scares us, but the mass murderer who has convinced Lucas to move into the scene of his crimes. In many ways, it is Lucas who is haunted. He is a true crime writer with a couple of best sellers and a long streak of nothing. His marriage is teetering on the edge of divorce and it is affecting his daughter who has taken a liking to the dark and the occult.

Cult leader and killer Jeffrey Halcomb is giving him the opportunity to interview him for a book but the price of admission is to live in the house where the murders took place thirty years ago. What happens next is a nightmare that threatens to destroy Lucas and his family and may revitalize the terror that was spread by Halcomb.

Lucas is not necessarily the most likable person but he is troubled by the most common challenge of just living and succeeding. It lends an air of believability when he takes resident in a house that would send most tenants fleeing in terror. The author, Ania Ahlborn, knows that desperation and insecurity can be more terrifying than the most awful demon and the most eerie ghost. Ahlborn is a skilled writer who realizes horror is more terrifying when you are immersed in the characters and slowly drawn to the scares rather than hit in the head by the proverbial hammer. The author uses alternating time lines to tell her story: the current time where Lucas is trying to make his comeback and ends up accepting a deal with a killer, and 30 years earlier, at the time of Halcomb's cult and its murders. In this narration of a previous time, we are introduced to Audra/Avis, who becomes our focal point as we discover how and why the killings took place. Halcomb and his followers are not based on any actual murder but seems to be a loose mix of Charles Mansion and Jim Jones.

But the strength in this tale is that Halcomb often feels like an enigma. We get no direct look at Halcomb in the present age but we learn about what the young 1980s Halcomb was like through the eyes of Audra. We follow the insecure Audra as she struggles with her role in this perverse family. That is what I really liked about this story: that in both timelines, it is the potential victim that brings us anxiety and scares. Villains are fun and Jeffrey Halcomb is an imposing villain but in this engrossing novel we connect with the victims and their strange but recognizable hopes and fear.

Lots of strange things happen in this haunted house and there are plenty of shocks for horror fans, but overall the psychological horror genre wins out and that is fine with me. Ahlborn deals in the more quiet and haunting chills and while she doesn't shy away from violence (especially at the end), it is not what keeps the reader. It is the cold and deep chills that keep us reading. *Within These Walls* stays with you. The characters stay with you. Ahlborn's meaty horror novel succeeds not just for the scares but as a psychological study of persons desperately and tragically seeking their role in life and ending in a nightmare. For that reason, it comes highly recommended.

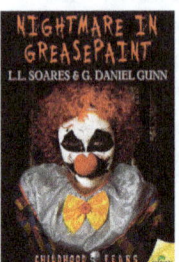

*Nightmare in Greasepaint: Childhood Fears*
**L.L Soares & G. Daniel Gunn**
**Samhain Horror**
**May 5, 2015**
**Reviewed by Tim Potter**

Everybody loves clowns. Right? No? Well, most horror readers at least loves to be terrified clowns and it's a theme *Nightmare in Greasepaint* uses to the fullest.

Another installment in Samhain Horror's Childhood Fears novella series, the book by L.L Soares and G. Daniel Gunn, successfully uses coulrophobia to evoke terror. Coulrophobia, the fear of clowns, is a theme found in horror fiction on a fairly regular basis, but that familiarity doesn't lessen its effect in this sharp new tale.

The passing of his mother takes Will Pallaso back to his childhood home to settle her affairs. The home is normal in every way to Will's wife and his son Billy, but the hidden terrors that linger from a horrific event in Will's youth soon become apparent. It starts with Billy's nightmares, which wake him screaming in the middle of the first three nights in the home. These fears are only allayed by the purchase and installation of a clown's head nightlight. What helps Billy get to sleep soundly only causes more anxiety for Will.

As the reader is drawn deeper into Will's backstory, they learn about the horrors of his youth and why they still reside within the house. The mystery of the makeshift altar in the basement and what it signifies are central to the story. Some of the greatest tension comes from the fact that Will's family have no idea what's going on and no idea why Will is so disturbed and upset. The story unfolds as the reader and Will's family learn what is really going on in the house.

The story takes an unexpected supernatural turn, which works for the most part though it's full potential is under realized. The conclusion is also satisfying though one character never gets fully resolved and some questions are left unanswered. Unanswered questions are okay, the ambiguity they provide leaves the reader with a sense of the mysterious. In this book, though, there were a few questions I wanted the answers to.

Will doesn't want to admit it to his family, but he has a very good reason to be afraid of clowns, and whether the reader is afraid of clowns or not, *Nightmare in Greasepaint* is a creepy and enjoyable.

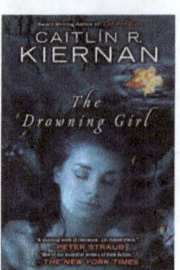

*The Drowning Girl: A Memoir*
**Caitlin R. Kiernan**
**Roc Books**
**Reviewed by Lucy A. Snyder**

*The Drowning Girl: A Memoir* is a fictional memoir of madness, haunting and loss written by Caitlín R. Kiernan. The novel was published in 2012 by Roc Books (an imprint of Penguin). It was nominated for the Nebula Award, the Locus Award, the Shirley Jackson Award, the Mythopoeic Fantasy Award, the British Fantasy Award, and the World Fantasy Award. It won the Tiptree Award and the Bram Stoker Award.

As you might suspect from all those award nominations, the novel is really damned good. I found something striking in nearly every paragraph. Trying to pick just one thing to focus on in my review was difficult, partly because it was like trying to pick the most valuable gold coin in a whole room full of dragon's loot, and partly because trying to separate everything out in this complex narrative is like trying to pull a single live octopus from an entire bucket of octopi: grab onto one slippery cephalopod and five more latch on and come with it.

To paraphrase the narrator, India "Imp" Morgan Phelps, the book isn't factual, but it's true.

According to her Author's Note, Kiernan was initially inspired to write the novel after she read a nonfiction book on the Black Dahlia murder. She also references and invokes the work of Lewis Carroll, Edgar Allan Poe, H.P. Lovecraft, and dozens of other writers and poets. She does not mention Chambers' *The King In Yellow*, but I could see its influence throughout her work, like snatches of a repeated motif barely audible in a layered, complex symphony.

One of the many things that struck me about this novel is its structure. At first, poor mad Imp's story seems random, disjointed like her memory and mind. But then I came to realize that the narrative is very carefully constructed. Painstaking is the adjective that springs to mind. The structure of individual pages reflects the narrator's obsessive mindset; sentences and paragraphs move in circles and spirals:

> *I didn't realize I was also insane, and that I'd probably always been insane, until a couple of years after Rosemary died. It's a myth that crazy people don't know they're crazy. Many of us are surely as capable of epiphany and introspection as anyone else, maybe more so. I suspect we spend far more time thinking about our thoughts than do sane people. Still, it simply hadn't occurred to me, that the way I saw the world meant that I had inherited "the Phelps Family Curse" (to quote my Aunt Elaine, who has a penchant for melodramatic turns of phrase). Anyway, when it finally occurred to me that I wasn't sane, I went to see a therapist at Rhode Island Hospital. I paid her a lot of money, and we talked (mostly I talked while she listened), and*

*the hospital did some tests. When all was said and done, the psychiatrist told me I suffered from disorganized schizophrenia, which is also called hebephrenia, for Hēbē, the Greek goddess of youth.*

On a chapter level, the novel has a much more disciplined structure, even though Kiernan maintains the illusion of disorder in the spiraling narrative. For instance, once you boil down Chapter One, it is an introduction to all the characters, themes and the essentials of the story the reader is about to embark on. Chapter Two launches the plot as Imp meets her girlfriend Abalyn and things start to get strange. The whole plot progression from chapter to chapter is quite logical and deliberate if you look at it on a macro level.

Kiernan changes things up in an interesting way by interspersing whole short stories written by the main character. The very first, "The Mermaid of the Concrete Ocean", is presented as being a fictional truth by the narrator. Its "outsideness" is emphasized by it not being labelled as a chapter but as an insert between Chapter Four and Chapter Five. Separating it from the rest of the narrative like that gives the impression to the reader that although Imp has just told us the story is true, it's still just something she made up out of her improperly medicated imagination and we shouldn't give it too much credence within this constructed reality. But "Mermaid" more than anything else foreshadows and illuminates the presented-as-real events at the end of the book. It's a brilliant bit of intentional misdirection. You reach the end of the book and realize the truth of it was hiding in plain sight all along.

In her Author's Note, Kiernan states that the structure of her narrative was partly based on the Neil Jordan film *The Company of Wolves* and partly on Henryk Górecki's *Symphony No. 3, Op. 36* (also known as *The Symphony of Sorrowful Songs*). She says that the structural mirroring of *The Company of Wolves* was unintentional until it was pointed out to her by her beta readers after the novel was complete; with the novel's dreamlike qualities, fairy tale narrative style and stories-within-stories structure, the resemblance is obvious. But I, too, missed it until she mentioned it in her note, even though it was right there in plain sight all along.

I had not heard Górecki's Symphony before reading Kiernan's novel, but I did study music, and so I could see the structural resemblance to some kind of orchestral opus. I'm glad to know what the model was. The symphony focuses on strings and a lone soprano and lacks the epic swell of percussion and horns that you'd find in, say, a Wagnerian opera. The book's macro-structure mimics the three movements of the symphony. Imp could be seen as the novel's soprano, and in the book you'll find no fantasy battles or other loud scenes; everything is intimate and personal and centered on loss and the fear of loss.

I've written stories inspired by individual songs, but to use an entire symphony as the template for a novel? That's ambitious. I thought the book was brilliant before, but I'm in awe of Kiernan now, particularly knowing that when she wrote this she was clearly holding enough sorrow to kill a person. Making complicated artistic choices is really quite difficult under those circumstances.

HELLNOTES

FICTION, MOVIES, AND ART
DEDICATED TO THE HORROR GENRE

IF YOU MOVE HOMES DON'T LEAVE YOUR DARK DISCOVERIES SUBSCRIPTION BEHIND!

E-mail your change of address to christophercpayne@journalstone.com

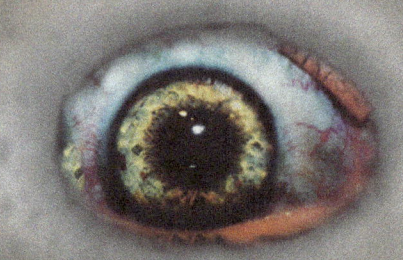
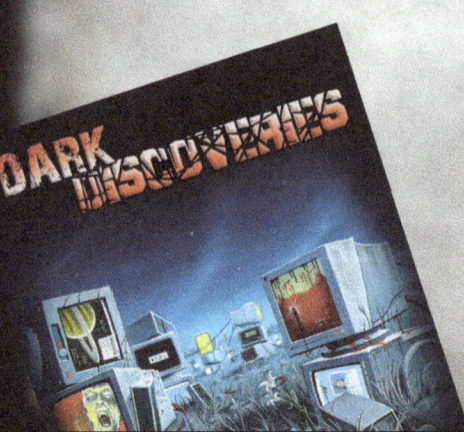